THE
WRONG
SIDE OF
KAI

First published in 2019 by Ink Road
INK ROAD is an imprint and trademark of
Black & White Publishing Ltd

Black & White Publishing Ltd
Nautical House, 104 Commercial Street
Edinburgh, EH6 6NF

1 3 5 7 9 10 8 6 4 2   19 20 21 22

ISBN: 978 1 78530 248 0

A CIP catalogue record for this book is available from the British Library.

Typeset by Iolaire Typesetting, Newtonmore
Printed and bound by CPI Group (UK) Ltd, Croydon, CR0 4YY

THE
WRONG
SIDE OF
KAI

ESTELLE MASKAME

INK ROAD

1

"So, what's Harrison really like?"

The vodka in my mouth almost ends up on the floor. I gulp it back and turn to face Chyna. She's perched on the edge of the countertop, surrounded by bottles, swinging her legs back and forth. She has an eyebrow raised high as she fights back a laugh. It's an abrupt change in topic from our previous pondering over where the other girls might have bought their cute outfits from.

I nonchalantly raise my drink to her, a mix of soda and too much cheap vodka, and shrug. "Above average. He definitely knows what he's doing."

Chyna releases that laugh. "I meant his personality."

"Oh, then kind of boring."

My eyes flicker back to the living room. I can't stand her, but Madison Romy does always throw a good party every couple months when her parents leave town for business. Right now, her parents are in Florida, so the Romy house has turned into a social hotspot. A lot of our senior class is here, too many bodies weaving around one another and too many voices yelling out at once. The music is loud, the bass thumping. Only Maddie Romy has a house big enough to host parties like this. The kind of parties where the alcohol never runs out, where no parents ever turn up, where everyone is game for anything. They were fun at first, but now they're just . . . predictable. And predictable is boring.

I lay eyes on Harrison Boyd. He's leaning against the far wall, chugging beer as he jokes around with some of the guys from the team. He scratches his temple. Like he always does. He looks up through the crowd and spots me watching him. A smirk toys at his mouth, and he flashes me a knowing wink. We've been hooking up for the past two months, so I know exactly what that wink means. It's become so familiar, so routine. It means we'll sneak upstairs at some point. It means his lips will find mine.

I smile back at him, deliberately coy, then flick my hair over my shoulder and turn away, focusing back on Chyna. Harrison isn't the only one who can flirt. "Do I keep playing hard to get?"

"You can keep trying," Chyna says as she slides off the countertop, "but you're going to crack as soon as he whispers sweet nothings in your ear." She deepens her voice and leans into me, angling her body against mine. "*Hey, Vanessa. It's me, Harrison. How you doin', baby?*"

I push her off me, trying to muffle my giggles. "Shhh!" Others in the kitchen are shooting us weird looks. It's not like my fling with Harrison Boyd is a secret, but I still don't need everyone all up in my business. I slam the rest of my drink then toss my cup into the trash. "I'm gonna go talk to him." I fiddle with my hair, fluffing up my bouncy curls, then pull out my lip gloss and apply it. I want to look my best for Harrison. We've been carefully avoiding one another all night, and yet again, *I'm* the one who has to give in and make the first move. It would be nice if he took the initiative every once in a while, but Harrison is a little too cocky to do the chasing.

"Go get it, girl," Chyna says, cheering me on. "Isaiah is picking us up later, so don't disappear on me, okay? Oh, and be safe."

"As always," I say, then pout my glossed lips and blow her a kiss with my hand. She catches it, pretends to slip it under her dress, then blows me one back. It's something we've always done.

In freshman year, Chyna's dad got a new job in Cincinnati and the day she left, we blew each other kisses and pretended to hide them so we could hold onto them forever. They dramatically moved away, but then her dad quit that new job three months later, and back home the Tates came. Chyna and I have never stopped blowing kisses to each other since.

I leave the kitchen and make my way over to Harrison. It's nearing midnight, so I don't have much time before Chyna's brother picks us up. Some people are already slumped on the couches, fighting to stay awake, while for everyone else, the party buzz has yet to wear off. I'm feeling upfront, and now it's time to make my move. Harrison and I always play hard to get, always flirt from a distance, always make out like there's nothing going on, even when we know that very soon I'll be tearing off his clothes and he'll be tearing off mine.

I touch the ends of my hair as I approach Harrison and his friends, adjusting my skirt to keep my hands busy. Hike it up a little higher, revealing more of my legs, but then—

Ow.

I collide against something, then a drink splashes onto me and a cup is crushed between my body and someone else's. My tunnel vision for Harrison breaks as I regain my full line of sight, the rest of the party comes back into focus, and my eyes shoot up to the person in front of me.

I don't instantly recognize the guy, which is unusual, because I have a pretty good awareness of everyone in my senior class. He takes a step back from me as he stares down at his jeans, clearly unimpressed by the sight of liquid seeping through the denim.

"Vanessa," I hear Chyna saying, her voice scolding as though I'm a toddler she's babysitting. She approaches me from behind, wraps a hand around my elbow, and yanks me back. "Sorry, she's a little clumsy," she says sheepishly on my behalf, then she leans in closer to my ear and mumbles, "You've got to watch where you're going, girl."

The guy lifts his head to look at me. Even though I can fully see his face now, I still don't recognize him. His blue eyes stand out against the warm bronze of his skin, and his curls are cropped short, shaved at the sides but heavier at the top. He doesn't go to Westerville North – if he did, he wouldn't be a stranger to me.

"Yeah, Vanessa," he says mockingly, and my name carries a certain weight to it, almost like he is amused rather than agitated. He narrows his eyebrows and I can't help but focus

4

on the one brow that has a slit shaved into it. "Watch out." His lips twist into a smirk, and then he saunters past Chyna and me before blurring into the crowd in the kitchen.

I sniff at the air, inhaling the lingering scent of his cologne before it evaporates, then blink at Chyna. "Who *was* that?"

"Does it matter?" Chyna says. She gestures in the direction of the lounge where I was supposed to be heading. "Are you going to get Harrison or not?"

Right. Harrison.

I take a second to compose myself then set off again. Harrison and his friends are still joking around together, and I elbow my way into the circle, pushing in between Noah Diaz and Anthony Vincent. Harrison's gaze instantly meets mine.

"Harrison, your booty call is here," Anthony teases, nudging his shoulder into Harrison's. Noah only glances down at the ground and swigs his beer. Not too long ago, I was fooling around with *him*. But it's not a big deal. The guys I get with know the score. They know it's only a fling and they know I come with an expiration date.

"Aw, don't be jealous, Ant," I say with a grin, then sling my arm around his shoulder and plant a kiss on his cheek.

"Hey," Harrison says, clearing his throat. He presses his lips together, feigning disapproval, though I watch his mouth twitch as he tries not to smile. The best part about flings? There's no jealousy. No trying to control someone else's behavior. We don't owe each other anything.

My gaze meets his and I tilt my head to one side, keeping my expression neutral. "Oh. Do you need something?"

Harrison cracks into laughter and reaches for my wrist, tugging me toward him. My chest presses against his, while his gaze mirrors mine and his mouth remains inches from my own. He places my hand on his neck, and I can feel the warm energy of his skin. "Have you been avoiding me for the past few hours?" he murmurs, his voice so low I hardly hear him over the music.

"I could ask you the same thing." I skim my lips over his, teasing. I'm trying to be seductive, so I bat my eyelashes a little more than usual. I can sense Noah and Anthony shifting away, giving us some privacy despite the fact that we're surrounded by other partygoers. No one cares, though. Parties were *made* for this. Hell, I'm pretty sure Matt Peterson and Ally Forde were groping each other on the couch a second ago.

"Okay," Harrison says abruptly. He cups my face in his hand, his thumb on my chin, firmly holding me. "Let's cut the crap," he murmurs softly, but I recoil a little from the smell of beer on his breath. His smile is lazy, cocksure, as he narrows his eyes. "Am I leading the way upstairs, or are you?"

I don't hesitate. I've been bored all night and I'm dying to spice things up. My hand is in Harrison's and I'm spinning around, pulling him across the living room with me. He tucks his other hand into the waistband of my skirt, his skin hot against mine. I spot Noah's eyes following us across the room. Other people's too.

"What the hell are they doing here?" Harrison says suddenly, his voice gruff as he pulls his hand free from mine. He pushes past me and storms ahead.

6

I stare after him, growing agitated as I wonder what could have possibly grabbed his attention more than me, and then I spot the fight brewing over in the kitchen. From what I can make out through the wave of people pulsing toward the commotion, some guys from our school's rival football team have decided to turn up. And clearly, they weren't invited, nor wanted.

The rivalry between Westerville North, Central, and South is all too real. Especially between North – us – and Central. Last weekend, we played against Central. Usually, I don't care for football much, but I went to that game only because I knew I was meeting Harrison afterward. We lost – no surprise; our team sucks – but the real highlight of the game, the only burst of energy, was the brawl that broke out on the field during the third quarter.

And it looks like that fight isn't quite over yet.

I elbow my way through everyone toward the kitchen, toward Harrison, but Chyna pops up by my side again. Her braids swing around so fast they slap me in the face.

"I will never understand why high school boys act like they're in the NFL," she says, but I'm only half listening to her. I'm on my tiptoes, trying to see the confrontation. "It's not that serious, but all these bruised egos sure do make for good entertainment."

"It's the Central guys, right?"

"Yep. Am I allowed to say that their team is hotter than ours?" She dramatically fans her face with her hand. "Russell Frederick, though. Phwoar. I wouldn't say no to that red hair."

Speaking of Russell Frederick, he's squaring up to Noah

Diaz. Because it just wouldn't be high school football if the quarterbacks from rival teams weren't the two fighting. I'm convinced these rules are engraved into a block of marble somewhere. Behind Russell, a handful of the Central players back him up. Behind Noah, there's our own players. Our North players. Harrison.

"That result was . . . harsh," I hear Russell say. He's built of stone, I swear. His shoulders are as wide as a bridge. Russell cocks his head at Noah. "I'd have cried too."

"You really want me to throw another dent into that nose of yours?" Noah fires back, and he's already curling his hand into a fist, ready to swing if he's triggered enough. There's a lot of muttering and grunting. Players exchanging insults and taunting remarks.

Yawn. I'm so stuck in this boring routine that even all this party drama posturing can't excite me anymore.

"Hey, Harrison, you wanna catch these hands again?" one of the Central guys calls out, and when I pinpoint the voice, I realize it's the sweet-smelling guy with the bronze skin I encountered a couple minutes ago. *That's* why I don't know him – he goes to Westerville Central, and he has turned up at this party in tow with the rest of the Central football team, ready to stir up trouble. And he's calling out Harrison, of all people.

Which is a bad idea. As per usual, Harrison lurches forward, provoked and looking for a fight. He busted his lip during that brawl last weekend when one of the Central players swung at him, probably this same guy who's antagonizing him now, but at least I got to kiss it better all night. Maybe tonight I'll do the same.

When Harrison throws himself toward the opposing team, it sets everyone else off. I watch, unimpressed, as Noah rams his body into Russell, as Anthony propels his fist through the air, as Harrison grabs this mysterious guy who clearly has a problem with him. *Boys.* I hate them sometimes. Their egos are too easily wounded; they're so desperate to prove themselves.

There's a lot of yelling and shoving, everyone cheering on our guys to kick the crap out of the Central team, everyone pushing to get closer to the action. A couple of girls are screaming at them to stop, but no one else is even pretending to be civilized. All I can focus on is Harrison. He's got that guy pressed up against the countertop in a headlock, but the Central player is quick and strong. He slides out of it, and he grabs the first cup he finds and slams the drink into Harrison's chest.

Maddie Romy's shrieking voice slices through the atmosphere, and she comes barreling into the crowded kitchen. "Stop! My parents will literally kill me if you guys smash up the house!" she screams. She's flapping her arms around and I don't expect anyone to actually listen to her pleas, but the brawl stops, each guy freezing on the spot. Harrison is staring down at his soaked T-shirt with rage. "Take this crap outside if you have to. This is a *North* party. Not a South party, and definitely not a Central party." Maddie wrinkles her nose and points to the door. I'm impressed by her sudden authority. "Leave if you aren't supposed to be here."

There's a lot of shoulder barging as the Central players leave. The guy who just threw that drink at Harrison smirks as he brushes past him, smoothing a hand over his hair. He glances up for a moment and I swear his gaze locks directly on me, bold and intense, causing my stomach to flip. Just as quickly, he looks away again. I wish I knew his name so that I could mentally refer to him as something other than hot-guy-whose-drink-I-spilled.

Like a pack of wolves, he and his teammates leave, slinking away and growling under their breaths. The second they disappear out the front door, it's like they were never here to begin with. The music bumps straight back up, the circle around the kitchen disperses, the voices and the laughter return.

"Now I have to go soothe Harrison's ego," I whisper to Chyna. She laughs and nudges me in his direction, wiggling her perfectly shaped eyebrows at me. I don't need much encouragement.

"Kai Washington," Harrison is muttering when I reach him. He motions down at his T-shirt, damp and clinging to his sculpted torso. "He's really starting to push me."

So that's his name, I think . . . *Kai Washington*.

I try to focus on Harrison, but I couldn't care less about his lame football rivalry, so I'm quick to cut in before he can say anything more. "Who cares? I'm taking that shirt off anyway." As the words leave my mouth, I grab a fistful of the soaked material and tug him toward the stairs, desperate to leave the dregs of the party behind, to feel his hands on my body. We're both buzzing with energy after the fight – Harrison because his adrenaline is pumping, and me because the powerful look Kai Washington gave me has sent an electric current through my body. I try to shake the unsettling feeling and concentrate on Harrison instead.

We stumble upstairs together. Whatever, we aren't exactly sober, but we both like it that way. Matt Peterson and Ally Forde have moved upstairs from the couch too, and they're making out against the wall. They're oblivious to Harrison and me as we slide past and disappear into the first room we arrive at. I don't even flick on the lights; don't even care whose room we're using.

I tighten my grip on Harrison's shirt and pull him toward me, slamming my chest against his at the same time as his mouth finds mine. We're off balance in the dark, bumping into furniture and stumbling over each other's feet. I can hear music echoing around the house, muffled and distant behind closed doors.

Harrison tugs at my lower lip with his teeth. My hands are in his hair, pulling roughly on the ends. He's squeezing my butt. I'm kissing him harder. We collapse back onto the bed and I'm straddling his hips, leaning forward to plant a row of kisses along his jaw and down his neck.

"Vanessa," Harrison suddenly says, gently grabbing my face with both hands and lifting my head. "Can I ask you something?"

He shifts beneath me, stretching over to switch on a bedside light. It brightens up the room and I can see him again, his chest rising and falling beneath me, his breath heavy. His tee's pulled up and I rest my hands on his bare chest and stare at him, bemused by the interruption.

It feels like his tone isn't that playful anymore, and the solemn way he's looking at me isn't his usual style either.

"Right now?" I laugh, then press my lips back to his to shut him up. I try to kiss him deep enough to distract him, but it doesn't work the way it usually does.

He pushes me away again and sits up a little beneath me, propping himself up on his elbows. He looks so serious that I wonder if perhaps he *isn't* drunk. "Listen," he says, and he flicks his blond hair out of his eyes. "Next month me and some of the guys are going skiing up Mad River Mountain for a couple days. Some of their girlfriends are joining us, and I was thinking maybe you could come too."

It sounds cool; I like skiing. But even so, panic grips me like a vice. Is Harrison . . . asking me out? Is he serious? He's asking me to go on a skiing trip with him and his friends, and that sounds pretty damn serious to me. It means only one thing . . . He wants to take things further. He wants more from me, for us to spend time together like a couple, but there's no way I can give him that. My stomach suddenly feels like the final spin cycle of a washing machine – it's now somersaulting around at full speed while I fight the urge to vomit.

The answer has to be no.

I can't let anyone into my life. Not like that. I can't take the risk.

So, brick by brick, I construct a solid wall of defense between Harrison and me.

"Woah," I say, sitting bolt upright. My hand is still pressed flat to his chest, and I can feel his heart beating fast. The room has fallen silent, and it's like the party around us has disappeared into a void. "You're asking me out?"

"I just think it would be fun—"

"No dates, Harrison Boyd," I say, wagging a finger at him with a coy smile to mask the panic that's got me tight in its grip. We already established this back in the summer when I first kissed him in his truck. He'd picked me up after we'd spent the entire day flirting by text, and we didn't hesitate to get straight to business. We made it clear at the time that we were only fooling around, and that there was nothing more to any of this. Purely fun. Nothing serious. "We're just keeping it casual, remember?"

Whether or not he knows it, I've just made the decision that this is the end of us. I have no choice but to bail if someone shows signs of wanting to take things further. I kind of like Harrison. He's hot and he knows how to work his hands and he's not *as* much of a self-absorbed jock as the rest of his teammates. But I don't like him like *that*. I've realized that "real" relationships scare the absolute hell out of me. They always end and someone will always get hurt when they do, one way or another. I can't shake the thought that you'll always, inevitably, lose the person you've fallen for.

I can't help it. Uninvited, my dad weaves his way into my head, and I see an image of him now, a man with ashes where his heart once was and a hollow emptiness in his eyes. I never want to end up like him.

Harrison groans, bringing my focus back to him. "You're so hard to read sometimes."

"Is *this* hard to read?" I ask, and I lean in close to him again, distracting him, pushing him back down against the bed. I cup his face in my hands and my nails brush against his cheekbones as I press my lips to the soft skin of his neck. I kiss a path down to his collarbone, making sure I leave a hickey that'll take forever to fade, something to remember me by because, after this, I won't ever be kissing him again.

"Vanessa," Harrison murmurs, his voice a low rumble, and he exhales as his body relaxes beneath mine. One hand is on the small of my back, the other is pulling at my hair, tangling it around his fingers.

We break apart only so I can pull off his damp shirt. I toss it to one side and sit back up again, this time smirking seductively down at him. My favorite part of all this? The teasing. The driving them crazy. The hunger that captures their eyes. The control I have over them. It feels like the only part of my life that I *do* have any control over.

But right now, my performance is as much a distraction to myself as it is to Harrison. I focus all of my energy on pleasing him so that I can stop the whirlwind of panicked thoughts spiraling through my mind.

I move against Harrison as he stares up at me, the denim of his jeans rubbing against the exposed skin of my thighs. I like to believe that I'm talented when it comes to maintaining eye contact – I never, ever break it. My gaze is locked on Harrison as I play faux-innocently with the ends of my hair, as I bite my lip, as I pretend I don't know *exactly* what I'm doing.

"You're so hot, Vanessa," Harrison is mumbling, "I can't handle you."

He's right, he can't. But at least he's finally enjoying this now, allowing adrenaline and desire to take over.

Then, "Smile," he says with a wink, and that's when I notice he's pulled out his phone and is holding it up suggestively. "How about you give me a show?"

And I do.

I smile straight into the camera, and give him a show that'll be worth remembering tomorrow.

2

I wake to Chyna snoring in my ear and slobbering over my shoulder. I push her away, shoving her to the other side of her huge bed so that I can get some peace. I don't know what time it is, but I know it's definitely not early. My stomach is grumbling too much for that.

I rub my eyes, my lashes thickly clumped together by the mascara I was too tired to remove last night when we got back here. I did remove my clothes, though, because when I slide out of the bed, the chill of the AC in Chyna's room hits my bare skin. I stand still for a second, testing out whether I'm still drunk, hungover, or miraculously fine.

My clothes are scattered on the floor, but when I scoop them up, they reek of last night. A sure sign that the party was good.

"Chyna?" I say, but she doesn't stir, only continues to breathe too heavily until suddenly she is snoring like a damn freight train again. On her bedside table there're three odd, mismatched cans of beer that she swiped from the party as we left. She won't have drunk them, but it's a totally Chyna

16

thing to do. She's been swiping stationery from classrooms all through high school.

I don't need her to be awake, though. I have spent the night here at the Tates' house so many times that I'm becoming a fixture. A part of the furniture, as permanent as the dining-room table or the TV. Sometimes it's easier to stay here when I can't bring myself to return to my own home. I quietly raid Chyna's closet, grab one of her camp T-shirts from five summers ago and a pair of shorts, and get dressed. They fit me just fine – I've grown almost too comfortable here.

My stomach won't stop growling so I leave Chyna to sleep while I head downstairs to the kitchen. It's almost noon, but I pour myself a bowl of cereal and sit up on the counter, legs crossed, slurping up the milk.

The house is unusually silent today. I stare at the clock on the wall opposite, listening to each second tick by. It's funny, how different silences can be. In my house, the silences are strained and full of unspoken grief and the absence of Mom, like the walls of my childhood home are about to implode on themselves. In Chyna's house, the silence is a welcome relief – a safe haven. I relax, enjoying my few minutes on my own without that cloud hanging over my head, until I hear footsteps enter the kitchen.

Isaiah starts when he sees me, surprised to find me perched up on his countertop eating a bowl of cereal at this time. He flashes me a smile over his shoulder – his teeth are misaligned in the most adorable way – as he pulls open the refrigerator. "Morning, Vans. No hangover?"

"I'm not sure yet." I focus intensely on a spot on the ceiling, tuning everything out so that I can decide exactly how I'm feeling. I'm still suspiciously okay for now.

"Lucky. I miss being seventeen and having a liver made of steel. That's why I don't drink anymore," Isaiah grumbles as he grabs a Gatorade and a bottle of water, then kicks the refrigerator shut behind him. There's something effortlessly attractive about Isaiah – maybe because he towers over me, all six feet, four inches of him – but he's also like my brother, so *ew*. I have adopted Chyna's family as my own and, luckily, they don't seem to mind. To me, the Tates are the perfect family – whole and complete.

"Was I drunk?" I ask, but given that I can recall all of last night's events, I already know the answer.

"Not really, just mega annoying," Isaiah answers, and his mouth transforms into a wide, sarcastic grin. "You kept leaning into the front of my car to change the music. *No one* turns off Tupac, so you should be glad I didn't kick you out." He steps forward and hands me the bottle of water, damp and as cold as ice against my skin as I take it from him. "Drink this."

Just then, Chyna slumps into the kitchen, her slippers scuffing the wooden flooring. She looks like she's been hit by a truck at full speed on the freeway, yet she has miraculously survived to tell the tale. She can barely hold her head up. "I want to die," she solemnly announces.

Isaiah's shoulders shake as he cackles with laughter, but he does the right thing and passes his Gatorade to Chyna. The stark height difference between the Tate siblings is insane – Chyna is just a fraction over five feet, and next to Isaiah, it'd be easy to assume she's still in elementary school.

"How come you seem fine?" Chyna questions, her eyes meeting mine. She gulps down the Gatorade as though her throat is on fire. "Surely you drank way more than I did."

I shrug, trying not to laugh at her misfortune. "I guess Harrison sobered me up." Which is true, in a way. We had a good time, but nothing sobers me up faster than being hit with the panic that a guy wants a *real* relationship. My heart beats faster even now at the thought of it.

"Aaaand, that's my cue to leave," Isaiah says. He grabs another Gatorade from the refrigerator and a massive bag of chips from the cupboard, then swivels around and promptly exits the kitchen. It's clear he's terrified of getting dragged into the conversation that's about to happen, which he should be – it's girl talk.

A few moments of silence pass while Chyna eyeballs me. She wants the gossip, as always, and despite not feeling great, she manages to perk up. "So what happened with Harrison last night then? Spill!"

"We hooked up, but . . ."

"Oh no. Why is there a *but*?"

"I need to end things with him tonight," I tell her. No point tiptoeing around the reality of the situation. It was always going to end at some point. That's the entire definition of a fling – it's temporary, casual. There's no way I can keep seeing someone who wants things to progress. The very idea suffocates me.

Chyna nearly chokes. "What? Already?"

"He invited me on a ski trip," I tell her. "That's pretty serious, right? Like, *girlfriend*-serious."

I run my fingers through the ends of my hair, static making them stick to my skin like weird little magnets. I try real hard to keep my gaze focused on Chyna, but it's difficult when I know she doesn't get it. I always think that Chyna is lucky in life; she's never even so much as experienced the death of a family pet – in fact, her family tree is made up entirely of *living* family members, both close and distant, and the only funeral she's ever attended was the one where I was sat in the front row. She doesn't *know* how awful it is to lose people. My guess is that she takes all of her relationships with the people she loves for granted, but that's not her fault. How could she do otherwise?

"And what's so bad about going on a trip with him?" Her big brown eyes bore into mine, and there it is, that simple innocence and inability to relate to my thoughts on the matter. I don't know how many times I have to tell her that I will *absolutely not* get into a relationship with anyone *ever*, but I can never find the words to convince her. "Harrison is at least one of the nicer guys on the team," she says. "You like being around him, don't you?"

I nearly grab my empty bowl and hurl it at her, mostly because a guy being nice can't ever be enough to change my mind, but I remain calm. Instead, I just laugh. All airy and fake. "Oh, come on. Can you seriously imagine me dating Harrison Boyd?"

Chyna thinks. "Okay, nope. You don't have that much in common."

"He was getting boring anyway." I shrug, sliding down from the counter and pulling at the hem of Chyna's camp T-shirt. "And the fun part is finding someone new," I say, steering the conversation onto safer ground. "Do you suppose Drew Kaminski is single?"

Chyna links her arm around mine and flashes me a sideways grin, her smile dazzling as it lights up her face, making her seem more like herself. "Isn't there only one way to find out?" she says with a laugh, and that's why I love Chyna. She doesn't always agree with my antics, but she doesn't ever judge me for them. We're young. We have our whole lives ahead of us. We're free to do as we please. We make our own decisions, and just because we're friends doesn't mean our choices have to be the same.

"Hold on," Chyna says, tugging me toward the refrigerator. She ransacks it, filling her arms with a variety of food, from cheese to cooked chicken. "I need to eat before I die of starvation."

For the past two years, I have grown to hate walking through the front door of my own house. It doesn't feel like a home anymore. It doesn't have that sense of warmth and security it had when Mom was alive. She used to always have candles lit around the house every evening in the fall and winter, and every room would smell of spiced cinnamon. You could always hear her singing too – while she did yoga, while she cooked dinner, while she dabbled in sketching. Without her, our home has no ambience. It's why I prefer to spend the night elsewhere whenever I can, absorbing the easy love of someone else's family. It's not just that, though. If I come back here I'm instantly locked in a battle with the awkward silences that are waiting in every corner of this house. And even if I don't come back, there's still a silence. I want Dad to wonder where I am for *once*. I want him to worry about me. To ask me where I've been and who with. Instead, he never seems to bat an eyelid.

I wave goodbye to Chyna from my porch as she drives off after giving me a ride home. I'm still wearing her clothes while holding a grocery bag full of my own from last night. My hair is matted. I haven't showered. I look like absolute trash, but it's not like our neighbors haven't seen me returning home like this on a Sunday morning before. Mrs. Khan, the old lady who lives on her own next door, scrunches up her face and resumes watering her plants when she catches my eye, so I don't even give her a smile. Instead I grit my teeth and push open my front door. The house is silent and reeks of stale smoke. But that's nothing new these days.

I head for the kitchen and find Dad huddled over our old dining table, surrounded by travel guides and scraps of paper and a pack of cigarettes. He's engrossed in something on his laptop, the glare of the screen reflecting off his glasses.

"Vanessa," he says without glancing up. He motions

for me to join him, but I don't budge an inch. "Come and check out these pictures. The Cliffs of Moher. Aren't they amazing?" He leans in even closer to the screen.

But I've seen it all before. He doesn't really want my opinion on the Cliffs of Moher or any other of the Emerald Isle's natural wonders. "I'm home, Dad," I announce, loud and clear so there's no doubt he's heard me. But he doesn't even blink, only keeps on clicking away on the laptop. He has yet to look at me. "I stayed out all night. I went to a party and I was drinking," I continue to explain, but in between my words, I'm fighting back a sigh. I know he isn't listening. It's like speaking to a brick wall. "Like, *way* too much," I exaggerate to get a reaction. I could probably tell him I'd committed a felony and it wouldn't even register. I give up on trying to get a reaction out of him and instead wander over to the dining table. "So why exactly are these cliffs so special?"

Dad reaches for a pen and scribbles furiously into a notebook. I flinch at the sight of his fingernails; they're overgrown and yellow with nicotine. It's the same notebook he's been compiling notes in for the past few months, crafting the perfect Irish road trip that he wants us to take next summer. "Oh, your mom would have loved this. The Doolin Cave is only a twenty-minute drive away, so we can do both of those in the same day. Look," he says without answering my question, and turns the laptop toward me. On the screen there're photos of sheer granite cliffs overlooking a clear blue sea as the sun shines down. I doubt it looks like that in real life. I mean, sunshine in Ireland? Seriously?

"Sounds great, Dad," I say, but the smile I force upon my face is so unbearably fake. One of these days . . . One of these days he *has* to lose it with me. One of these days he has to freak out when I don't come home at night. One of these days he has to act like my father. And that's when I'll tell him *I'm sorry, Dad, you're right. It worries you when I sneak around behind your back and don't come home. I won't do it anymore.* Except it doesn't worry him at all, and that's the problem. How am I supposed to grow up and take responsibility for myself if I don't have a father to set some boundaries for me?

"Okay, I'll keep organizing it," he tells me, turning the laptop back. He squints at the screen for a few more seconds, and just as I'm about to give up and retreat upstairs, he sits up straight and pushes his hair off his face. "You went to a party?"

Oh, so he *did* hear me. "Yep. It was pretty wild," I say. Inside, I'm practically begging him, *Stop worrying about cliffs and caves and worry about me instead!* I'm desperate for him to ground me. To react. To do something *normal.*

"That's good. I'm glad you're having fun," he says instead, and he gives me a sincere, inane smile before huddling back over that stupid fucking notebook again.

I stare at him in disbelief.

He looks – and smells, *ew* – as though he hasn't showered in days. His hair is an untamed mess that constantly gets in his eyes. He hasn't shaved in a couple weeks either – right now, his stubble is essentially a beard that extends all the way down his throat. And how have I never noticed how skinny he's become? The pounds have been falling off him, and now his faded, tatty-at-the-edges sweatshirt hangs from his gaunt body, drowning him. I can't remember the last time he bought himself some new jeans or went for a haircut.

My dad is so far gone, so lost in his own head that it feels like he never notices me anymore. He doesn't care. I've lost count of how many times I haven't come home over the past year, and even when he has no clue where I've been, it's still not enough for him to come out of his own bleak world and pay me any attention. I clench my jaw, digging my nails into my palm as I storm out of the kitchen and up to my room. I know I'm being dramatic, but I bet he doesn't notice that either.

I rub at my temples as I throw the bag of dirty clothes into my room, my bed still made from yesterday morning. I don't stay, though, because I can hear Justin Bieber's sweet, sweet voice calling out to me from Kennedy's room. I thought the Bieber hype died years ago, but nope, not for Kennedy. I cross the hall and push open the door to her room, strolling straight on in without knocking. We don't need to knock. We're *sisters*. We bathed together until I was, like, eight, so it's not like we need to be shy with each other.

Kennedy is sitting at her dresser, carefully applying a coat of red polish to her nails underneath a small spotlight. Theo, our family tabby cat who adores my sister but despises me for some reason, is curled up asleep on the windowsill. Kennedy stops mouthing along to Justin and glances up. At first, she seems surprised to see me.

25

I groan and throw myself down onto her bed, sprawling out on my stomach and grabbing a pillow to rest my chin on. "If Dad mentions *one* more thing about Ireland to me, I'm moving out. You coming with me?"

Kennedy gives me a small, understanding smile over her shoulder then continues painting her nails. She hasn't bothered to turn down the music yet. "Where did you go last night?" she asks. Her voice is curious, but also doubtful. At least someone around here cares enough to wonder whether or not I was lying dead in a gutter somewhere. Even if it is only my little baby freshman sister. She may only be fourteen, but she's so incredibly wise for her age.

"A party."

"Aaaand?" she urges, dipping the brush back into its pot and swiveling her chair around to face me. "Did you kiss anyone hot?" Her eyes are wide, because she knows the answer already.

"Harrison Boyd. Again." I haven't mentioned Harrison to her directly, but it's not like she doesn't know I've had a thing going with him for the past couple months. Secrets are never really secrets in high school, are they? Gossip travels fast around here.

"Oooo," she squeals, as though she thinks Harrison and I are actually going somewhere. Nope. The only place we're going is onto one another's list of exes.

My phone buzzes in my pocket, and my chest tightens a little when I reach for it and see Harrison's name on my screen. Of course it's him. "Crap, I guess I summoned him."

> Just woke up and you're already on my mind. Last night was fun. Wanna repeat it later? My place. I'll let you know when my parents are asleep.

"Summoned him to say what?" Kennedy asks.

Looking at her eager face, I'm sure she's hoping he's declaring his undying love for me or something. She's been a hopeless romantic since birth, thanks to her obsession with Cinderella when she was a kid, and thinks I'll end up marrying every boy who so much as smiles in my direction.

"He wants to see me tonight," I say. I don't mention the rest. There are some things I can't talk to my little sister about, and what Harrison Boyd and I do behind closed doors is one of them. Nuh-uh.

Her eyes grow wide. "Are you gonna see him then?"

"Yep, but only to end things with him." I type back a reply, my nails cracking too loudly against my screen. It's short and simple:

> Can we just go for a drive instead?

"What?" Kennedy shoots bolt upright in her chair, looking utterly disgusted at my choices. "But he's *so* fucking hot! And if you got together you could fix me up with his brother. And then we could go on double dates. And then we could go on vacations together to the Bahamas." Her gaze wanders off, her mind wrapped up in innocent fantasy.

My phone's still in my hand and I can barely look away,

chewing at my lip while I wait for Harrison's reply. I wonder if he can tell by my message that something's up, that I'm not as keen as I usually am. "Hey. You're right, he totally is hot, but drop the cussing," I tell Kennedy, flashing her a scolding glance. "And you're way too young to be *fixed up* with anyone."

She rolls her eyes and blows on her freshly painted nails. "Okay, Dad."

The irony is that Dad would never give her trouble for casually dropping an F-bomb like that. It's not just that, but it feels like I do all the parenting around here, at least for the past couple of years. I was the one who ran a mile to the store to grab sanitary pads when she first started her period and was a sobbing mess in the bathroom. I was the one who took her on a marathon shopping spree around Target to pick out school supplies ahead of starting high school in the summer. I was the one who held her in my arms when she experienced her first breakup and thought she would never be happy again. I promised her she would be, even though I know we will both forever have a broken heart. And not because of boys.

Mom is gone and Dad may be around physically, but emotionally, he couldn't be more absent if he tried.

Kennedy turns back to her dresser, examining her nails underneath the spotlight, checking for blotches. She doesn't know it, but when Mom died, I made a promise to myself that I would always protect her no matter what. It's a lonely place to be, because I'm now the only one who can.

My phone buzzes again.

I like your thinking . . . Pick you up at nine.

"I'm going out, Dad."

Dad glances briefly over his shoulder. He's standing in the kitchen, laptop open and a pot of ramen noodles boiling in front of him. His gaze is so empty, a deserted wasteland every time he looks at me. "Do you want dinner?"

"I already ate," I say with a shrug. Guess he didn't notice the microwave spaghetti and meatballs I was scarfing down an hour ago a mere fifteen feet away from him. I can't cook to save my life – and no one in this house is going to fix that anytime soon – but at least I keep myself and Kennedy fed with microwave meals, which is more than he tends to do. "And so did Kennedy."

"Oh. You guys did? Okay." He turns back to the pot and keeps on stirring in silence. His voice used to be so vibrant and booming with joy that it would piss me off if he spoke for too long. Now I would give anything to hear him talk for hours on end the way he used to about the thrill of a big drugs bust at work, or his dream of owning a Porsche 911, or how he'd beaten his friends at poker again.

I hover for such a long moment that it hurts. This waiting for something, *anything* is agonizing. Why can't he just give me a firm warning not to stay out too late? Even just a reminder that I have school in the morning? But I get nothing. *Nothing*.

And I have been used to *nothing* for so long, but it still hurts every time I find myself faced with it.

So, I don't say anything more either. I grab my keys, slip my feet into a battered pair of Converse by the door, and head outside. It's just after nine, and of course, Harrison is bang on time. His truck is parked outside, its engine purring and its headlights illuminating the street. I bet he can't wait to see me, which makes this suck even more. But it's not like I haven't done this before. Breaking boys' hearts has almost become standard.

I have to protect myself, but I've even made it more bearable for him. No makeup, so my eyes are sunken and tired. My hair thrown back into a ponytail with too many loose strands to count. An old hoodie with a hole in the sleeve that's three sizes too big for me. My worst-fitting jeans. Not a single spritz of perfume. I figure it'll hurt him less if I look like crap.

My steps are lethargic as I trail across the lawn and pull open the door of his truck. I yank myself up into the passenger seat, then look over. God, Kennedy is so right: he *is* gorgeous. Like, Greek-god gorgeous. A groan rises in my throat, but I fight hard to suppress it. *Why* couldn't he have been happy with just hooking up and nothing more? Now I have to turn down those bright blue eyes, chest made of stone, and sandy blond hair.

"I like this carefree vibe you've got going on," Harrison

says, his eyes sweeping over me, taking in my newfound style. I dress casual at school, but I never dress *scruffy*. "Makes you look young. It's cute."

"What?" I'm literally trying to be the exact opposite of desirable right now. I sit up straight in my seat and angle my body to face him, narrowing my eyes. I wonder if he can tell by the abrupt tone of my voice that I'm not here to fool around. "And you seriously think I look cute without eyelashes?"

Harrison pouts, disappointed by my attitude. "You're no fun tonight. I'll fix that."

Obviously, he doesn't notice that I'm not in the mood for fooling around. Doesn't notice that I haven't flashed him my coy smile yet. Doesn't notice that I haven't instantly placed my hand on his upper thigh. "Heritage Park should be a nice spot to park up," he says as he begins to drive.

Great. Heritage Park, Westerville's prime hookup spot on the edge of town where half the school hangs out on weekends in the backseat of their moms' cars. At least Harrison's truck is his own. But what does it matter? There will be absolutely *no* action for us tonight, that's for sure. Not because I don't want to, but because I'm determined not to give Harrison false hope that there could ever be anything more between us than late night kisses.

"Harrison . . ." I say, but he doesn't hear me because he's already turned up the music. He places his hand on my knee, his grip firm, and I stare at the grazes on his knuckles while he drives. Somehow I can't resist placing my hand atop his, intertwining our fingers. My other hand is in my hair, massaging my head as I think. Could it hurt to kiss him one more time? I told myself last night was it, never again, but . . .

God, I hate myself for even getting into these situations in the first place.

"So . . . Did you enjoy the party last night?" Harrison asks after we've driven in silence for a while. We don't talk, not really, and if we do it's only ever to flirt. I don't know much about him, just that he's Harrison Boyd, that he's on the football team, that we've shared classes over the years, and he must be smart because I've never once seen him fail a test. We don't talk about anything important. I don't actually *know* him. He doesn't know much about me either.

I'm still staring at my hand on his, trying my hardest not to flirt, not to deliberately turn him on even now. "Yeah. Did you?"

"Yeah."

More awkward silence. It's like we're trying to pass time until we're able to get our hands on each other, because we don't know how to interact when we're stone-cold sober and not making out. It makes me question why Harrison would even invite me on that ski trip with him. What would we even talk about? How cold the snow is?

Out of habit, I lift his hand and kiss those grazes on his knuckles. I know I shouldn't be leading him on, but I'm going to miss this. I'm trying to appreciate it while I still can. Harrison drives with one hand on the wheel, the other interlocked with mine, letting me kiss my way down his bare arm. He glances at me out of the corner of his eye every once in a while, his gaze growing more and more heated.

We make it to Heritage Park and follow the quiet road up through the trees to the secluded parking lot, and there's only one other car parked in the distance. Lights off. Shadows moving inside. I look away, back to Harrison as he rolls the truck to a slow halt, tires crunching against the gravel. I know I should tell him right now, before things go too far, but when his smoldering eyes meet mine, I can't resist.

I drop his hand and reach out for him, pressing my lips to his. In another world, one where I didn't believe that all relationships were doomed from the get-go and where I wasn't so terrified of losing the person I loved, perhaps I'd be more open to getting to know Harrison better. Maybe I'd even be excited about the idea of heading off on a ski trip together.

Harrison might not know much about me, but he knows how to do everything right. His fingers are tangled in my hair, teasing more strands loose from my ponytail, and he's tugging at my waist, desperate to bring me closer.

We've never hooked up in his truck before, and I feel awkward and clumsy as I climb over the center console and onto his lap. How do people do this? I'm locked between his chest and the steering wheel and I'm wondering how the hell the logistics of this can even work when I remind myself that, no, I'm not doing that. There's no seduction here. I am *not* hooking up with Harrison tonight.

"Harrison, listen," I say, breathless between our kisses. I hold his jaw, keeping his mouth away from mine so he can't shut me up with his lips.

His hands are already winding their way under my hoodie, caressing my chest. He can't fight that sexy little smirk that always makes an appearance whenever we start touching each other, and he manages to bury his face into my neck, his breath hot against my skin as he leaves a trail of kisses behind.

"Harrison," I try again, but it's more like a groan. I tilt my head back, giving him more access, closing my eyes. His mouth feels so good, his hands feel so good . . .

No. I need to stop this.

Abruptly, I push him away until he's facing me. His lips are parted, his eyes glistening. "Listen to me," I say, and then I let it all spill: "We can't get together anymore. It's over. We're done."

The warmth of Harrison's hands disappears from my body and the truck goes silent. All I can hear is his heart thumping, or maybe it's mine. He blinks at me as though he can't quite process what I've just told him. "What are you talking about?"

"I'm sorry," I say, and it's true: I am. "But I can't . . . I don't want to . . . date you."

He writhes beneath me, shoving me roughly off his lap, like I'm a parasite clinging to his body. When I slide back into the passenger seat, he grips the steering wheel, his jaw clenched.

"Is this about the ski trip?" His voice is seething, dripping with a bitter humor that I can't make sense of. "Because I wasn't asking you on that trip as a *date*, Vanessa," he snorts, like it's the most absurd thing in the world. "I only wanted you to come on that trip so we could hook up. As if I'd want to date you either."

Oh.

So he didn't want our fling to be anything more than it was . . . *Why* did I read more into that ski trip idea? We could have continued exactly as we already were, but now I've made the whole thing beyond awkward. I fold my arms across my chest and sit back in the seat, trying to process this. I feel so stupid.

"And even if I *did* want to date you . . ." Harrison continues, sitting forward to glare at me. "How come you get to just jump into my truck, kiss me like that, then tell me it's over? Seriously, Vanessa?" He's angry now. His eyes have lost all their sparkle, and suddenly he's no longer that sexy, confident football player who I thought was so cool until approximately four seconds ago. "If that's how easy you think it is to drop me, then there's no way I'm signing up for this."

"Harrison, chill out," I say, keeping my cool despite how massively uncomfortable he's making me. I can't look at him straight in the eye. "I misinterpreted something. It happens. Now can we just get back to doing what we're good at?"

"Nah, screw you, Vanessa. Get the fuck out." He points, nostrils flaring, and I hear the click of the doors unlocking.

My eyes widen with shock and I glance outside. That car from before is still parked, but there's no one else around. It's dark, it's late, and I'm miles from home. I look back at Harrison, my brows drawn together. "What? You're kicking me out of your truck?"

"You seriously think I'm giving you a ride home? After you want to mess me around? No way. Like you said, we're done, *babes*," he barks with laughter, shaking his head as he starts up the engine again.

I look down at my fists clenched in my lap. How is he throwing this back in my face? "And what exactly are you going to do without me to keep you company?" I challenge, angry now too.

"What – you think you're the only girl I've got on speed dial?" he mutters under his breath, but I know he wants me to hear it, and of course I do.

That's what gets me out of the truck. I throw open the door, but not before I grab a handful of fast food wrappers from the glovebox and throw them at Harrison. *Dick.* I've barely slammed the door shut again before he speeds off, wheels screeching on the gravel. I grab a fistful of rocks and hurl them at his stupid goddamn truck before it can disappear, but once his taillights have faded away, I heave a sigh into the darkness. I really didn't expect Harrison to explode on me like that.

I sit down on the gravel and watch the lone car that remains here. Pretty sure it's shaking in a very obvious rhythm. Pretty sure I look like a pervert. I call Chyna, because I know by now not to rely on Dad to be my savior, but she doesn't answer. I try her a second time but to no avail, and I realize I have no other options. Sometimes I wish Kennedy was the older Murphy sibling so that she could rescue me at times like this, but no, she can't freakin' drive yet.

Ughhh.

Nice one, Harrison. Abandoning me in the middle of nowhere. Now I feel really stupid for even agreeing to see him tonight.

I bury my head in my hands and massage my fingers into my hair. I'm deep into the park and it's at least a mile walk to the exit, which I'm not psyched to do on my own. It's too secluded, whereas at least here in the parking lot, I have company. I steal a peek at the car again, wondering if I can ask them for help, but then the buzzing of my phone grabs my focus. I've never felt so relieved to see Chyna's name flashing on my screen.

And with no questions asked, she promises to be here within fifteen minutes.

She turns up within ten, and when I climb into her car and am faced with her eyebrows raised expectantly, all I say is:

"Fuck Harrison Boyd, man."

3

"I heard someone smashed some super sentimental vase and her parents flipped," Chyna muses on the drive to school, subconsciously moving her hands as she speaks. A bad habit of hers, one that nearly kills us every morning because her hands never seem to actually be on the steering wheel. "What if her parents get home from their trip and ban her from throwing another party? Imagine that. No more Madison Romy parties. A Westerville tragedy." She places a hand on her chest, in a parody of mourning, and I reach over and grab the wheel, jerking the car to one side to avoid us knocking down a streetlight.

"You know what would be an even bigger tragedy? Us dying when we we're T-boned by a truck because you flew through a stop sign," I deadpan. I have my own license, but I haven't yet bought a decent car and I refuse to drive Dad's old clunker to school. Mom once named it "The Green McRusty." Because, you know, it's verdant green and a total rust-bucket. The name has stuck ever since.

"Oops," Chyna says, blushing. She grips the steering wheel a little tighter. "Do you think Harrison will talk to you?"

"Nope. Probably just shoot me death glares across the Biology lab." I shrug and pick at my nails. One of my acrylics is barely hanging on. "I'm already over him, though."

I guess it'll be awkward at first when I see him again, but the school is big enough that I can avoid him if necessary. Enough different hallways to take alternative routes. Only one class together today. Totally bearable.

We pull into the school parking lot and straight into an empty spot, diagonally and mere inches from the car next to us. I don't even point it out, just grab my backpack and squeeze out the car without dinging anyone's paintwork. When we return at the end of the day, there'll be a "Learn how to park, sucker!" note stuck under the wiper just like there always is.

"I gotta run. I have a meeting with Mrs. Moore before class. She's helping me finalize my college application," Chyna says. "I'll catch you later." She retreats, binder tucked under her arm, and blows me a kiss. I catch it and tuck it into the pocket of my jeans, then she turns and dashes off across the courtyard.

My first class is at the opposite end of the building, so I head for the south entrance. It's a low sun, crisp air kind of morning. I love it. The winter, the cold. The summer was unbearable, but balance in Ohio is always restored when our extreme humidity is switched for bouts of snow. The first snowflakes have yet to fall, but soon our streets will be glistening white, coated in a thick, icy blanket, and the thought of it makes me feel warm and fuzzy inside. Truly ironic.

I walk with my head down, my eyes on my phone, refreshing

my social media for what feels like the thousandth time this morning. Harrison hasn't made any attempt to contact me after kicking me out of his truck last night, which means that we are finally done. I exhale in relief.

I glance up from my screen only because I nearly collide into Ryan Malone, the appointed creep of our senior class, because, well, he is. In sophomore year he was suspended for repeatedly barging into the girls' locker rooms "by accident."

"Hey, Vanessa," he says, and I stop dead in my tracks because Ryan Malone has never once dared to open his mouth and say a single word to me before. I look over my shoulder at him and his chapped lips twist into a pervy smirk that immediately puts me on edge. Why the hell is he talking to me? "I just wanted to let you know that . . . That I think you look great. Really hot." *What?* It's definitely not an innocent compliment; his tone is sickening.

"Gross, Malone. Fuck off." Scrunching up my features in disgust, I pull my jacket around me, trying to cover up before he can get an eyeful. Absolute freak.

I leave Malone behind, my strides wide and too fast because I don't want to be anywhere near him, and I only slow down again when I'm inside the building and making for my locker. There's a few minutes until first period, so everyone is milling around in the hallways, a constant buzz of voices as everyone talks about the killer weekend they just had. My guess is that Madison Romy's party is the hot topic. Half the senior class was there, and those Westerville Central football players turning up and kicking off a brawl definitely makes for some serious gossip.

But I notice something is off. As I squeeze my way through bodies, I can feel it. The pressure of a thousand eyes on me. I keep my head down, trying my best to ignore it, pretending I'm imagining it.

But no, I'm seriously not.

I slow down, lifting my gaze to look around. Even so, it's not immediately obvious. People are moving around, pushing past me, groups of friends leaning against lockers lost in their own conversations. But I still catch the quick glances. The subtle sniggers. The one group of junior guys that busts out into laughter as they all turn to look at me. What the hell?

I give myself a quick once over just in case I've been walking around with my bra on show or the zipper of my jeans open – at least that would explain Malone's weird remark – but nope, nothing. Did news spread that Harrison and I are done? That he kicked me out of his truck and left me behind at Heritage Park? Sure, it's gossip, but it's not *that* big of a deal. It's not like we were actually dating, and I didn't think people cared *that* much about Harrison and me.

I keep my head down and continue along the hallway to my locker. My heart is beating faster than usual as I fumble with my combination. I taped a mirror to the back of my locker door in freshman year, and it's always been a lifesaver. I scan my appearance once more, but my hair is fine, my makeup is fine, my clothes are definitely fine, everything is *fine*. So why the hell is everyone looking at me so weird? And now that I think about it, why have I walked the entire length of this hallway without anyone talking to me?

"Looked like you had fun at Maddie's party," a deep voice says from behind.

I spin around so fast my elbow clunks against the metal lockers and I find myself face to face with Anthony. Noah is by his side, a few other guys from the team huddled in close behind them, pretty much trapping me against the lockers. It's suffocating, but I'm not surprised. They're Harrison's friends. They're going to taunt me the same way they did when I first cooled things down with Noah. That's what guys do – it's that dumb pack mentality they have.

"Um, yeah, I did actually," I say, and they all snicker, their laughter ringing hollow in my ears. My eyebrows furrow as I watch them exchange knowing looks, rolling their eyes and generally behaving like the dicks they are. I'm not sure what's so funny.

"How come you never once gave *me* a striptease?" Noah asks, leaning in close as he juts out his lower lip like a kid feeling left out. He places a hand on my hip, and the smile he gives me is gross. "I would have been cool with that, you know." Anthony and the guys cackle, their laughter howling down the hallway so loudly that it echoes.

I grit my teeth and shove Noah's hand off me. Fucking Harrison telling all his friends about our business. It's not like I don't know guys talk about this stuff. Hell, I do the same with Chyna, but still. The thought of half the football team knowing what gets me off makes my stomach churn.

Slamming my locker shut, I push my way around Anthony's bulky frame and walk away from them, my pace quick. My heart is thumping too hard in my chest. I'm freaked out.

"Oh, come back, Vanessa!" Noah calls after me. I know most of the people in this hallway are listening at this point, and my cheeks are scorching red with heat. "Anthony wants his turn on the Murphy-Go-Round! He's heard it's a great ride."

Assholes. I hate what they're insinuating. Sure, I like to fool around, but what's so wrong with that – besides inevitably dumping any guy who ends up asking for more from me? It's fun. I can take my pick of the hot guys. I like the excitement. The guys act as if I have a list with a hundred different names on it, when the reality is there's only a few. I'm pretty sure Noah has hooked up with too many girls in this school to count, including me, so to hell with him and his double standards. Those standards aren't mine, but I've learned to accept that they're just the way things are. I make sure the remarks I get every once in a while don't bother me anymore.

But they bother me today.

As I push my way down the hall, I hear that stupid word: *Slut*.

I don't catch who says it. Some girl, but I don't even try to pinpoint who the voice belongs to. My mind is in a whirl. Something's going on. Something bad. I can *feel* it in the air. An odd sense of me versus the world, like everyone in this goddamn school is against me. I feel powerless, exposed; my skin is as thin as tissue. What's worse is, it's usually the exact opposite. I don't know where this feeling has come from, but suddenly I want to curl into a ball, making myself as small as I can be, and hide.

I have my fair share of people who aren't exactly my best friends, but it's never felt as pronounced as it does right now. Most people like me, and I like most people. That's why I have a big circle of people I can hang out with and be part of. Or at least I thought I did. Right now, the usual distinct line between friend and enemy is a total blur. The circle is closed. Everyone feels like an enemy.

I round the corner and nearly collide with Chyna. My chest sinks with relief at the sight of her. Walking through these hallways alone right now is too much to handle, and I'm pretty sure it's because Harrison has been running his mouth. Maybe Chyna will know what he's been telling people about me.

"Oh, thank God. I've been looking everywhere for you," she says, the words rolling off her tongue at lightning speed. Her eyes are wide, panicked. "I've just tried calling you like a million times!" She grabs my arm and pulls me into the girls' bathroom at the same moment the bell for first period rings out. The few girls who are in the bathroom make a swift exit, but Chyna and I don't budge from our spot in front of the sinks.

"Shouldn't you be at your meeting?" I ask once we're alone. I can hear the rumble of commotion out in the hallways as everyone rushes to their classes. At this point, I've already accepted the fact that I'll be late for Bio.

Chyna doesn't answer. Instead, she grabs my shoulders and stares straight into my eyes, her expression almost wild with concern.

What the hell's going on?

"Do you want to skip classes? I'll ditch with you. Let's get out of Westerville. We'll head into Columbus and ..." She pauses to shake her head. "Or let's hit up Cleveland. Anywhere that's not here. Sound good?"

"Chyna, slow down," I say. I'm confused. Is she upset about something? Why is she so desperate to leave? "Why do you want to skip class?"

Chyna's face floods with horror. "Oh my God." She drops her hands from my shoulders and her body seems to deflate. Her voice is almost a whisper as she says, "You haven't seen it yet."

"Seen what?" My heart rockets back and forth in my chest while my words feel like sandpaper in my throat. An immense feeling of dread slices through me as pieces of this morning's puzzle start to slot together. "Chyna? What haven't I seen yet?"

"Shit," Chyna groans, collapsing back against a sink. She presses her hands to her face so that she doesn't have to look at me. "I thought you'd be the first person it got sent to ... I'm sorry. I really don't want to show you this, but ..." She straightens up from the sink and pulls out her phone, scrolling for a few seconds before she hands it over to me. "I'm sorry," she says again. "I'll slash Harrison's truck tires for you."

I stare at Chyna for a moment, her phone in my hands. I have no idea what I'm about to see, but a wave of sickness is building in the pit of my stomach and my hands are trembling. My heart feels as though it's been squeezed to a pulp.

It's a video.

I swallow and tap the screen, pressing play, and all the air is sucked straight out of my lungs.

It's a video of *me*.

A video of me at Maddie Romy's party on Saturday. It feels as though I've been sucker-punched right in the gut.

In the video, I'm upstairs in that bedroom, sitting on Harrison Boyd's lap. I smile at the camera, straight into the lens like a total sucker.

I feel the color drain from my face as the scene unfolds in front of me. I'm staring at Vanessa Murphy as though she's some stranger. She climbs off Harrison's lap and gets to her feet. She dances to the low background music, her hands in her hair, as she slowly peels off her clothes. The video loses focus as she slinks her way back to Harrison.

"You don't want to watch the rest," Chyna says, snatching her phone back. I'm relieved. She's right: I *don't* want to watch the rest. I already know what happened that night. "Trust me," she adds. "It doesn't last much longer, and you can't really see much, but—"

My mind goes dark with fury. "He fucking leaked a video of me *stripping*?" I nearly tear the damn sink off the wall, and I slam my hand down against the smudged and cracked mirror above it. Just how long was Harrison recording for? My body ignites with so much rage that I'm convinced I'm about to burst into flames right here in this bathroom. Heat radiates from my core like an erupting volcano.

How could Harrison do this to me? Is he seriously that pissed about me ending things that he's set on ruining my life? I know how these things go. They do ruin your life.

When Kristen Rogers's nude selfies were leaked around school a few months ago, it was all anyone talked about for days. Me included. Because if it's not you in the firing line then these kinds of things are easy entertainment . . . People might gossip about my sex life, but I've never been that unfortunate girl who's texted private photos to the wrong guy. I used to roll my eyes at how stupid those girls were, but now . . . now I'm one of them, and it's definitely not funny. It's horrifying.

It's clear now why everyone was acting so weird out in the hallway. It's because they all *know*. They've all seen it; I can guarantee that. Stuff like this spreads like wildfire. And all around Westerville, and probably all over Ohio too. Maybe even further, but I make my brain shut down at that.

"Chynaaaa," I wail, throwing my hands back into my hair. I blow out fast breaths of air, trying to calm myself down from the sheer dread coursing through me. There's nothing she can say to fix any of this. The video is out there. I need to find a way to hold my head up high as I walk out of this bathroom while knowing that every damn student in this school has now seen my naked body.

But that's nowhere near the worst part.

The worst part is that Harrison has absolutely no right to share such an intimate video, and yet he *has* shared it. All around school. To my closest friends. To people who barely even know me. To *everyone*. Whatever trust we had between us has been shattered into a million pieces. I didn't want a relationship with him, but that doesn't mean I didn't care about him. But he clearly doesn't care about me, and if he could do something like this, then he must have *never ever* cared about me at all, not even from the beginning. Because if he had a single shred of respect for me, then he would never share what we both knew were private moments.

It's the worst betrayal possible.

My palms are clammy as I run them over my jeans, blinking down at a dirty patch on the floor. My breaths are labored and rapid, my heart is palpitating and suddenly I feel lightheaded, the entire room blurring around me. Am I actually going into cardiac arrest?

Chyna puts a hand on my shoulder to steady me. "He's such an asshole," she says, putting her phone away. She gives me a small, sympathetic smile. "But for the record, I think you look hot as hell in the video."

It's beyond inappropriate, but I love her for it. This is why we're best friends. No judgment. Ever.

My mouth mirrors hers, though inside I feel like I'm crumbling. It takes all of my energy not to faint on the bathroom floor. "If there's anything worse than having your sex tape leaked, surely it's having a *bad* sex tape leaked. So hey, it could be worse, right?" I say, trying my hardest to display a cool exterior, but inside I am rocked by the shock. I don't believe my own words – this is as bad as it gets.

My eyes are damp with tears that threaten to fall, but I'm fighting to hold myself together. I'm flooded with so many different emotions, but the only one I can focus on is fury. I'm going to hunt Harrison down, I think, realizing I know exactly where he is. "He's in my Bio class," I blurt, and before

Chyna can speak, I'm bursting through the bathroom door and into the empty hallways.

That feeling of betrayal is pulsing through me, fueling my steps.

It's always alright for the guy, I think as I race down the hall. Sure, Harrison is in the video too, but no one cares about him. No, they're all judging me. Judging me for hooking up with him at that party. Judging me for being easy. Not like they didn't already think that, anyway. But now they have proof. They have something to use against me. Something they can use to break Vanessa Murphy, which I'm sure is what a lot of people have been waiting for all these years. I'm perfectly aware that the girls in this school, even the ones I'm friends with, secretly judge me for the attention I get from guys. I've never dwelled on it too much, but I guess it's because of their own insecurities, their jealousies and fears. Who knows? I don't want to hurt anyone, but I'm not playing those games. And the guys . . . well, some of them don't like the fact that I would never look twice in their direction, while others don't like the fact that I've ended the flings I've had with them. I've always got what I want, and that's rubbed people up the wrong way. Now it's payback – for them at least. Now they can gang up against me, glad it's time for things to not go my way.

I'm walking faster and faster. I need to have this out with him.

"Vans, wait!" Chyna calls after me, her worried voice echoing down the deserted hallway. But I don't want to wait. I want to get my hands on Harrison, and I don't care what the consequences are for assaulting someone on school property.

Mr. Lee's classroom is in sight. My rage is burning, adrenaline surges through my veins. I push open the door to a sea of faces that all swivel toward me, but I'm only searching for one.

"How nice of you to finally join us, Miss Murphy," Mr. Lee drawls from his desk. "Please take your seat while I fill out your detention form."

I don't listen to him. I lock my eyes on Harrison instead – slumped at his desk in the back corner of the room, slowly straightening up as he sees me. He drops his hand from his face and exchanges a glance with Anthony who's sitting next to him, his features flashing with panic. I bet he expected me to be crying in a bathroom stall or something. And, to be fair, I just was. I bet that's exactly what he wants – for me to be too ashamed, too mortified to show my face again.

"C'mon, give us a show!" Anthony calls out, shaking his chest at me, then grins as my classmates release a hushed symphony of laughter that dances around the room.

With my hands balled into fists by my side, I march across the room, weaving my way around desks and ignoring all of the other murmured remarks. My fiery glare is still set solely on Harrison, and his face turns pale as I near him.

"Vaness—" he tries, but the whip of my hand against his cheek cuts him off.

"I've spoken with Principal Stone. You're *very* lucky that you aren't getting suspended right now," my school counselor, Mrs. Delaney, informs me as she walks back into her cramped office.

"So you can't be suspended for self-defense. Good to know."

"Vanessa, let's not joke about this," she says, firing me a stern look as she sinks down into her chair opposite. I look at her graying hair and then down at her bright red Crocs. She's too old to be a high school counselor, really. What does she know about teenagers? She doesn't get our humor, that's for sure. "Why exactly did you raise a hand to Harrison Boyd? Is there something the school should know about?"

"Because he's a douchebag," I say, flippantly waving her away. I don't like the soft, concerned tone of her voice. This isn't some therapy appointment. "Can I go now? I accept that I shouldn't have hit him, so just give me the detention form or whatever and I'll get out of here."

Mrs. Delaney just stares at me. "Vanessa," she says with a small shake of her head. She almost looks hurt by my lack of participation, but I refuse to confide in my school counselor about the hell that my life has suddenly become. "You hit a fellow student. Why? Did Harrison provoke you?"

I nearly laugh in her face, but I think better of it and keep my features under control. "Seriously, it's just personal drama," I say, growing frustrated. The last thing I want to do is discuss the fallout from a leaked sex tape with a woman who could be my grandmother. I just want to get out of this stuffy office. I rise to my feet, prepared to leave. "We shouldn't deal with our issues on school property. I get it. Please can I just have the detention form?"

Mrs. Delaney reluctantly signs me up for two weeks of after-school detention, and I almost have to pry the damn form out of her fingers before she allows me to leave. I head out of her room and into the main office. It's quiet, the majority of the desks empty, the doors to most private offices closed. Must be a busy morning at Westerville North.

I heave a sigh and glance down at my hands to examine the damage. I lost two nails slapping Harrison, and another in Mrs. Delaney's office from digging my fingers into my palms so hard, but scheduling an appointment with my nail tech is the last thing on my mind right now. All I can think about is how *embarrassed* I feel. I'm not going to classes today. It's all so fresh, the drama and the gossip. Hell, if it was any other girl in that video, I'd be talking about it too. Scrutinizing her. Mocking her. So, I'm skipping the rest of the day. Chyna is already waiting outside in the parking lot for me, and although we're not going to run off to Cleveland, we *are* going to go get ice cream from our favorite ice cream shop uptown.

"Aren't you the girl from that video?" a voice says, cutting through the silence, and I stop in my tracks in the middle of the office. I look over at the row of chairs against the wall, only to find a guy slouched back in one with his hands hanging between his legs. Totally nonchalant, totally couldn't care less. I don't recognize him as one of my fellow students.

"Yep, that's me," I say. Better to own it, I decide. Less awkward than trying to deny it. "No, I won't give you a private show."

"I hear it's been kicking up a storm." The boy studies me curiously as he sits up, his interest piqued. "But I wasn't going to ask. Trust me, you're not my type."

"Ah, I get it," I say, as I flash him a knowing grin. I may as well play the part. "You like the sweet innocent type, right? Not trash like me."

"Actually, I just prefer blondes."

My eyes close shut and a groan rumbles in my throat. I run my hands back through my hair as I take a couple of slow breaths. "Sorry. It's been a rough morning," I admit. "I don't mean to take it out on everyone else."

"I bet," he says. "Can I ask you something?"

"No, the sex wasn't worth it."

He smiles again and waits for a beat, almost like he's trying not to let himself laugh out loud. "Actually, I was going to ask if you spill people's drinks often."

I stare at this stranger while my mind catches up. Everything is lagging – my thoughts are dominated by Harrison and that video and the fear that I may still pass out – but suddenly the boy comes into focus and I realize I know *exactly* who he is.

He was at Maddie's party on Saturday when he turned up

uninvited with the rest of the Westerville Central football team . . . and I collided into him. I *did* spill his drink on his jeans, and he told me to watch out, and then he had that stupid brawl with Harrison.

I may be stone-cold sober right now, but the thoughts that cross my mind are similar to those when I was buzzed that night. It's like I'm seeing him for the first time all over again. I go quiet for a few seconds while I assess him, his presence that's working wonders at distracting me from the ball of shame thrumming painfully in my chest.

The curls of his hair, the warm bronze of his skin, the stark blue of his eyes . . . I focus on the slit in his eyebrow again, so I don't find myself staring at his ridiculously perfect lips.

"Yeah . . . I'm sorry about that," I eventually muster, my voice sounding much more like my own now. "What are you doing here?" I ask, glancing around the Westerville North main office as though to remind him that he doesn't attend this school.

"Just transferred from Central. It's my first day," he says, lips curving into a smile that reveals his immaculate teeth. My heart is still pumping fast, but it feels like it's for a different reason now. "I was just curious about something," he goes on. "It's Harrison Boyd in that video, right? He leaked it?"

"Yeah, and he can go to hell for all I care."

"If it makes you feel any better, you're not the only person he's screwed over." The guy stands and takes a step closer to me, and I rack my brain for his name. I remember Harrison telling me it . . . but my memory is hazy. I'm quiet as I wait, staring up at him. He towers over me, suddenly all ominous and mysterious. "I've got a lot of things to say about that guy, and they aren't nice."

I have no idea what he's talking about. "Do you have some weird football rivalry with him?" I ask, lamely.

"It's more personal than that," he says, his tone ambiguous. His eyes darken as he looks down at the floor, the smile wiped from his face, his jaw clenched tight.

I'm not exactly sure why this guy is talking to me right now, let alone telling me about his beef with Harrison, but I'm strangely glad to see him again. I figured he would just be one of those gorgeous guys you encounter once and then never cross paths with again, but here he is – standing in *my* school office, telling me that he hates Harrison Boyd too.

"Are you going to elaborate?" I ask. My skin's tingling, but I'm also trying not to sound like I'm being coy.

"Nope," he says, popping his lips. He glances around the office, but everyone has yet to return to their desks. "Just wanted to let you know that you aren't alone. I know the kind of guy Harrison is, and trust me, I probably despise him more than you do."

This is all pretty mysterious. Harrison can be a macho jock at times, but he's generally well-liked. He's on the school football team, gets good grades and plenty of girls see him as a bit of a sweetheart – oh, how wrong I was about that. But now it seems I'm not the only person Harrison has messed with, because the guy standing in front of me appears to have his own personal grudge against him. I'm not sure why, but it *is* nice to know there's someone else out there who isn't falling for Harrison's Mr. Nice Guy charade.

"I'd so love to mess up his life," I say, deciding that he doesn't deserve to have things easy. "Revenge would be sweet."

The guy tilts his head to one side, and those blue eyes smolder at me. "Revenge," he echoes, and he lets the word hang in the air for a while. He furrows his brows, his gaze never leaving mine. I'm feeling an intense presence around him. "That's not a bad idea, you know."

"I was kidding," I say, though I definitely wasn't.

But he ignores me. "Just think about it for a second. You're pissed at Harrison Boyd; I'm pissed at Harrison Boyd. We really could screw with him," he says, as though he's voicing his thoughts out loud. He looks off into the distance as though the gears in his mind are shifting. "A good old taste of his own medicine. It could be fun. We could help each other."

My pulse begins hammering in my head. Put like that, it's an enticing suggestion. He's right: maybe toying with Harrison *could* be fun, especially if I don't have to do it alone. This morning's been grim and it's not going away anytime soon. Harrison deserves to suffer too.

The guy's gaze finds mine again and all I can do is look blankly back at him. *Goddamn, what is his name?* "I'm not sure we've been properly introduced," I say stiffly, as if we're at a business meeting.

"Well, I know you're Vanessa," he teases me, extending his hand. The smile he gives me is mischievous, a little bit devious, but somehow still entirely charming. "What do you say? Partners?"

I stare at his hand for a moment. This could be interesting. It feels like the final shreds of my dignity were abandoned at Maddie's party, so what is there to lose? I slip my hand into his and he squeezes mine firmly back, his skin smooth and warm, his touch sending a bolt of electricity all the way from the tips of my fingers to the base of my spine. "Partners, I guess."

I hear a door swing open, and Mrs. Delaney's voice bounces around the office. "Kai Washington? Sorry to keep you waiting."

"No problem," he tells her, looking over my shoulder.

My hand is still in his and he grabs it, turns my palm toward him, pulling a Sharpie out from the pocket of his jeans. It tickles as he scrawls his phone number on my skin, and I can't help but stare at the way my hand fits into his. *Kai Washington*, I think, repeating his name in my head.

"Call me," he murmurs, then steps around me and heads off into Mrs. Delaney's office with her.

I stare after him, bewildered. My body tingles as a thrill runs down my spine. There's something enchanting about his calm, cool presence. And I know it should be the opposite – I should know that this guy means trouble and I should run a mile in the opposite direction, but I can't help feeling drawn to him the same way I did at the party.

My eyes drop to my hand and I roll my eyes at what Kai has written there. I pull out my phone and add the number to my contacts.

I save it as: *Kai Washington (Partner)*.

4

"So you meet up with this weirdo from the school office who you know *nothing* about, and he lures you out of town, kills you, then dumps your body in a ditch behind some trees. Which song would you like played at your funeral?"

I glare Chyna down. We should be at school, but instead we're sitting in Rollies eating a second helping of ice cream. We're both on good old chocolate chip. "He's not a weirdo," I say with disapproval. "He's from Central, remember?"

"Oh, even *worse*," Chyna groans, slamming her head down toward the table. I love it when she goes all dramatic on me. It makes me laugh, and I could really use some of her humor today.

"Honestly, he seemed ... intriguing," I say, stifling a laugh as I reach for Chyna's arms and pull her up from the table. I stick my tongue out at her before I scoop up another mouthful of ice cream, and I can't help but replay my interaction with Kai in my head all over again. I have such a damn soft spot for tall pretty boys, especially when they have blue eyes and an exuberance of confidence. *Oomf.*

He's been a welcome distraction in the mess of today. "And he's smoking hot too," I tell her.

Chyna snaps her fingers in front of my face. "So, is this about getting revenge on Harrison, or is this about you meeting a new hot guy?"

"The revenge, for sure," I say. No lie there. Having a hot partner-in-crime just so happens to be a bonus in this mission. I point my spoon at her. "You mentioned slashing the tires of Harrison's truck. I like that idea. I'll keep it in mind."

"Vans . . . Are you sure you want to do this?" Chyna questions, looking worried. She doesn't seem entirely convinced about the morality – or legality – of my plan. She's good like that. Always nice, always sensible. Except for her magpie stationery habits. "Sure, go ahead and get even, but don't get into trouble."

Honestly, what with the ice cream and the encounter with Kai, I'm managing to squeeze thoughts about that video being shared all around town out of my head for a minute or two at a time. Instead I'm focusing on getting my revenge on Harrison and all the possible ways to do it. It's almost thrilling. I'm realizing that it's much easier to channel my energy into payback rather than to let myself be consumed by the hurt and the betrayal, the shame and the embarrassment. "Do you have any other ideas?"

"I don't know about trucks, but I *am* good with computers, so just holler if you need me to do any hacking rather than slashing," Chyna murmurs under her breath, picking at her ice cream as though she's wary of getting involved now that the idea's caught fire in my mind. She glances up. "It's lunch period, you know. Call this hot weirdo. I want to find out what he says."

I glance up at the vintage Hershey's ice cream clock on the wall, watching it tick on for a few seconds. It's only been a couple hours since I met Kai in the office. "Shouldn't I wait until tonight?"

"Call him," Chyna orders, more firmly this time.

I don't put up much of a fight. I'm desperate to know exactly how my arrangement with this guy is going to play out. Like, what's first on our agenda? Is he on board with potentially slashing some truck tires? "Okay. Okay. Calling him." I grab my phone and pull up the number for *Kai Washington (Partner)*, then call it before I can hesitate.

It rings for so long that I think it's going to go to voice-mail, but then someone answers, "No, I don't want to claim your free prize for some contest that I never entered, and no, I'm not prepared to disclose any of my info."

Maybe Chyna's right. Maybe he *is* a weirdo. "Kai? It's Vanessa," I say, but my voice sounds pathetic. I sound ... nervous. Which is crazy. I'm used to calling up guys and making my voice sultry while I flirt, but maybe that's the problem. Maybe I'm not used to talking to a boy under more platonic circumstances.

"Hey, partner," Kai says, and now he's totally unsurprised to hear from me so soon. His voice has a smooth, husky undertone to it that I notice more over the phone than I did when he was standing in front of me. "Should we have code names for each other? I'll be ... Captain Washington for now until I think of something cooler. You?"

Okay, definitely a weirdo. "Um ..."

"Nessie, then," he says without a pause.

"Excuse me?"

"Listen up, Nessie," he continues. "Captain Washington here. We should meet up tonight to discuss our battle plan. My place or yours?"

I blink, taken aback by how forward he is. For all that we are total strangers to one another, Captain Washington sure does move fast. He's calling me nicknames and inviting me over to his house already?

"I hope this isn't just some ploy to get me upstairs with you."

"Again, Nessie, you're not my type," Kai says firmly.

Right. He likes blondes, and I'm the darkest shade of brunette you can get. Chyna is on the edge of her seat across from me, eyes wide, impatiently waiting for my feedback on what Kai's saying, but I quickly shake my head at her. I can feel a smile playing on my lips as I turn to face the window.

"Let's meet somewhere more public," I say. I'm not worried about Kai murdering me or anything. I just don't want to go to a stranger's house, and I certainly don't want to invite him into the unwelcoming, cold house that is mine.

"Okay. Meet me at the library at eight."

"The library?" I snort. I've never once stepped foot inside the library. I stare out the window – I can see the library from here, just across the street. Uptown Westerville is only a small district of the city – most people just head to downtown Columbus instead.

"It's low-key, isn't it? Who do you know that would ever go anywhere near the library at night?" he questions, and I go quiet. "Exactly," he says. "And Operation Harr-assassinate is strictly a secret."

"Operation Harr-assassinate?" Did he seriously just say that? Either way, it makes me laugh. He's taking this way too seriously, but he's being playful about it too. I didn't know plotting to screw with someone's life could be so ... fun. "Okay. Library at eight. Wear all black. Don't forget a dark hoodie and gloves, Captain Washington,"I say, joining in with his charade. Two teenagers hellbent on revenge, conjuring up a secret masterplan from within the silent depths of the Westerville Public Library ... I can roll with this.

"Roger, Nessie. See you at the library," Kai declares. "Captain Washington, over and out."

He hangs up and the line goes dead, but yet I keep the phone pressed to my ear for a while, so lost in a trance that I'm blissfully unaware of the couple of hipster dog-walkers outside the window who think I'm grinning at them.

When I snap out of it and turn back to Chyna, she looks utterly horrified. "Surely I need to get my hearing tested because there's no way in hell you just called that guy *Captain Washington*, right?"

"Sorry, private information," I tease, clamping my lips shut for dramatic effect.

Chyna looks like she might hurl the remaining slop of her ice cream at me, but her attention is diverted when her phone buzzes on the table. She reaches for it and sighs. "My dad," she says. "Time to explain why I haven't been in classes. Don't worry, I'll just say you're going through some guy drama and you needed your best friend for moral support." She answers the call and angles away from me.

I glance down at my own phone, like I'm expecting a call from my dad to come through any second. I should know better. I can't remember the last time my father so much as texted me. A couple weeks ago, maybe, and that was only to ask me to drop by the store for milk. I would do anything for him to call me up right now and yell at me down the line. I would do anything for him to demand to know where I've run off to. To know why I'm stuffing my face with ice cream rather than taking notes in English Lit. And I would do anything for him to ask me if I'm okay, because then maybe I could take a chance and tell him that I'm not.

The Green McRusty isn't in the driveway when I get home later that afternoon. It's a good thing. It means Dad's at work – he quit the intense cop game when we lost Mom and now strolls around Kohl's every day as a Loss Prevention Officer – and not huddled over the dining table adding to his obsession with this dream of a trip to Ireland. I know he's not all there anymore, so I worry about him. The new job doesn't ask anything of him, and I wish he saw his friends more, but I don't think he has any left. It feels like he's cut ties with them. We have a huge extended family, but us Murphys are scattered all over the Midwest, so any visits are few and far between. I figure he's lonely, too wrapped up in his own head to notice, until one day I'm guessing he will glance up and realize he's pushed everyone away. Long gone are the days when he'd take Kennedy and me out for dinner and a movie every Thursday, and the nights where he'd have a poker game going with his friends in our kitchen, and the romantic weekends he'd whisk Mom away on. All of those moments are lost forever.

The house is quiet when I walk through the front door. Kennedy is cross-legged on the couch in the living room, noticeably tense, staring at a paused TV screen.

"Hey," I say as I pass, but I come to a halt when I don't get a reply out of her. I turn back around. "I said hey."

"I know about the video," Kennedy states, her tone blank. She can't bring herself to turn around to look at me, but it's okay because I can't look her in the eye either. "All my friends were talking about it. They were calling you a—"

"I know," I cut in, my heart sinking in my chest. I don't want to hear my sister say it. I can fill in the gaps myself. "But I didn't do anything wrong. That video was supposed to be private between Harrison and me. Did you . . . did you watch it?"

"Only the first few seconds," she says. "I didn't believe them, so I had to check."

A new rage storms up inside of me, a new fury at Harrison for putting my sister through this too. She attends Westerville North – she will hear all the snickering and the gossiping, and I can't think of anything worse than my own sister being humiliated because of *me*. At least she hasn't watched the video. The thought of her watching it . . . I shudder.

"Can you do me a favor?" I ask quietly as I sit down on the arm of the couch, bumping my knee against hers. "Talk to me about it as much as you like, but . . . please don't mention it to Dad."

"Like he'd hear me, anyway," she mumbles, and I stare helplessly down at her still figure.

She knows it too: we're both invisible to him. Talking to Dad is like throwing your words out into an empty void. No matter how raspy your voice gets, no matter how badly your lungs hurt, you can scream for all eternity and never get a response. He's a shell of a man, like his entire heart and soul was ripped out of his chest when Mom took her last breath, leaving nothing in its place.

"Thanks," is all I say, and I squeeze her shoulder in solidarity. A sisterly gesture to remind her that I know exactly how she feels. "And just a heads up, I'm getting Harrison back for this. So, your life lesson for the day is to never let a guy screw with you. And if he does, then you screw with *him*."

I squeeze her shoulder again and, finally, Kennedy looks up at me. "How are you going to do that?" she asks, a curious shine to her gaze.

"Haven't figured out that part," I admit, "but I do have some help from an outside source who seems willing to do whatever it takes."

She groans out loud. "Oh, you're *so* gonna get yourself in trouble."

"Good thing Dad doesn't care then, huh?" I wink, and we both snicker. We've grown all too used to this kind of dark humor. Easier to joke around than admit that what we really want – what we need, now our mom is gone – is for our father to act like one.

"I guess this means I'll never get to date Harrison's brother," she says. "Thanks for that, sis." She heaves a sigh as she resumes watching her TV show and I roll my eyes as I head for the stairs. But not before reminding her to switch off the TV and finish her homework in five.

I feel mentally drained yet energetic at the same time. Mentally drained, because so many different thoughts have been running through my head all day, like what if some of my teachers watch that video? What if someone posts it to some porn site with a billion subscribers? What if it *doesn't* blow over and people are still making snide remarks about it until graduation? What if the video follows me all the way to college, and beyond, where I'll forever be haunted by the fear of someone discovering it? I've heard the stories of heartbreak and lawsuits. I know that these throwaway moments ruin lives.

That's why I'm buzzed on the idea of ruining Harrison's too. He doesn't get to do this to me and come out the other side unscathed. No, he's going to pay, and I can't wait to think of all the wicked, twisted ways to do it. Mess with his truck? His friends? His place on the football team? His family? So many possibilities . . . And I don't care that payback makes me just as bad as he is. I want revenge, and I'll do anything to get it. It's the sweet price he'll pay for such betrayal.

I climb the stairs, but I come to an abrupt halt on the

landing. On the wall in front of me is a photo of Mom when she was a teenager. Young and beautiful, grinning into the camera with her smile that was always too wide and a hand touching the ends of her bouffant of hair, those permed curls hairsprayed into a style that she swore was cool and fashionable back in the 1980s. I look at that picture every day. Every morning when I leave my room, every evening when I come home ... but my heart feels heavier than usual today, too heavy for my mom's fashion fails to make me smile. I know it's because I feel guilty. If she were here, she'd be disappointed.

I think back to sixth grade. The day every parent received a letter home from school reminding them to warn their kids about the dangers of social media. Mom sitting me down in the kitchen. Going over some simple rules with me. Never curse online. Never say anything nasty about any of my peers. Never give out private information. Never take inappropriate pictures of myself ...

I've broken every single one of those rules. How would she feel now if she knew there was a video of me circling around social media and into the far reaches of the internet? How would she handle that shame – both mine and hers – knowing I didn't listen to her advice? That I've betrayed her trust, I've been stupid and reckless, and I haven't lived up to the standards she set for me before she was gone?

I cringe with shame. I regret it now. I knew what Harrison was doing. It's so easy in hindsight to know that I should have told him to put that phone away, to stop recording something so private. But I thought it was sexy. I thought it was intimate. I thought I could trust him.

I wish Mom were here. Even if it meant she would yell the house down at me. Even if it meant she would ground me forever. Even if it meant I would slam my bedroom door in her face.

At least she would care.

At least she would be alive.

5

I grab the car keys and leave the house without saying a word to Dad. Why waste my breath? I leave him in the living room with a cold cup of coffee and a cigarette in hand as he stares at the ceiling. God, I wish he would do *something* to prove that there's still some life left in him. I wish he'd go see his friends, maybe grab a beer with them, because there is nothing worse than feeling *pity* for my own father.

It's approaching nine, and there's a weird, jittery feeling in my stomach at the thought of meeting Kai. I still don't know *exactly* what I'm getting myself into. What is Kai's definition of *revenge*? What if he wants to take things further than I do? What if his operation includes crazy plans to, like, get Harrison kicked out of school? Beaten up? Arrested? I guess I'll find out.

I climb into the Toyota SUV that's older than I am and internally groan as the Green McRusty's antique engine struggles to come to life. I only drive this piece of junk under the cover of nightfall when no one can see that it's me behind the wheel. Talk about social suicide. Although right now, I doubt I have much of a social standing anyway. Dad wants to run this heap into the ground before he considers an upgrade, which is why I have a totally rational fear of the whole bucket of rust exploding into flames while I'm cruising down the highway one day.

I pull out of the drive and head toward Uptown Westerville. I must live in the only suburb in the world that refers to their downtown area as *uptown*. It's like how Westerville Central is actually further north than Westerville North. Westerville is just . . . odd. But it's cruel of me to make fun of Westerville, because I do actually like living here. We're twenty minutes north of downtown Columbus, so city life is right on our doorstep, yet Westerville continues to feel like a quaint town with a certain charm to it. A safe college town with a close-knit community. Which is usually a good thing so as long as you behave. In a tight community like ours, there's no room for mistakes.

When I get uptown, I'm not surprised to find the streets quiet. It's late on a November Monday – too cold and dark for casual strolls down our little main street. It's the kind of downtown area that movie sets are based on. The kind where most of the stores and restaurants are independent, old-fashioned ones that are loved and supported by the community. I can see the ski and outdoor gear shop on the corner of the block, and I grip my steering wheel tighter.

Our library is just across the street from Rollies where I sat with Chyna this morning, shoveling chocolate chip ice cream into my mouth. I've never been here before, so I take a minute to scout out the building as I approach. I pull around back into a parking lot where only a handful of cars sit. Kai was right. The library isn't going to be packed an hour before closing on a Monday night, and anyone who *is* there won't be under the age of twenty-five, most likely. Maybe one of the cars is Kai's? I abandon the Green McRusty across two bays because I'm too lazy to straighten up, then lock up and apprehensively head toward the building in search of the entrance. Do I need a library card to even step foot through the door?

I shove my hands into the pockets of my leather jacket. Black, of course, to match my jeans. Like a gangster, lurking around town late at night. I keep my head down and shuffle past the main desk, but the intense silence in here makes me feel as though there's a giant spotlight shining over my head. There's no librarian at the desk, thank God. There's a woman stacking books onto shelves over in the children's area. A man typing ferociously on one of the computers. A girl browsing the crime section while balancing a tower of paperbacks in her arms.

"*Pssst.*"

I glance over, and I spot Kai peering at me through a gap in the shelves of the self-help section. He glances around as though any of the three other people here are actually paying attention, then waves me over.

Seeing Kai's blue eyes again makes my heart pump a couple beats quicker. I walk over to meet him behind the shelves, and I bite back a smile when I discover his attire. He's wearing a black Nike hoodie, ripped black jeans, and black sneakers. He got my memo. "Excuse me, where are your gloves?" I say, folding my arms across my chest and feigning disappointment.

Kai reaches into the front pouch of his hoodie and pulls out a pair of red football gloves. "Do these count?" When I laugh, he puts them away again and runs a hand along the spines of the books to his left. "Unfortunately, there isn't an idiot's guide on how to exact revenge. We'll have to do the hard work ourselves."

"I have ideas," I say. "I just need your help executing them."

"Well, damn, call me The Executor." He clears his throat, pulls a tiny notepad out of the back pocket of his jeans, then reaches for the pen he has resting behind his ear. It's all very serious. "Let's get started, Nessie."

I have yet to decide if his attitude is entertaining or annoying. It's refreshing, for sure. The guys at Westerville North aren't like this. Maybe it's a Central thing. Maybe they're more laid-back. Maybe they couldn't care less about trying to impress. Or maybe this is just Kai.

I follow him over to some tables in the center of the library floor and he pulls out a chair, straddling it. I sit down next to him, leaving a safe gap of a single empty chair between us. At the end of the day, I don't even know this guy. Personal space is a must.

"Can you stop calling me the name of some mythical Scottish legend?" I say before we get started. I mean, seriously? *Nessie?* When has that *ever* been an acceptable nickname for Vanessa?

Kai sets down the notepad and clicks his pen, arching a brow at me. "You thought of a better one?"

"No, but . . ."

"Ideas, Nessie," he says, cutting me off. He hovers the pen patiently in mid-air and smiles at me the same way he did in the school office. A devious smirk, yet the warmth in his blue-gray eyes makes his expression seem less ruthless. "Share them."

My shoulders sink. Nessie it is, I guess. "Well, I want to slash his truck tires," I admit, propping an elbow up on the table as I watch him scribble down my words in the notepad. His handwriting is steady and neat, making my heart tilt as I remember how he held my hand to write on it earlier.

He looks up from the notepad. "What else?"

"Can we hack into his phone? Or at least mess with his social media accounts somehow? My best friend can help."

"We would need to get our hands on his phone in the first place, but it's definitely an idea." His smile widens and he begins to write again. Without looking up, he quietly asks, "By the way . . . How's the backlash? You know, after today?" The concern in his words surprises me.

But I also want to scream at the reminder of that stupid video. I sink further into my chair and shrug, casting a quick glance around the library to make sure no one from school has suddenly turned up. As if anyone would. "I skipped classes and I haven't opened Twitter all day, so honestly, I've been running from it. But it doesn't take a genius to know what everyone is saying about me." As I watch Kai write down some notes, chewing on his lower lip, an awful

73

thought creeps into my mind. A curiosity that I need to indulge. "Did you watch it? That video?"

He glances up, his expression blank. "No."

"No?" I echo in disbelief. It feels subconscious, the way I pull my jacket shut around me, shrinking into it. I'm almost afraid to look him in the eye.

"Not everyone is a jerk, you know," he says, his voice soft and reassuring, and it stuns me when he places a hand on my shoulder – even makes me gulp. He leans in closer and offers me a smile that eases the tightness in my chest just a little. "I promise you, hand on heart, that I haven't watched that video and I don't plan to. Captain Washington doesn't judge, but Harrison is a scumbag for leaking it. That's why we're gonna inflict some serious damage in return." He takes his hand from my shoulder, focuses his attention back on the notepad.

It's oddly comforting that this stranger with zero loyalties to me chose not to watch the video and bask in my misfortune. He could have sneered just like everyone else, but he didn't. It gives me hope that perhaps there are others at school like him, that there *is* a small minority out there who are capable of taking a moral stance even when everyone else is so quick to grab a moment's amusement at someone else's misery. I was never one of those people – but now I wish I had been. What goes around comes around . . . Ugh.

"You haven't told me what *your* reason for doing this is," I say with an edge to my voice, hoping I can coerce him into telling me. "You said it wasn't a football thing. What, then?"

Kai smirks, but doesn't look up, only inks *Operation*

Harr-assassinate in 3D writing so that it looks like graffiti on the page. "I also said it was a *personal* thing."

"And you don't think my sex life is personal?" I fire back, pursing my lips at him. "C'mon, you know my motive. Now tell me yours."

"I've got an idea," he says with great enthusiasm, avoiding my question and changing the subject back to the real matter at hand. "Do you know where Harrison lives?"

"Over in Brookstone. I only ever saw his basement."

Kai raises an eyebrow, then shakes his head. "I don't even want to ask," he says, then adds the name of Harrison's neighborhood to our notes. So far, the page could do with some more details; it's looking a little empty. "How easy do you think it'd be to get inside his house?"

I stare at him. Is he kidding? "I mean, not that hard ... but why do we need to get inside? Can't we just throw eggs at the windows or something?"

"Too easy," Kai says, placing the pen between his teeth, chewing thoughtfully. "We need to steal some of his stuff. Like sentimental stuff that can't be replaced."

An uneasy feeling bubbles inside of me. Is it too harsh, too cruel, to do this to Harrison ...? But then I remember that he didn't care when he shared that video. He didn't care that it would hurt me. He didn't care what it would do to me. I have too much anger inside of me that needs to be released somehow – and this is how I'm going to do it.

"His parents are super strict. He and his dad grab dinner at Bob Evans every Wednesday," I blurt. It's about the only personal detail I know about Harrison's life away from school, and the only reason I know this tidbit of information is because we never met up on Wednesdays.

"Write this down," Kai urges, pushing the notepad across the table. He hands me his chewed-up pen, which I reluctantly take. "Anything you know that could give us opportunities. Anything that we could use against him. Like, does he still sleep with a stuffed bear? That kinda stuff."

I still sleep with a stuffed bear, so I hunch over the table and write down exactly what I just said: that Harrison's parents are your typical wealthy folks, and that every Wednesday he and his dad go for dinner together. I also write down that he has an older sister in college and a younger brother in freshman year, and I'm pretty sure he once mentioned a Chihuahua, but I clarify on the notepad that I don't want to drag the Boyd family pet into this war. I also write that Harrison has football practice most days after school, loves his truck to death, and hangs around almost exclusively with Noah Diaz and Anthony Vincent. As I write, I realize that it hurts just *thinking* about Harrison right now.

When I'm done, I sheepishly hand the notepad back over for Kai to study. He nods a couple times then rises to his feet. "We can add more to the list as and when we think of ideas. First things first, it's time for action. Let's go slash some tires."

There it goes again: that knot in my stomach, the feeling of guilt and dread. It's all fun and games *planning* to mess with Harrison. But actually going ahead with it? I didn't exactly imagine we would, and especially not tonight. Is this the kind of stuff Kai always does for kicks? I stand up from the table, but my balance feels off.

"You got a car?" Kai asks, shoving the notepad into the pocket of his jeans and placing the pen back behind his ear.

Oh, Lord, please, please, please don't make me admit that I own the Green McRusty. "Don't you?"

"Nope," he says, smiling. "Biked here, and unless you want to ride on my handlebars, then I'm relying on you to provide our battle vehicle."

"Fine," I mutter, already feeling my cheeks heat with the incoming embarrassment. I turn for the door and say over my shoulder, "But please don't judge."

"Nessie, didn't I already tell you that Captain Washington doesn't judge?" he says as he keeps up with my pace, teasingly nudging me with his elbow. I shoot him a sideways look, but I still don't understand his playful expression. Where did this guy even come from, other than out of absolutely freakin' nowhere? And he still hasn't told me – why does he hate Harrison Boyd?

Apprehensive, I point a finger and mutter, "It's the green SUV over there." Why the hell don't I have my own car yet? I make a mental note to prioritize my hunt for a vehicle that isn't a total embarrassment.

I steal a glance at Kai, but he's staring silently at the SUV as though he's waiting for me to tell him I'm kidding. When I don't say anything at all, he thoughtfully rubs his chin. "How do you expect us to lay low if our battle vehicle is a green SUV that rolled off the production line when Reagan was in the White House? I have a spare bike in my garage. You can use that."

I snort. I haven't ridden a bike since I was, like, twelve and the thought of me whirling across Westerville on two wheels is laughable. "You want us to ride around on bikes?"

"Yep. Why not? More discreet than a car, can dump them anywhere, and they make for a fast getaway because we can ignore all the traffic lights." Kai walks off to grab the bike that's propped up against the building. I didn't notice it when I first arrived. He carries the bike over in one hand and looks at me expectantly. "Well? Unlock the Hulk and let's get going."

"It's actually called the Green McRusty," I tell him, but instantly I wish I could shove all those words back in. Why did I even say that? Way to embarrass myself by openly admitting that I have a lame nickname for an even lamer car. "Get in." I unlock the door and climb in behind the wheel while Kai shoves his bike into the back seat, muddy wheels and all, but I honestly don't even care.

"I think we're going to make a great team," Kai announces as he slides into the passenger seat next to me. Buckles up, gets comfortable.

I study him out of the corner of my eye. "And why do you think that?"

"Because you're someone who has a nickname for their car, and in case you hadn't noticed, I like nicknames. That tells me everything I need to know. You're a fun person to be around." Kai's mouth twitches into a smile as he looks at me, and his voice is smooth and sweet, just like honey.

An unfamiliar shyness creeps through me – mostly because

78

when guys say that I'm fun, they mean that I'm fun in the bedroom, and not fun because I refer to my dad's car as "The Green McRusty." It's such a tiny thing for Kai to point out, but it lets me know that perhaps he sees beyond my reputation. My thoughts on Kai were pretty touch-and-go until this second – I couldn't decide if he was some obnoxious football player, or a troublemaker, or a straight-up weirdo. Now I'm thinking he's actually not that bad.

"Let's get this show on the road," he says. "Parkland. Drive there."

I do as I'm directed and put the car in drive, peeling out of the library parking lot and onto our main street. Uptown Westerville isn't an expansive area littered with endless stores. It doesn't need to be. It's the damn suburbs. Couple stores here and there, a few restaurants dotted along the way. Within minutes, we're already crossing through residential neighborhoods toward Parkland. It's not too far from my own house. In fact, I realize that it's a ten-minute drive between Kai's neighborhood and mine. It sometimes blows my mind that you hardly know any of the people who live around you, even in a small community like ours. How have I grown up in Westerville my entire life with Kai living ten minutes away and never having met him until now? Circumstances, that's why. Circumstances determined that we wouldn't meet until that party, and then circumstances brought us together again in our school office, and now here we are, creeping around town late at night in a crappy SUV together. I'm used to sneaking around late with guys, but not quite like this.

"I hope you know how to ride a bike," Kai says, eyeing me dubiously. Do I seriously look like I can't ride a bike? But before I can shoot him a snarky reply, he sits forward and points out the windshield. "That house up there. With the pumpkin mailbox."

I give him a weird look, but he isn't kidding. It really *is* the house with a mailbox disguised as a pumpkin. The house with the skeletons in the yard. The ghosts hanging from the drainpipes. The clown sitting on the porch. I'm almost too scared to drive any closer, but reluctantly I pull up outside the freaky-ass house and cut the engine, unable to tear my eyes away from the decorations. "Wasn't Halloween two weeks ago?"

"We're not here to talk about that," Kai says gruffly, and gets out the car. He yanks his bike out from the backseat while I walk around to join him. Despite his words, he goes on to explain, "It's for my little brother. He absolutely loves Halloween. So my parents keep the decorations up until Thanksgiving when we replace the pumpkin mailbox with a turkey mailbox. And I seriously wish I was kidding."

"They're weird, aren't they?"

"Yeah." He shakes his head, his expression dismayed. "I told them to at least get a clown that looked like Pennywise. And to put it on the lawn near the gutter."

"I meant younger siblings."

"Oh. Yeah, they're weird too." He guides his bike up the walkway toward the house and I follow. "You got one?"

"A sister. Kennedy. I'm basically her parent." I laugh when I say it, but I realize that it really hurts to admit it. I don't *want* to be the parent. I'm seventeen. I'm still a kid.

"Jackson's only seven," Kai says in response. "Big age gap. But that only makes me more protective. So, sure, the Halloween decorations make us the laughing stock of the neighborhood, but they also make Jackson smile every time he gets off the school bus."

We head through a gate into the back yard, and Kai dumps his bike on the grass. It's dark and there're no lights in the yard, so I squint after him as he disappears into the shed. There's a lot of rummaging and clinking of metal, then Kai reappears, wheeling another bike across the grass toward me. "This is my dad's bike," he tells me, "so you can take mine, and I'll take his. But listen. Pop a wheel? Scuff any of the paint? Get makeup on my handlebars? Then you're dead to me." He grins wide, revealing his teeth, his expression sweet.

The back door to the house suddenly swings open, bathing the yard in light. "Kai, is that you?" a voice calls out. A woman stands at the door, hugging her dressing gown around her, squinting out into the cold. She's slim, her blond hair pulled back into a scruffy ponytail. "What are you doing out here?"

I try to keep my head down. I really shouldn't be here in the first place. I'm a stranger, just some girl from school who literally only met Kai today. I don't want his mom to get the wrong idea.

"Grabbing the bikes," Kai calls across the yard. I notice the way he angles his body to hide me, pretending I'm not there. "I'm heading back out, but I won't be late. Don't wait up for me."

"No later than midnight," the woman says, her voice firm. She sighs – I can see her breath in the cold air. "And can't you wear a helmet?"

Kai cocks his head to one side and pats his curls. "Not unless I want to mess up this hair."

"Goodnight, Kai," she says, ignoring him. Her eyes move to me. I expect her to give me a dirty look – *who's this girl sneaking around my back yard with my son?* – but instead she gives me a small, friendly smile. "Actually, why don't you come inside first? I want to meet your friend." She disappears back into the house, leaving no room for argument, the door wide open behind her.

"She really doesn't make me seem cool, does she?" Kai scoffs. "*Wear a helmet?*"

I laugh with him, but I can't help but think about how I'd actually rejoice if Dad ever told me to wear a helmet.

Kai rests his dad's bike down on the grass next to his own and exhales, dragging his feet toward the house. I follow close behind him and, for a second, I deliberate over whether or not this is all worth it. I don't *need* to meet Kai's parents – I could shrug my shoulders, tell Kai I'm out, and walk away right now. But something keeps me moving forward, all the way across the yard and through the back door into Kai's home.

His mother has her head in the refrigerator, fetching us two cans of soda that she seems overly pleased to present us with. It feels weird meeting a guy's mom.

"So, Kai?" she urges, leaning back and folding her arms. Her smile is expectant as she gives me a pointed glance, patiently waiting for Kai to explain just exactly who I am. "Introduce us."

"This is Vanessa," Kai mumbles as he kicks the back door closed. This is unbelievably awkward, mostly because Kai and I don't know a single thing about one another besides our names. Hell, I doubt he even knows my last name. "Vanessa, this is my mom. Obviously."

His mother looks at me, her smile widening. "Yep, I'm the mom. Cindy. I assume you go to Westerville North?"

I nod and rotate the cold can of soda around in my hands, my eyes flitting around the room, unable to look at her directly. The kitchen is warm and inviting, clean yet cluttered with precious knickknacks scattered here and there. Personal. "Yeah, I do. Go Warriors," I pathetically joke. Kai plays for the rival team, the Westerville Central High Warhawks – or at least he did before he transferred, for reasons unknown, to Westerville North.

"It's nice that Kai's made a friend already," Cindy muses, and the look of death that Kai shoots her is hard to miss. It makes me bite back a smile because I can just *feel* his embarrassment. It's kind of cute.

Mom used to embarrass me all the time, but only because she cared and I thought that caring was lame. Like that one time I scraped my knee out on the sidewalk and Mom came running outside with a first-aid kit and a look of panic as though I'd broken a bone. I felt like a complete baby in front of my friends and I hated her for it. I didn't appreciate back then that she was just overprotective because she loved me – and because she felt my pain as much as if it had been her own and then some.

Now I would give anything for Mom to baby me in front of my friends again.

"Yeah, and we have a class project that we need to work on together, so can we go?" Kai asks. It's not really a lie. We *do* have a project that we're working on together.

"I didn't know we were having a guest over," a deep voice remarks. There's a creak in the wooden floor as a man wheels himself into the kitchen. Kai's father, I assume. He has the same curls and bold features. Broad shoulders, chiseled jaw that's lined with dark stubble. Bright brown eyes. He rests his hands in his lap and looks at me from his wheelchair. "Hello there."

"Neither did I. This is Vanessa, a friend of Kai's," Cindy tells him. She rests a hand on her husband's shoulder and the two of them look at me. Suddenly, there's too much pressure.

"Hi," I force out, not quite sure whether to offer my hand to shake. I do a feeble wave instead. I say the only thing I can think of. I tell them, "I like your Halloween decorations." And I instantly want to melt into the floor.

"Yeah, I like 'em too. When it's actually Halloween," Kai's father deadpans, then rolls his eyes as Cindy swats at his shoulder.

"We're heading out," Kai interrupts, bringing the subject back around to the fact that we want to leave. I don't think he wants his parents to get to know me, because it's not like we're actually friends. After we deal with Harrison, we'll probably never talk again, and his parents will wonder why I never came back around. "We just need to grab some textbooks from my room."

Kai gives me a look that makes it clear I need to follow him, so I squeeze past him on our way to the stairs and I make sure to give his parents a polite smile on my way. They seem caring, and they're both still alive. Two things Kai should appreciate.

"Car accident," Kai says quietly over his shoulder as I follow him upstairs.

"Huh?"

"My dad," he clarifies. "Truck slammed into him on the freeway a few winters ago. He's paraplegic. There, now I saved you the awkwardness of having to ask. It also means he won't notice that his bike is missing, 'cause it isn't like he uses it these days."

"That's rough," I say. These facts are also a little personal, especially because I wasn't going to ask anyway.

"Yep, and between medical bills and Dad having to go freelance, we're pretty much broke," Kai says as we reach the landing. He stops and turns to face me, and his willingness to share such intimate information with a complete stranger makes me feel uncomfortable.

"You don't have to ... You don't need to tell me this."

"Well, actually I do, because you're going to wonder why my room looks the way it does," he says, then smiles slightly as he turns away again. He pushes open the first door on his left and I stare at him, confused and unsure what to expect.

Because when someone warns you that they're broke, you might expect their room to be bare, with essentials only. Not totally cluttered with hundreds of miscellaneous items spread over the floor and a small child on the bed.

"Hey!" Kai says. "Stop playing in here, man. You can't touch this stuff."

The boy – I assume his little brother, Jackson – is sitting cross-legged on the bed, a handful of action figures in his lap. He freezes at the sight of us, then tosses the action figures away and scrambles off the bed. His hair is a cute explosion of curls that gets in his eyes as he whizzes past us and disappears down the hall into another room.

Kai groans in frustration, then shuts his door and carefully steps around the clutter on the floor. "That was Jackson, so now you've met the whole Washington crew," he says. He grabs the action figures from his bed and reaches up to align them all back on a shelf mounted on the wall. I notice there's an ancient Captain America figure, and I wonder if that's where Kai's inspiration for his code name came from.

"Those action figures are yours?" I question, watching the way he takes great care of positioning all the figures on the shelf, like there's a certain order to it.

"Don't laugh," Kai says, glancing defensively over his shoulder at me. "They're from my childhood, and I don't have the heart to toss them. It's not like I actually play with them."

"And is all this stuff souvenirs from your childhood too?" I scour the floor again, and the desk space, and the window seat. There's stacks of old CDs, video games, a couple TVs, and college textbooks.

"Not exactly," Kai says, scratching his temple as he walks back over. He kicks a few CDs out of the way. "I hang out in thrift stores and go to yard sales a lot, and I flip shit on eBay for easy cash. Helps my parents out on the money front. I'm not a hoarder, I swear."

Oh. There's a lot of stuff here. Definitely a few hundred dollars' worth of stuff that needs sold, and I think how it's super cute that Kai does this to help out his parents. He must care about them a lot. They're an actual family that looks out for each other. I miss how that feels.

"Speaking of your parents . . ." I say, nervously shoving my hands into the pockets of my leather jacket. "Should I really be in your room right now? I don't want them to think . . ."

"That we're up here grabbing a knife to slash some tires with?" Kai stares intensely at me, his mouth twitching into a smirk. I stare right back at him, just as intensely, before he turns and heads to his closet. He searches through his clothes for a few moments, until finally he retrieves something. He comes back over to me and holds out his hand, presenting a small Stanley knife. "Ready to mess with Harrison Boyd?"

So, we're really doing this. We're really about to declare war on Harrison. I swallow the lump in my throat as my eyes meet Kai's. "As ready as I'll ever be."

6

It's kind of thrilling, you know. Whirling down the middle of the road with the wind in my hair, kicking up leaves as we track our way across Westerville's quiet streets. There's a nip to the air that bites at my nose and ears. I'm riding the hell out of Kai's bike, like a kid at Christmas, whizzing too fast around corners and standing up in the pedals because I'm suddenly convinced it makes me look cool. And if the cops saw us now, two teenagers in hoodies and leather jackets racing across town on bikes, I'm sure they'd have some questions. Honestly, I was so glad to abandon the Green McRusty back at Kai's place.

"I hope your parents don't report it for suspicious inactivity and have it towed," I said as we pedaled away from his house.

"No guarantees," he replied, with a wink over his shoulder as he flew past me at speed.

But it's me who's in the lead now. I'm guiding the way to Harrison's house, but the closer we get to his neighborhood, the more my head begins to spin. I'm shaking, but with nerves and not the cold. I like to think I really don't have any fucks to give these days, that I'm someone who does whatever she wants. It's an attitude that makes life easier. Living by my own rules. Not caring. But yet, as I cycle toward Harrison's house, I find myself wondering if maybe it's wrong to slash his tires. Plus, it's a crime. Would it be a step too far? He loves his truck. But his family has money, and I know he'll have a fresh set of tires fitted within twenty-four hours. It'll be more of an inconvenience than anything else. And I think Harrison deserves to be inconvenienced, after all. He put my body on display to the world. *He* caused this anger, so he can't blame me for being irrational.

"You keeping up?" I call back to Kai.

"Yep. Got a nice view worth keeping up with," I hear him yell back, his tone easy.

Instantly, I slam my butt back down onto the saddle and fire him a glare over my shoulder. I nearly run into a street-light. "Please wait until tomorrow at least before making remarks like that. That video is still raw." If today had been any other day, his comment would have made me wonder just how much Kai likes what he sees. But I'm too numb, too protective of my body to entertain his comedic remarks this soon.

"Sorry, Nessie," Kai says. He rolls up alongside me and when I glance over, he's mock-pouting like a little kid who's been caught with his hand in the cookie jar. It's clear he's teasing me and wants me to forgive him, but I remain seated.

"It's just around this corner," I say, feeling those nerves coursing through me again. I've never done anything like this. Never been much of a wild child, so this is all new to me, and I can't tell if I hate the way it's making me feel or if I'm enjoying the rush.

A car passes us, angrily honking its horn because we're biking down the middle of the street, but Kai just flips them the finger. I don't think he gives too many fucks either. Maybe that's why we're going to make a good team, because neither of us cares too much about the consequences of our actions. We might be a good team, but we're probably a bad combination.

"Ah, how the rich kids live," Kai remarks as we turn onto Harrison's street. We gradually slow down, silently rolling past the rows of American-dream homes. The white picket fences. Actual driveways with more than one car parked in them. No loose trash accumulating in the gutters, no broken streetlights. Perfect homes inhabited by perfect families. "Maybe we *should* egg his house."

"I bet a street like this has some sort of neighborhood watch in place," I say. "Keep your head down."

"Okay, partner." Kai pulls his hood up over his head. "Let's do this."

I brake sharply outside Harrison's house. His lawn is so huge, his house is actually set a hundred yards back from the sidewalk. I've been here a couple times. Never inside the house itself, though. Always the basement. Harrison didn't want his parents to know he had a girl over. Not a girl like me, anyway. They would have lost their shit if they'd ever caught us, apparently.

"I guess they're home," Kai comments, nodding at the driveway full of cars. Harrison's truck is among them.

"Gotta be extra sneaky now." He gets off his father's bike and dumps it behind the oak tree on the sidewalk, then crouches down. I follow suit, huddling behind the tree next to him.

"Plan of action?" I whisper, hyper aware of his shoulders nudging mine.

"Slash the tires, then maybe – oh, I don't know – run like Usain Bolt?"

I narrow my eyes at his deadpan expression until he chuckles under his breath, rolling his eyes at me. I guess the plan was obvious. It's not like we're going to hang around to get caught.

He pulls out the Stanley knife from the front pouch of his hoodie and encloses his fist around it. The fact that we're biking around town with a knife only makes this feel way more wrong than it already did, and a lot more serious. "You're my lookout, okay? But first, full disclosure. You're aware this is a crime, right?"

"So is sharing indecent videos of a minor," I say flatly, staring evenly at him. I can play his deadpan games. "Now shall you do the honors or shall I?"

Kai smirks, then pulls on the drawstrings of his hoodie to conceal his face before he dashes off across the lawn. He disappears behind Harrison's truck, then a few seconds later, I spot his head pop up. I glance all around the street – listening for approaching cars, searching for wandering neighbors, checking the house for movement. There're lights on inside. Colors from a TV screen flash from a room downstairs.

My gaze flickers back over to Kai, and I nod to give him

the go-ahead. I still don't know why he's doing this, but I can't help but admire his commitment to the cause.

Immediately, he ducks out of view again. I wait by the tree, listening for some sort of loud bang or something, but all I hear is silence. And then the quiet hissing of air. And then a thunderous *bang!* makes me jump half out my skin.

Suddenly, Kai is sprinting toward me, his hood blowing down as he runs. "GO, GO, GO!" he hisses, gesturing wildly at me with his hands. He shoves the knife back into his pocket and jumps onto his bike. I stumble to swing myself onto mine, the adrenaline rush rendering me useless, and I panic even more when Kai catapults off without me. He's standing tall, cycling at his hardest, a shrinking figure in the darkness.

My blood is rushing to my ears, my heart pounding as I clamber onto the bike, desperately trying to find the pedals. I hear the front door open and a deep voice calls, "HEY!" across the lawn. I'm convinced I'm having a heart attack because *none of my limbs are working*, but then I finally burst into motion. I cycle so hard my legs go numb as I race off in the direction Kai went, leaving Harrison Boyd's house behind, never glancing back.

The wind blows my hair into my eyes, obscuring my vision, but I just keep on pedaling, my legs powered by fear. Was that Harrison who came outside? Or his dad? I pray with everything in me that it was his father. Harrison would have recognized me, although when he discovers his vandalized truck, I'm sure he'll know in an instant that I'm behind it. Either way, I'm screwed. I start thinking about jail cells and extortionate bills and the criminal charges that the Boyds will press against me.

"Nessie!" I hear Kai call, and I skid to a stop. My heart is beating so hard it hurts. I move my hair out of my face as I search for my partner-in-crime, and my shoulders sink with relief when I see Kai perched on the edge of a low wall. His bike is on the ground.

"What the hell, Kai? Teammates? You left me behind!" I yell, panting my words. I clamber off my bike – or his bike, whatever – and walk it over to him. I throw it down hard onto the sidewalk and watch him squirm.

"I'm here waiting for you now, aren't I?" he says, cocking his head. He doesn't make any comments about me possibly damaging his bike. "Teamwork also means *not* getting the other one caught. Sorry, but you sucked back there."

He's not wrong. I just couldn't get myself away from the scene; it was like I was glued to the spot, a sorry excuse for a criminal. With my head hung low, I sit down next to Kai and sulk. We're in the next neighborhood over, but it doesn't feel far enough. I'm worried the police are going to come whizzing down the street, lights blaring, any second.

And then what? What if Dad had to pick me up from the station because I'd been charged with a crime? Would that be enough to shake him out of his numbness?

"I got the front tires cut, but the rear one burst. Nearly blew my damn brains out," Kai tells me, running his hands through his hair. "But at least now Harrison has one wrecked tire and two that'll be totally flat by morning. Does that make you feel a little better?"

I look sideways at Kai. He gives me a gentle smile. "Yeah, it does," I admit. Harrison deserves to have a shitty week. I can picture him now – standing around his truck with his parents in shock, examining the damage. He was probably already pissed at me for hurling gravel at his paintwork last night. But who cares? He and his precious truck can go to hell.

Kai leans back on his hands and stares up at the cold sky, dark and dotted with stars. "It's fun, right? Doing the wrong thing," he says almost wistfully.

"Sounds like you're used to doing the wrong thing."

"Only lately," he says.

"Why's that?"

"No one worth doing the right thing for." He slides off the wall and yanks his bike up from the ground, turning his back on me. I get the sense that he doesn't want to elaborate, so I don't push it. "We should turn in for the night. The plan is to start off easy, then ramp up the pressure until Harrison cracks."

We get back on the bikes and head off, making our way to Kai's place so that I can, unfortunately, claim back the Green McRusty. It's nearing eleven, so Westerville is pretty much dead to the world. At least in these neighborhoods. We cut across lawns and fly through cross sections without looking, feeling indestructible. Kai and I don't say much to one another, not until we're nearing his house.

"Damn, no one stole it," Kai says, tutting in dismay at my horrible SUV still parked up outside.

I slide off my bike and pull out the keys from my pocket,

pausing next to the car. I think my heartbeat has only just returned to normal. I look at Kai as I hold onto the handlebars, waiting for him to take his bike from me. "I guess I'll see you at school."

"No, you won't see me at school," he says matter-of-factly. He's still sat on his dad's bike, feet planted on the ground to keep his balance. When I stare at him with confusion flashing across my face, he rolls his eyes as though the explanation is obvious. "We're not friends. We don't know each other. We're not associated. So, don't look anywhere in my direction. And keep the bike. You'll need it for next time."

"Uh. Okay." I go quiet, still perplexed. I'm searching Kai's expression for something more, but I can't get past his calm, cool exterior. "You trust me enough to give me your bike?"

"What are you gonna do, Nessie? Pedal off into the horizon with it?"

I purse my lips and shove his bike into the backseat, slamming the door shut. I turn around once more, only to be polite, and give Kai a smile that even *feels* awkward, so I don't know how it must look to him. How do I say goodbye to him, a stranger but one who I'm now complicit with?

But the stranger does it for me. "Goodnight, Nessie. I'm sorry for leaving you behind."

"It's fine. Goodnight, Kai."

He pulls a face, shaking his head. "No, Nessie, that's not how this works. I want to hear you say it."

"Goodnight—" I grit my teeth and lower my voice "— *Captain Washington*."

Kai's face lights up with that childlike glee again, and it

makes me wonder what he meant when he said he hasn't been doing the right thing lately. Other than witnessing him literally slashing someone's truck tires thirty minutes ago, he doesn't seem all that bad to me. But then again, would someone who *wasn't* that bad really set out to ruin someone else's life? I guess we all have different sides. Right now, I just so happen to be seeing the wrong side of Kai.

We turn our backs on one another. Kai cycles off into his back yard and I climb into my car, and I definitely don't dither. In a matter of seconds, I'm speeding away from his house, heading back to my own. As I drive alone in silence for the few minutes that it takes to get home, fatigue sinks in. All of the emotional stress from today has exhausted me.

My head is a war zone, so many different thoughts fighting with one another; the minute one comes out top, another jostles for position and shoves it to one side. The conflict of feelings is relentless.

I'm feeling fury at Harrison for betraying me by sharing something that was for no one else to see. But also anger at myself for being so stupid, for letting him record that video in the first place. But was I really so wrong to trust him to keep it to himself? A small part of me wants to believe I'm innocent, that I'm a victim in this, but it's no match for the voice in my head that's insisting it's all my fault. Like, if I wind it all back to the start, I should have never hooked up with Harrison in the first place. That action was the trigger for all this.

It's strange the way life works. You can feel comfortable about your decisions, content with them, yet the outside world can turn a single, unthinking moment into something so awful that you're forced to regret it. I feel disgusted at myself – not for the hookup, but for not realizing what I was letting myself in for – even when yesterday I didn't. What we've done to Harrison doesn't wash that disgust away, not one bit.

I park outside my house and grab Kai's bike from the back seat. I don't want Dad heading off to work in the morning and spying it in the rearview, so I dump it in the yard and hope for the love of God that no one steals it during the night. Our neighborhood isn't particularly sketchy, but we do get some weirdos roaming through on their way uptown. I don't think Kai would be too impressed if I told him some stranger had taken his bike.

The front door is unlocked when I reach it. Dad always forgets to lock the front door at night, but I like to pretend he leaves it unlocked on purpose because he's worried I'll forget my keys or something.

"Dad?" I gently call out. All the lights are still on, so Dad must still be up. I walk into the living room, and there he is, standing on a step ladder and trying to balance some artwork on the wall.

"The painting fell down again," he says without looking over his shoulder at me. For once, it seems he's actually heard me come home. He stretches up higher and the ladder wobbles. "It's a goddamn ugly painting, but Debra loved it, so I need to get it back up." He tucks the artwork under his armpit and begins fiddling with the hooks in the walls. True, the painting doesn't come close to matching our color scheme *and* it used to give Kennedy nightmares when we were younger, but our living room wouldn't be the same without that murky lake with human faces beneath the water that Mom bought off one of her quirky art friends a decade ago.

I glance at the clock on the wall. It's after eleven. Now is not the time for DIY. "Just do it in the morning, Dad."

"No, Vanessa!" Dad snaps, his head swiveling around. His cheeks flare red as he clings onto the painting while balancing on the ladder. "Can't you see that I'm trying to fix it? I'm almost done."

Maybe, I think in despair, things would be different if Mom's health had gradually deteriorated over time, if we *knew* what was to come. Maybe that extra time would have allowed us to prepare ourselves mentally for such a loss, but it didn't happen that way. On the Wednesday evening, Mom was yelling at Kennedy and me for fighting over the TV remote and reminding us to bring our laundry downstairs. By the Thursday afternoon, she was pronounced dead in the ambulance. She didn't even make it to the hospital. Our entire world changed in that moment. We had no time to prepare. No time to learn how to accept it. I just remember being pulled out of school and how all the air in my lungs was knocked straight out of me when my grandparents choked through sobs that my mother was gone. When we arrived at the ER, Dad was an inconsolable, untouchable heap on the floor, his knees hugged to his chest and his head in his hands. It was the first and only time I've ever heard anyone wail.

I stare at Dad now, totally mute. He loved her so intensely

that he can't seem to grasp how to continue through life without her. It's like he's stuck in limbo, frozen in an endless, eternal loop of time. He can't seem to step out of it and move forward. At least Kennedy and I are trying.

Dad returns to the wall, trying to place the painting back where it belongs, and I feel my throat clenching tight as my eyes sting with tears. He wants so hard to keep her memory alive. I know he hates that painting too, but he's fighting to nail it back in its prominent spot, but it won't stay up, and it keeps falling back down, and Dad is growing more and more exasperated . . .

And then he grabs that ugly painting and throws it across the room in a wave of fierce, unprecedented rage.

I stare at Dad wide-eyed as he steps down from the ladder and fumbles in his jeans pocket for his pack of cigarettes. He has totally lost it. He's grumbling under his breath as he walks over to the kitchen, pushing past me as though I'm invisible – which, figuratively speaking, I guess I am.

"The painting can just stay down, Dad," I say gently, following him into the kitchen.

He slides open the patio doors and leans against the frame, lighting a cigarette and blowing the plume of smoke out into the cool night air. Mom never used to let him smoke inside the house, but she's not here to enforce that rule anymore. Half the time, he doesn't even make the effort to smoke at the back door. That's why our house reeks of tobacco, and why Chyna rarely comes over more than once a week because she's tired of her asthma flaring up as soon as she walks through the front door.

"She'll be disappointed," Dad mumbles with a cough. "She loves that picture."

She'll also be disappointed that he's smoking in the house, so why does an old painting even matter?

"But Mom's not here," I say. "Things are never going to be as they were."

He cranes his neck to look at me, appalled at my bluntness. Dad doesn't like it when we say factual stuff like that. Half the time, he still talks about Mom in the present tense as though she's off traveling the world and will return soon with gifts and hugs and tales of faraway adventures. If only.

"You can't think that way," he mumbles. "We still need to make her proud."

And how exactly are we doing that? I think.

Mom wouldn't be proud of Dad right now. She would want him to be happy, to be the man she fell in love with, and not some tormented, grieving, shabby recluse. And she definitely wouldn't be proud of me either. The daughter who messed up, who can't get a handle on her own behavior; the daughter who's desperate not to be shamed as her sex life circulates around school, and beyond, on some screwed-up video.

For a second, I think about telling Dad. I imagine opening my mouth and confessing the truth, then asking him, as my father, to help me fix this mess. I want him to reassure me that everything will be okay, that he's going to help me resolve this, and that *I'll* be okay. But I know he's no longer capable. He is numb to everything except his own pain.

I leave him smoking by the patio doors and run up to my room, taking the stairs two at a time. I grab my MacBook, collapsing onto my bed as I log in while tears break free and roll down my cheeks because the realization that I'm alone in this misery is too much. I don't turn on any lights, only let the glare of the screen illuminate my face as I pull up my internet browser. I open a couple new tabs. Twitter. Facebook. The first social media I've seen all day.

I check Facebook first, only because I know it's the safest. No one uses it these days, so the likelihood of me seeing anything about myself on there is pretty much nil. But I scroll through my newsfeed anyway, searching and searching for my name, but all I see are photo uploads from distant relatives and middle-aged locals airing their dirty laundry.

My focus shifts to the Twitter tab. The most ruthless social media of all. It's a cooking pot when it comes to gossip and high school drama – everyone has something to say, because it's just so *easy* to say it, and everyone feeds off one another's posts, fueling heated discussions, fallouts and unwanted opinions. I'm not stupid. I know exactly what I'm about to see as I log in, because I know what I'd be saying if it were anyone else, but it still shocks me to my core as soon as the posts come up on my timeline.

what a whore
hasn't every guy in Westerville North already seen that body anyway?
vanessa murphy really has lost it
#smileforthecamera
oh my godddd gross!!

Only a couple of the tweets mention my actual name, but it's so clear that every post is about me. Every post from seven this morning up until right now, tweet after tweet shaming me, humiliating me, my peers from school basking in the sadistic glee of tearing someone else to pieces. They're just so freakin' glad it's not them who's in the firing line, because it's always more fun being the one laughing than being the one laughed at. What hurts worst of all is that last week most of these people were talking to me in the hallways at school. They were joking around with me at Madison Romy's party. They were sitting with me at lunch. It feels so clear now that they have never really liked me at all, that they most likely already had these opinions about me, but never had the courage or the opportunity to express them. But people grow brave – and vicious – when they're in unison with others. I'm usually a part of it too, but now it feels so wrong.

I wanted attention, sure, but not like this.

I make my account private and slam my MacBook shut.

The total unfairness of it sends tears streaming down my face. But there's a purpose galvanizing behind my tears. Now I'm craving payback more than ever.

There wasn't a single mention of Harrison's name. Not a single insinuation *about* Harrison. But I already knew that too. I knew this morning that it would be me who'd be subject to all the backlash. Harrison doesn't have to worry about being tortured online or his social status being torn apart – but he does have something else to worry about.

Kai and me.

7

I sleep in late for school. Admittedly, on purpose. I can't bear the thought of walking down those hallways again. To think that yesterday I was blissfully unaware that everyone around me had that video on their phone. *What a sucker.*

I did shoot Chyna a text telling her not to pick me up, and I promised her I'd be at school by noon. No matter how much I dread facing everyone at school, I don't want to ditch Chyna during lunch. We have our own table in the cafeteria that we share with some mutual friends, but Chyna is more reserved than I am, someone who's happy to be in my shadow, so she'll panic if I don't turn up. That's why I have to show my face at school today. For my friend's sake.

Second period is drawing to a close as I pull up to our campus. But, oh no, not in the Green McRusty. Dad took it to work this morning, so I had to improvise. I'm on Kai's bike. Embarrassing, sure, but nowhere near as humiliating as a leaked sex tape. I've discovered that it's quite freeing, really – feeling so exposed already that it doesn't matter what you do next, because it's not like you can sink any lower.

I stopped by the hardware store on my way here to buy

a bike lock, because nothing is ever safe on this campus. And right now, I'm the prime target for abuse, so if anyone catches me pulling up on this bike, they'll most likely break the chain and then toss it in the dumpster just to spite me. And then Kai will kill me.

There's no one around, though. I chain the bike up to a rack and study the others already there in search of Kai's father's one, but I can't remember what it looks like. Kai's is painted a dark blue and the tires have a red trim, but his dad's was more subtle. I keep checking the bikes until it occurs to me that what I'm really doing is trying to figure out whether or not Kai is at school.

Of course he's at school. Why wouldn't he be? It's only his second day. I don't even know *why* Kai transferred here from Westerville Central. I need to ask him, but apparently I'm not allowed to talk to him in public.

The bell for lunch period rings out, echoing across the deserted school campus. It's my cue to pluck up some courage and enter the building. I take a deep breath, several of them, and head for the door. I'm wearing a pair of baggy jeans and a hoodie, because I know it'd be like feeding time at the zoo if I turned up today in my usual style. I like tight jeans and low-cut tops, because *I* like the way they look, but I know that drawing attention to my body wouldn't do much to help my cause right now. So, another middle finger up at Harrison for forcing me to change the way I dress.

Students spill out of the building and I have to fight against the current to get inside. I ignore the whispers, the laughter. It doesn't mean they don't hurt. No amount of trying to tough it out can save me, not really, not deep down. I keep my head up and my eyes set ahead, lips clamped firmly shut. I can't look at the sea of faces in the hallways as I drift past them. It's all a blur. I don't want to see Harrison or his friends. I don't want to see Kai, because right now, other than Chyna, he feels like the only other friend I have, so I'm worried I'll run straight to him. And I've no way of knowing if I can trust him. Plus, he's made it clear that he doesn't want us to be seen together.

When I reach the cafeteria doors, I brace myself for impact. The cafeteria is always toxic – it's where arguments that have been brewing all day finally break out, it's where jock-level disagreements are settled with fistfights, it's where Judgment Day takes place for those of us who have made mistakes and sinned against the rules of the school.

I follow a couple of freshmen girls through the doors and into the boxing ring that is the Westerville North cafeteria. It's a buzz of noise, mindless chatter laced with laughter, bodies milling around with trays. At first, as I weave my way around tables toward my own at the back, I'm praying that everyone is too self-absorbed to notice my arrival. But then the hushing starts. It's subtle, the volume of the cafeteria dropping by only a notch or two, but it's there. Eyes latch onto me. Tongues wag.

It's hard not to tune in to what they're saying, and I flinch, but it's easier to bear once I finally spot Chyna at our table. She's on her own, picking silently at her food, which is weird. Our table is usually packed full, and on the odd occasion that there is an empty seat, it doesn't take long for some desperate soul to fill it. As I approach, Chyna glances up, her face lighting up with relief.

"You're here!" she says, her smile wide and beautiful. She stands from the table and pulls me into a tight hug that I know means much more than her just being grateful that I've turned up. It's a hug full of love and reassurance, a hug that reminds me that she's here for me. I squeeze her back, burying my face in her braids, fighting back tears. Sometimes when I look at Chyna, I see pieces of my old self in her. Happy, passionate, loyal – hopeful for all that's ahead of us. The past couple years, I have become someone entirely different, but yet we have never grown apart. It's corny, I know, but that's how I'm sure we'll be best friends for life.

We sit down at the table together, side-by-side, and I look around at all those empty seats again. I feel a thousand eyes burning into me. "Where is everyone?"

Chyna shrugs and turns her eyes down to her lap, but we both know where our friends are. Nowhere near me, that's where. Refusing to be associated with the school tramp. Well, screw them. Fake ass friends. Chyna slides her tray over to me, offering me some of her grapes in consolation. "I'm sorry," she says.

"It's fine," I lie, and pop a grape into my mouth. I guess I already knew she was the only real friend I had anyway. I have my back turned to the cafeteria, refusing to glance over at anyone, instead staring aimlessly at a dirty smudge on the windows. It's really not fine. Is this what it feels like to be a social outcast? I bet even creepy Ryan Malone has more friends at his table than I do right now.

"You still haven't told me what happened last night with Kai. What went down?"

I look at Chyna. It's probably not wise to admit that I was an accomplice in a misdemeanor crime, but she's my best friend. "We rode around on bikes, went to Harrison's house, and messed up his truck," I say under my breath, leaning in close to her. I manage to flash her a devious smile. "Thanks for the suggestion."

Chyna's eyes go wide and she nearly bursts out of her seat. "You actually slashed his tires?!"

"Shhh!"

"Sorry. But holy shit."

"It was Kai who did the dirty work," I explain, taking the heat off myself like a coward. "I was just the lookout. It was . . . fun." I think back to last night, remembering the terror, but also the rush of exhilaration and adrenaline, and I wonder what move Kai and I will make next. It feels like we're playing a video game.

Chyna folds her arms across her chest, giving me a stern look up and down. "Don't tell me you're about to fall off the rails and end up in jail or something."

"You don't have to worry about me," I say, rolling my eyes. If I can survive losing Mom, then I can survive anything.

"Yeah, I kinda do." Chyna's expression turns serious. "Are you okay?"

I just nod, forcing a smile onto my face. We both know it's fake and we both know that no, I'm not okay. But what can I do other than just bear the next few days, weeks, or months until attention shifts to someone else's mistake?

#SmileForTheCamera is scrawled onto my locker door in bright red Sharpie. I hear people around me snicker as they watch me discover it, but I swallow and continue to open up my locker and fetch my books. Was that written by the same person who tweeted that hashtag on Twitter yesterday? Or has it simply become the agreed phrase for all my peers to taunt me with?

I slam my locker shut again and turn around, but a gasp escapes my mouth when I find someone standing directly in front of me.

"Vanessa," Harrison says, his voice low. He glances at the words painted on my locker and grimaces. His eyes meet mine and he steps closer. "You didn't happen to slash the tires of my truck last night, did you?"

"I've got no idea what you're talking about," I state calmly, then barge my shoulder into his as I push past him. I can't even look at him. I *hate* him.

A firm hand grasps my arm and yanks me back. "Vanessa," Harrison says again, more aggressively this time. He squeezes my arm too tight and his glare becomes threatening. "Don't fucking touch my stuff."

"Don't leak our private business," I bite back, then widen my eyes and add, "Oh wait," before giving him a bitter smile. Roughly, I pull my arm free from his grip and we glower at one another, two lovers turned enemies.

It's only then that I realize we have an audience. *Of course* we do. Everyone is watching our every move, listening to our every word, desperate for new developments in this scandal. I don't want to give them any more juicy gossip, so I grit my teeth and walk away despite how badly I want to kick Harrison to the curb.

With my English Lit books hugged to my chest, I walk to class at full speed and arrive just as the bell is ringing. I'm one of the first inside the class, which means I get first dibs at the desks. Everyone tends to stick to the same seats, but it's not a rule, so there's no way I'm willingly taking up position in my usual spot. I share this class with Noah, and we sit next to one another on the back row where we engage in mindless bickering and flirting – or at least we did. It's how we started hooking up in the first place, but after I called things off, we didn't talk as much. Yesterday he was a dick to me, so I refuse to sit near him and be subjected to a barrage of verbal abuse. I steal someone else's desk right up front by the windows instead.

The rest of my classmates filter into the room, their judgmental gazes unable to avoid peeking over at me, and it slowly occurs to me that every desk around me is empty. No one wants to sit near me. It's like being that kid in middle school who hasn't discovered deodorant yet, like I'm too disgusting to come within a five-foot radius of. I close my eyes, inhale. *All these people, all their phones with that video . . .*

A body slouches into the seat next to me. My gaze flickers over. It's Kai. He's wearing a Cleveland Browns snapback backward on his head and he gets comfortable, dumping a textbook on the desk. His every mannerism is effortless, languid, and, as he glances quickly over at me out of the corner of his eye, I swear I catch him smiling.

"Hey," I mumble, angling toward him. The only friend I have in this room. Thank God he's in this class – hopefully he's in some of my other classes too. There is suddenly hope that maybe I can survive the next hour.

"Undercover, Nessie," Kai hisses, his lips unmoving. He stares straight ahead at the blank projector screen on the wall. I can't tell if he's sitting next to me by choice or because there aren't many options left.

I sigh and turn back to my own desk, drumming my fingertips against the wood while I wait for Miss Anderson to show up. My phone buzzes in my pocket. I pull it out and raise an eyebrow at Kai – it's a new message from *Kai Washington (Partner)*. He won't look at me, and I can see the great effort he's making to blatantly ignore me.

I told you not to talk to me.

Oh, nice. He was actually being serious about that. I text back quickly, honest as I admit:

Sorry. Got no one else to talk to.

I watch Kai out of the corner of my eye as he reads my message on his own screen, then types back a reply, his fingertips moving fast.

Stay back at the end of class and we'll talk once everyone leaves. I've got an idea for what to do to Harrison next.

"Hey, anyone got a camera in here?" a voice booms across the room, and when I look up, Noah is strolling into class. "Just in case someone wants to start stripping and give us a show?" His eyes flash over to meet mine, and he grins, crooked and sadistic as the class cackles with hushed laughter. He walks to his desk at the back of the room, shaking his head at the empty spot next to it. "C'mon, Vanessa, get back to your usual seat. Maybe we can have some fun when Miss Anderson isn't looking. Look, I'll even make it easy for you." He undoes the button of his jeans, then bursts into laughter when some of the other guys from the team corral around him, fist bumping and high-fiving. The entire room is in fits of laughter. Laughter at *my* expense. I used to find Noah attractive because of his class clown personality, but being the one used for his punchlines isn't so funny.

My cheeks burn with rage, a hot fire that starts in the tip of my toes and spreads throughout my body. I turn to the screen at the front of the room again and try to tune it all out, but I'm so tensed up, my jaw so tightly clenched that I fear I might explode any second. With what emotion, I don't know. If I open my mouth, I'm not sure if I'll burst into tears or if I'll pummel someone. I think of all the nasty remarks I could throw back at Noah, but I clamp my mouth shut.

Kai is looking at me now. Our eyes lock and I realize

he's watching me with concern, chewing his lower lip as he contemplates whether or not to comfort me. And then he does the most bizarre thing – he doesn't comfort me at all, he *defends* me instead. He twists in his chair and looks back at Noah, coolly telling him, "I don't think she wants to catch your crabs."

Noah's laughter falters and the room falls silent with him. He's sitting on the edge of his desk, nostrils flaring as he sets his sharp glare on Kai. "And who the fuck are you?"

"The line runner on the team that beat your ass last weekend," Kai says with a challenging smile, and I can see the realization dawning on our classmates that Kai is from Westerville Central. They're most likely wondering the same as I am – what's a Central kid doing here in a Westerville North classroom?

"You don't need to act tough to impress her, you know," Noah says gruffly, slumping into his chair. He looks at me with hatred in his eyes. "Just ask her. She'll ride anything with a pulse."

"Silence, please!" Miss Anderson says, clapping her hands together as she whirls into the room. We all do as we're told, everyone going quiet as she jumps straight into where we left off on Friday.

Everything was different on Friday. I was back at my desk, musing to Noah about Maddie Romy's upcoming party, daydreaming of the drinks I would enjoy and the music I would sing along to and the kisses I would share with Harrison Boyd. If only I had known how that party would mark the beginning of the end of Vanessa Murphy.

I try to catch Kai's eye throughout the class, but he pretends to be engrossed in Miss Anderson's teachings, chewing on his pen the same way he did last night at the library. Unlike him, I can't focus, too paralyzed in fear that Noah will find an opportunity to crack more jokes to the room. But he doesn't, thankfully, and when class ends, I remain rooted in my chair while everyone makes a beeline for the door. Kai is deliberately slow to pack up his books, both of us waiting for the room to empty before we engage in conversation.

Noah makes his presence known again by walking through the middle of mine and Kai's desks. He bumps his shoulder into Kai's, stares him down, then smiles at me. "You did this to yourself," he says with a sneer, then walks out.

I stare after Noah. My late-night thoughts from yesterday set in again. The guilt, the blame. If I hadn't gone to that party ... If I hadn't been with Harrison ... If I hadn't been too buzzed and carefree to tell him to put his phone away ... If I hadn't *lived* my life, then none of this would have happened. But I was doing exactly that. I was living my life the way I wanted to. Do I deserve to be shamed for all of eternity because I had fun with a guy I was attracted to? Everyone seems to think I do.

Once everyone has left the room, including Miss Anderson, I turn to Kai, both of us standing up from our desks. My expression is blank. "Why did you do that?"

"Well, *you* weren't gonna say anything," he says. He takes off his hat, runs a hand through his hair, then sets the snap-back back on. Still backward. "And I couldn't resist making a dig at a North player."

"In case you forgot, you're a North guy yourself now."

"Central blood, Nessie. Central blood," he says with great passion, holding up a clenched fist, squeezing his eyes shut. When he opens them again, he smiles and lowers his voice as he says, "I hope you're free after school, because we're staying back. We have locker rooms to sneak into, and a phone to steal. Bring your A-game. None of this apologetic crap. You're really gonna let that team of douchebags do this to you? Fight back, Vanessa."

I stare at him, my real name sounding foreign on his tongue. "Vanessa?"

"I'm not talking to you as a partner anymore," Kai says. He leans forward and delicately places his thumb under my chin, tilting my head up. The movement is so careful, and my breath catches in my throat as I look up at him. "I'm talking to you as a friend now. And I'm telling you to keep your head up and keep moving forward." He gives me a nod of reassurance, like he really believes I have the strength to ignore all of the torment being thrown my way, and then he tucks his books under his arm and walks away.

I swallow hard, then run my fingers over my skin where traces of his touch remain.

8

I lock myself inside a bathroom stall at the end of the day until everyone has left the building. It takes twenty minutes after the final bell has rung, constant commotion in the hallways as everyone dumps books in their lockers and catches up with friends. When I haven't heard any noise from outside the bathroom for a while, I kick open the stall door and stick my head out into the hallway. My head swivels back and forth, like a cartoon secret agent, checking that the coast is clear before continuing with my mission.

There's a janitor mopping the floor at the end of the hall, so I stroll out of the bathroom and head for my locker. When I reach it, Kai is already there. A Sharpie in hand, adding to the words scrawled all over my vandalized locker door.

"Is this your attempt to convince everyone we're *not* friends even though you admitted earlier that we are? By writing abuse on my locker?" I ask as I approach, folding my arms across my chest. I don't really care what anyone writes, so my expression is neutral, more curious than anything else.

Kai starts at the sound of my voice echoing down the

empty hallway. He looks over, pen hovering in the air. "Actually, I was fixing it."

I stop next to him and look at my locker. The hashtag from before – #SmileForTheCamera – has been totally scribbled over by Kai's permanent marker to look like an ocean, and peering out of the ocean is . . .

"The Loch Ness Monster?"

Kai grins, proud of his crappy art skills. "Nessie. Clever, isn't it? Hiding your secret code name in plain sight."

"Not really," I say, squinting closer at my locker. Kai's interpretation of the Loch Ness Monster is pretty terrible – an awful-looking reptile with one huge, googly eye. "Everyone is going to assume someone is calling me a snake."

Kai looks at his drawing again. "Shit," he says, and scribbles over Nessie too, leaving my locker door a total inky mess as though a three-year-old was given free rein with a black pen. It's not as bad as that hashtag, though. And I guess it's kind of cute that he was trying to make my locker look a little better. "Okay, let's focus on the mission at hand. The locker rooms. How do we get to them?"

I lead Kai down the hallway and out the main entrance, passing the school offices where we met for the second time yesterday morning. It feels like days ago now. Would Kai have gone out of his way to find me after that party if I hadn't conveniently been placed in front of him again? Or was I simply an opportunity that presented itself to him? I don't know, but I'm glad I'm not doing this alone.

We step outside into the student parking lot where only a few cars remain, most likely owned by students who are stuck in detention or staying late to cram in some extra study. Chyna's car is gone. I told her not to wait around for me, that I had some extracurricular activities that needed to be done, and she didn't bother to ask anything more. I'm not sure if she agrees with what Kai and I are doing, so I don't think she wants to know what we're up to.

"Where's the Hulk?" Kai teases as he follows me around the building.

"I told you. My vehicle's name is the Green McRusty," I say defensively, furrowing my brow at him. "And I rode your bike here."

Kai abruptly comes to a halt. "Excuse *me*," he says, aghast, "you did *what*?"

"Rode your bike here," I repeat, but I keep on walking until he jogs after me. There's another low sun today, the air crisp. My favorite weather. Cold, sunny days where you can wear sunglasses while still hugging a jacket around you.

"And what gave you the right to ride *my* bike to school?" Kai asks, indignant. As we move across campus in fast strides, he walks close by my side, his elbow brushing against mine. I try not to focus on it too much, because I doubt he is doing it intentionally.

"You did," I remind him.

"I gave you my bike to use on secret missions only."

"And aren't we on a mission right now?" I look sideways at him. "A mission that you still haven't told me about."

Kai sighs, defeated. "The Warriors – who suck, for the record – have practice right now. I overheard some guys from the team talking about it in the Chemistry lab this morning. So, we know exactly where Harrison is right now, and we know that his stuff will hopefully be in an unattended locker room," he explains.

"So, we're going to steal his phone, and . . .?"

"Hack it," he finishes. "Somehow."

I like the idea of having access to Harrison's phone, even if it only means deleting that wretched video from its source. It won't stop the video spreading – I know everyone has the video already – but it might make me feel that *slight* bit better. Maybe I could read all of Harrison's messages and pray to find some incredibly embarrassing information about him, something I could use to humiliate him as much as he's humiliated me. His entire life will be on that phone, every detail, from the good to the bad – and there's so much I could do with access to it.

I take Kai around the back of the school toward the football field. I can hear the grunting and the yelling before we even see the field, and as we round the corner, I reach for Kai's arm and gently pull him behind a car. We peer over the hood, analyzing our surroundings and our options. The Westerville North High varsity football team is out on the field, running drills and hurling footballs around. The players are distant figures, tiny from this far away.

"Sorry, I don't know which locker rooms they use," I say, my shrug apologetic. I've only ever gone to a couple of games, and only because I was begged to by the guy I was hooking up with at the time. Like Noah last fall, and Harrison this year.

"I do," Kai says, and he points out across the field to a

small building by the bleachers. "Those are the visiting team lockers. I've used them before. So—" he points to another building a few hundred feet directly in front of us "—that's where we need to be heading."

"Easy," I say, and just like last night, I scour the area to check for any witnesses before I dash out from behind the car and sprint across the asphalt toward the locker room. Kai is close on my heels, both of us running while slightly hunched over as though it'll make us look smaller, and therefore, less noticeable. If anyone saw us now, they'd seriously laugh.

"I think you're starting to enjoy this," Kai says as we slam ourselves against the wall of the locker house building, shielding ourselves behind it.

"I'm enjoying the thought of putting Harrison through hell," I correct, but Kai is right: this *is* kind of exciting. We're in a game – us versus Harrison Boyd. The prize? The last laugh. "Please, please don't be locked . . ." I mumble under my breath as I reach for the door, and I exhale a breath of relief when it swings open.

"Man, it would have been more badass if we had to break a window," Kai says, slapping his thigh in disappointment. "But it's probably better that we *don't* vandalize anything else."

The locker house is silent and polluted with so much man-strength deodorant that I nearly choke. There's bags and clothes scattered all over wooden benches, and shoes kicked carelessly across the floor. There's also a lot of lockers . . . and a lot of locked combinations. Damn.

"His phone's probably in a locker," I state in dismay, scrutinizing the lockers for some sort of clue as to which locker belongs to who. No names, only numbers, which I assume correspond with each player's jersey. If only I'd paid attention at the games, maybe I would know what Harrison's jersey number is. "Well, we tried."

"Not so fast," Kai says. I watch him closely as he slinks around the locker room, rubbing his chin while he thinks. "What was Harrison wearing today? Did you see him?"

"Yep, he cornered me in the hallway." I don't mention that Harrison accused me of slashing his truck tires last night, because it's no big deal. Harrison will most likely know that I'm behind everything that's about to go wrong in his life over the next few days, but what can he really do about it? Nothing. That's why it's so satisfying. "Black jeans," I say after a minute of consideration.

Kai grabs the nearest pair of black jeans and rummages through the pockets, pulling out a wallet. He checks the student ID inside – it's not Harrison's. Sighing, he tosses those jeans back onto the bench and moves on to the next pair. I join in the search, grabbing a pair from the floor and sticking my hands into the pockets. I pull out a phone and a wallet, but I don't need to check any ID to verify that this stuff is Harrison's – I know it's his phone by the screensaver. A picture of his fucking truck. Weirdo.

"I found it!" I tell Kai excitedly, presenting him with the phone. It's locked with a passcode, *duh*, but still. We at least have the phone in our possession, which is one step closer to cracking open Harrison Boyd's life.

Kai dumps the jeans he's searching through and rushes over, taking the wallet from my other hand. He pulls out a driver's license and holds it up, grinning as we confirm that yes, we do have Harrison's phone now. Kai slips the driving license back inside the wallet, then swipes thirty bucks, to which I raise a questioning eyebrow. "No one would steal his phone without stealing his cash too. Besides, I think we deserve some monetary compensation from him," Kai says.

We shove the wallet back into the pocket of Harrison's jeans and then return them to where I found them. I carry Harrison's phone like a trophy – he stole my dignity, so I stole his phone. We're leaving the locker room, amazed by how easy this all is, when I hear footsteps behind us.

"What are you two doing in here?" a gruff voice questions, and Kai and I freeze on the spot.

I slip Harrison's phone into the pocket of my hoodie and turn around along with Kai, and we come face-to-face with Coach Maverick as he approaches us. He stops a few feet away, hands on his hips. He's old, verging on retirement, but he's a permanent fixture at Westerville North. Kind of a legend and basically part of the furniture. He furrows his thick, graying eyebrows at us.

"Hey, Coach Maverick," I say with a polite smile. "This is my friend, Kai Washington. He just transferred here, and he plays football, so I thought I'd show him around. Sorry." It's almost a convincing lie, and I see the creases of suspicion on Coach Maverick's forehead fading away.

"You aren't supposed to be in here," Coach says, but then turns to Kai with keen interest. "Where did you transfer from?"

Kai looks down at the floor and blushes a little as he admits, "Central, Sir."

"Ouch," Coach says, placing a hand on his chest as though he's been wounded. An enemy player standing in his own locker room . . . "You guys beat us good last weekend," he acknowledges with an appreciative nod. "If you're interested in playing for us, I'm sure I could find a spot for you. I'm not sure my guys would like it, though."

"No thanks, Coach," Kai says. He glances up and smiles. "I'd much rather get hit by a bus."

Coach Maverick's mouth parts in shock, but then it slowly transforms into a smile. "Alright, you guys really need to get out of here. Don't snoop around again without my permission first."

He doesn't need to tell us twice. Kai and I set off like rockets, bursting into a sprint the moment we walk out of the locker house. We're laughing as we run, enjoying the thrill of our getaway, and we only slow to a stop when we're back outside the school entrance. I bend over, hands on my knees, trying to catch my breath between giggles.

"Good work on the quick thinking," Kai compliments, leaning back against the wall of the school building for support. He's breathing heavily, his lips parted. "I thought we were totally busted there for a second."

I straighten up, finally recovered. "He totally believed me too. I swear, you can get yourself out of any situation just by feigning innocence."

"Let's hope so," Kai says. "Never admit anything, huh? I think this calls for some food." He pulls out the swiped thirty bucks from his pocket and passes the notes to me.

Our hands brush together and we both freeze in the moment, caught out by the feeling of his skin against mine. I stare at our hands together, only the cash between them, and wonder what it would be like to *really* hold his hand properly. I fight the urge to drop the dollar bills and interlock our fingers.

We both glance up. Kai gives me that smirk again, the same one he gave me when we met in the office yesterday, though I swear I see him blush as he pushes the cash into the palm of my hand and then steps back.

"It's on Harrison."

9

"I'm sure I could find a hacker on Craigslist," Kai muses in between mouthfuls of his cheeseburger.

We're sitting opposite one another in a booth in Delaney's Diner. We're just past the outskirts of Westerville, south of the Outerbelt, the interstate that circles Columbus and serves as a border line between the city and suburbia. We biked here, sticking to the sidewalks during daylight hours to avoid the traffic, and now our bikes are locked up to a mailbox outside the diner.

"Chyna is smart when it comes to computers," I say, remembering her offer. Chyna's sort of a tech whizz. Last year when my Mac seized up, she managed to remotely move my entire database over to an external hard drive so that I still had access to all my files. How much harder could it be to do that with an iPhone? Easier, I bet. "She already said she could help."

"And who is Chyna?" Kai asks, giving me a blank stare.

"My best friend."

"Do we really want to bring her in to this?"

"She already knows," I say sheepishly. Was I *not* supposed

to share Operation Harr-assassinate with my best friend? Chyna always gets to know everything. That's just how it works.

Kai rolls his eyes. "Of course she does," he mumbles as he bites into his burger again. He chews slowly for a few seconds, then swallows. "Okay, we can try your friend first. Then Craigslist. Then the dark web. And if none of that works, then I'm smashing the phone."

I nod in agreement and return to the buffalo chicken sandwich I ordered. It tastes even better knowing that we're paying for this with Harrison's money. "Can I ask you something?"

"Sure."

"Why did you transfer to our school?"

Kai leans back in the booth, sipping his Pepsi. He's quiet while he studies me, like he knew this question was coming. "Got kicked out of Central."

I kind of guessed that. You can't just up and transfer for no reason. Usually, it's because you have no choice – like when you're expelled. "You're going to have to give me more than that," I say.

"Got kicked out of Central for fighting." When I still stare expectantly across the booth at him, he groans and sets his drink back down. "Okay, fine. I already got suspended once in sophomore year for fighting, so when I was involved in that brawl at the game last weekend, I didn't stand a chance. Two strikes and you're out." He shrugs nonchalantly and tosses a fry into his mouth, but I don't buy his cool attitude. I see a flicker of regret in his eyes that suggests he cares more than he's letting on about getting kicked out of school.

"So why *did* you get involved in the brawl?"

"Because I couldn't resist the opportunity to deck Harrison Boyd," he says flatly, then abruptly holds up his hand to me. "And I swear to God, if you ask me why . . ."

I smile. "Why?"

Kai glares at me, the golden afternoon sun streaming in through the windows and lighting up every fleck of blue in his eyes. "Because Harrison ruined a good thing for me. He took something that was mine." His mouth is fixed into a frown.

It's all very ominous, and my head spins with possibilities. It's clear Kai still doesn't want to talk about it, so I don't push the matter. I return to my sandwich instead, silently forking up a mouthful.

"Can I ask *you* something?" Kai says suddenly, and I glance up, mid-chew. I give him a nod. It gives Kai the go-ahead to ask: "Why were you, you know, hooking up with him?"

I almost choke on my food. I reach for my iced tea, chug a bunch of it, then stare at Kai in mortification. He waits patiently for an answer, despite asking an incredibly personal question. "Because I . . ." I start, but I realize I don't have an answer that would make sense if said out loud. I was having casual fun with Harrison because a no-strings relationship is the only kind of relationship I can fathom having with a guy. Even just the idea of simply going on a date with a boy makes my palms sweat. I don't want an emotional connection with anyone, because I don't want to *lose* them. I can't deal with any more loss in my life right now. "Because I wanted to," I finally admit. It's a cop-out answer. There's no way I can even begin to explain my fears to Kai without sounding utterly crazy.

"But why Harrison?"

"Why Noah Diaz? Why Blake Nelson? Why Nick Foster?" I shoot back at him. Harrison wasn't special. He was just like the others. "Because they're hot, that's why. Because I thought they didn't want a relationship either."

Confusion crosses Kai's defined features. "And that's a good thing?"

"I don't believe in relationships."

"You don't *believe* in relationships?" he repeats, echoing my words with an air of disbelief.

"Nope, because someone always gets hurt one way or another. You always get your heart broken. You either break up or one of you dies first," I explain, trying to keep my voice casual as though my opinion on the matter is a totally rational one. I've been against the idea of a relationship ever since Mom died. My heart is already too broken. "Nothing about that sounds great to me." I picture my dad now – pacing the aisles at work, his lifeless eyes staring into nothing, his heart crushed into a million tiny pieces that are lodged in his lungs, making it impossible for him to breathe. I don't want to be like that, and the only way to ensure that doesn't happen is to never let anyone get too close to me. Who even *wants* a soulmate if you know you're going to be left heartbroken when you lose them?

"You're going to have to give me more than that," Kai

says, copying my earlier words. He cocks his head to one side and studies me.

I try to piece my wave of thoughts into a single coherent statement that sums up my feelings, but it's incredibly difficult. It may also be the first time I've admitted it out loud to anyone other than myself. That's why my voice sounds distant and far away when I finally say, "I don't do relationships, because if I let someone in ... then I lay myself open to the possibility of losing them."

Kai lets my words sink in for a minute, mulling them over in his head. His eyes narrow while he thinks, his gaze never breaking away from mine, like he's trying to see straight into my soul. I'm not sure if anyone could ever understand how I feel, no matter how hard they tried. Eventually, he says, "I'm not really into relationships at the moment either."

Silence ensues because the conversation has gotten too awkward and neither of us knows how to navigate it. I'm just glad he doesn't push me to elaborate any further, because I'm not sure what else I can say. We both return to our food; Kai picking at his fries, me picking at my side salad. Minutes pass where neither of us say a word.

Suddenly, a pair of manicured hands slaps themselves down on the table. My eyes fly over from Kai to find Madison Romy glowering over us. She glances back and forth between Kai and me for a few seconds, studying Kai suspiciously. "So you're the new kid who was fighting in my kitchen." Her gaze shifts to me. "And you made a sex tape in my little brother's room. What's going on here? Were you both deliberately trying to create a scene at my party? Trying to embarrass me?"

"Not everything is about you, Madison." I brazen it out, not even looking at her, only taking another drink and exchanging a look with Kai. I'm pissed off by her interruption, whereas judging by the shine in Kai's eyes, he seems to find it amusing.

Maddie squeezes into the booth next to me, and I blink at her. What is this? A visit from the morality police?

"Everyone's been talking about my party," she says. "More so than usual, and everyone keeps asking when I'll be throwing another one. Can you guys turn up again and cause some drama? Make it another party worth talking about?"

"That's literally the most self-absorbed thing I've ever heard in my life," I say, pressing my hand to my forehead. I can't believe she's for real. Is Maddie that desperate to be popular that she's seeking outcasts to cause a scene at her parties just to get more attention?

"Will you pay us?" Kai queries, leaning in closer over the table. "What if I make out with her in front of everyone and then we break out into an argument? I'll even punch a hole in a wall for extra dramatic effect. Lots of cussing."

"Kai," I hiss, and he bats his eyelashes at me.

Did he seriously just bring up the idea of kissing me? In public? He's only messing around . . . surely?

"That would be perfect!" Maddie yelps, nodding enthusiastically.

"Maddie, it's not happening," I snap. I massage my temples, searching for the will to survive this conversation.

Maddie Romy is a nightmare even on a good day, so right now, I really can't cope with her high-pitched squeals and pleas for popularity.

"My parents are still in Florida until next week, so I'm thinking of throwing another party on Saturday," she says, talking casually, as though Kai and I are her friends. It's not that I *don't* like her, not really. She's just one of those girls who floats back and forth between groups of friends. A girl desperate to be liked.

"Already? Haven't you filled your annual party quota?" I remark.

Maddie angles toward me and crosses her arms over her chest. The ends of her blond hair are softly curled, bouncing around every time she moves her head. "I don't like the way you're talking to me."

"I don't like the way you're hoping to use us for your own gain," I say without missing a beat. I lock my eyes on hers and stare evenly back.

"Ladies, ladies," Kai says, his smile charming as he leans even further across the table toward us. I break eye contact with Maddie to glare at him instead.

"Harrison Boyd is telling everyone that you vandalized his truck," Maddie blurts. Her smile is smug as though she's hit me with a devastating, wounding blow.

"That's because I *did* vandalize his truck," I say coolly. Technically, it was Kai who did the actual vandalizing, but I'm more than happy to take the blame.

Maddie's face falls. "Wait. You actually did? Why?"

"What do you mean *why*?" I stare at her. As if she doesn't

know. I bet she has that video on her phone – I bet she even posted something nasty about me online.

"What Vanessa is trying to say," Kai cuts in, "is that she's incredibly pissed at Harrison for sending out that video, and now she's embarking on a journey of revenge to gain some personal fulfillment. I'm sure you understand."

Maddie contemplates for a moment. "Maybe I can help."

"We don't need your help," I say, rolling my eyes. Is this a lucid dream? Why is Madison Romy now offering to help us mess with Harrison?

"Did you forget that I volunteer in the school office? The school office where everyone's files are kept?" she says. "More specifically, Harrison's file."

Kai and I look at each other. His expression becomes even more keen. This could potentially be useful and we both know it. So does Maddie.

"And what exactly do these files entail?" Kai questions.

Maddie gets up from the booth and dusts off her skirt before giving us an ultimatum: "I'll only pull his file if you both promise to turn up to my party on Saturday."

"Done," Kai says without hesitation.

Maddie gives him a beaming smile, then we both stare after her as she walks away, fetching a to-go bag of food from the counter and twirling out the diner door.

My expression is twisted. "What just happened?"

"I think we just blew our cover, but may also have recruited a third accomplice," Kai says, grinning. He leans back in the booth and smolders his eyes at me. "And I think I may have to kiss you on Saturday."

I avert my gaze, unable to look him in the eye. I'm fighting the blush that's rising up my neck and onto my face. The thought of kissing Kai … It makes my body tingle, but it's not as though the thought has never crossed my mind before. I've stared at his lips way too much already, because I was drawn to him the moment I looked up after bumping into him at Maddie's party on Saturday. I knew then that he was undeniably hot, but being around him for the past two days has only heightened the attraction. Even his brazen personality is attractive now that I'm getting to know it, so of course I would kill to feel his lips against mine. But everything between me and Kai so far is unconventional, so gauging how he feels in return is a lot harder than it is with other guys.

I force myself to look back at him across the booth.

"You at least better kiss me good," I manage to joke, trying to play it cool, like kissing Kai is simply mechanical and nothing more. My lips against his. That's all it is.

Except the mere thought of it is still making my stomach do somersaults.

Kai's smile is gorgeous, and he gives me a teasing wink. "I don't offer anything less." But as soon as the words leave his mouth, his expression goes taut and his body stiffens. He stares past me, blinks fast, then abruptly gets to his feet. He pulls out Harrison's thirty bucks from his pocket and dumps the bills on the table. "Gotta go, Ness," he says quickly, his voice low. "Call me later."

I don't get a chance to ask him what's wrong, because he's already walking away, exiting through the back door of the diner. I watch him as he leaves, utterly perplexed by the speedy getaway. I spot him again through the windows, grabbing his bike and cycling off into the distance.

"Excuse me?" a voice says gently, pulling my gaze away from the window. I glance up so fast that, at first, the blur of blond hair I see makes me think Maddie has returned. But it's not her.

Someone new has decided to drop by my booth this time. A girl around my age is studying me carefully while I analyze her in return. She has delicate skin and poker straight blond hair, and her makeup is flawless as though it's been professionally applied at Sephora. Over her shoulder, I can see a group of girls settling into a booth over in the corner, all of them looking this way. I don't recognize any of them, so they definitely don't go to Westerville North. Which means they recognize me from somewhere other than school, and it's not hard to figure out where they must have seen me before.

"Yep, I'm the girl from the video," I say, hoping to come across all blasé and indifferent. I reach for my napkin and wave it in the air, giving this nosy stranger a sardonic smile. How hard is it to eat my food in peace? "I can autograph this napkin for you."

The girl's perfectly shaped eyebrows pinch together, and she stares at me in silence for a few moments, only intensifying the awkward air between us. She looks perplexed, like she has no idea what I'm talking about, and I realize then that I could be wrong. Maybe she *doesn't* know about that video at all. She steps more into my line-of-sight and places a hand on the edge of the table. "Did I just see Kai sitting here with you? Kai Washington?"

"Uhh. Yeah. He just left," I say, dropping my eyes to her hand on the table – *ugh*, her nails are gorgeous too while mine are broken and gross – then glancing back up. I'm curious now. "Do you know him?"

"Yeah, I know him." She smirks and looks at the ground. "Are you guys, like, dating?"

"No. We're just working together on something . . ." I say. I'm unsure now, growing suspicious. What is this, twenty questions?

"Okay," she says, giving me a wide smile that reveals her teeth. "Thanks."

Thanks for *what*? I stare after her as she walks back over to her friends, the same way I stared after Maddie and the same way I stared after Kai, full of confusion and questions.

10

Did you steal H's phone, you stupid little bitch?

I stare at the message, and laugh. Like, laugh so hard all of my organs hurt.

I'm sitting on my bed next to Kennedy and Chyna, all of us in fits of giggles at the barrage of abuse being texted my way from Harrison and his buddy Noah. Harrison has called me a thieving piece of trash. Noah is calling me a stupid little bitch. And the best part? They *know* I'm in control. They know I'm fighting back. That's why they're throwing crass insults my way, but they have absolutely *zero* effect on me.

I glance over at Harrison's phone now. It's on my dresser, charging, because the battery died as soon as I got home from the diner. Kai is on his way over, and between him, Chyna and me, I'm sure we'll find a way to hack the phone.

"You should reply," Kennedy says, stroking Theo, who's sprawled across her lap.

"And say what?"

"*Screw you, dick face,*" she suggests, and I swat at her,

scolding her use of words. Mouth like a trooper, that one. But I'm no better.

"Noah's a jerk," Chyna says. "Total nice guy when you were interested in him, total douche once you stopped." She's sitting at my dressing table in her pajamas and fluffy bunny slippers, carefully styling her hair. She removed her braids this afternoon after having them in for six weeks, and it's an all-night procedure – she isn't happy that I've dragged her over to my place. I do love the luscious scent of shampoo wafting around my room, though. Along with her hair products and styling tools, she's also brought her laptop with her. We'll need it.

My phone buzzes again. Chyna and Kennedy both watch me as I open up the new message, waiting to hear which of Harrison's friends have texted me this time, but it's from Kai. He's outside my house and doesn't want to knock on the front door.

"Kai's here," I announce, clambering off my bed, tangled up in my sheets. I nudge Kennedy's knee. She knows all about Kai and our plans for revenge. "You gotta go. And take your laundry downstairs while you're at it."

"Ugh," Kennedy groans, reluctantly getting to her feet. She carries Theo in her arms and leaves my room, though I have no doubt she'll be spying on us all from afar. She'll want to see Kai with her own eyes, especially because I let it slip how gorgeous he was. I'm trying my hardest to focus on our mission together, but his charm and good looks are impossible to ignore.

"Oh my God," Chyna says, panicked. "Mr. Hottie is about

to come in here and my hair looks like *this*!" She throws her head back in exasperation and I throw a pillow at her.

I steal a quick glance at my own reflection in my mirror as I leave the room to fetch Kai – sweatpants and a tank top, my hair in a high ponytail, this morning's makeup blotchy and smudged. I don't really care, though. We aren't heading out anywhere tonight, so comfort is the way forward. It's like having a sleepover with your best friends, except no one is spending the night, and only one of my guests *is* actually my best friend.

I take the staircase too fast, tucking loose strands of hair behind my ears as I rush downstairs. Ever since I left the diner earlier, I haven't been able to stop thinking about kissing Kai. That's why I pause for a second in the hall before I let him in, adjusting my sweatpants and massaging lip balm into my lips – yesterday I would have thrown the door open without hesitation. Suddenly, everything I say and do around him feels like it matters.

When I open the door, Kai is standing on my porch, looking out over my lawn. He's wearing black gym shorts and a T-shirt, with that same cap from earlier today still on his head, and I spot his bike resting against the porch. He turns to face me. "Hey," he says, touching the bill of his hat and giving me a courtesy nod.

Lord, have *mercy*. I tear my eyes away from his chest and concentrate on maintaining eye contact instead. I realize that it's the first time I've invited a guy over to my house. "Hi."

Kai stares at me expectantly, his smile widening. "So, can I come in or do you need me to stay out in the yard?"

"Come in," I splutter, stepping back from the door and motioning him inside my cold, empty house. My heart beats a little faster as Kai steps over the threshold, kicking off his Jordans and carefully pushing them to the side. He keeps his eyes on me, waiting for guidance on what to do next, his smile growing more strained the longer I'm silent. "Sorry," I say, shaking my head. *Snap the hell out of it*, I tell myself. "We're upstairs in my room."

I head for the stairs again, taking the few moments of silence to pull myself together before I do something embarrassing that I'll regret, and Kai follows close behind me. I can sense him looking around, studying my home.

"Vanessa?" a voice calls from the kitchen. It's Dad. "Who are you talking to?"

Oh, so *now* he wants to pay attention to me? I pause, one foot on the staircase, and look over at Dad as he walks over. He's drying his hands with a towel, glancing back and forth between Kai and me, his expression blank as ever. That's the thing with Dad – he's *emotionless*.

"This is Kai," I tell him quickly. "We have a homework assignment together, so we'll be upstairs."

"Hey," Kai says, flashing Dad a polite smile and giving a little wave. I bet he wants to sink into the floor.

"Okay," Dad says. He doesn't smile in return, only throws the dishtowel over his shoulder and pads back into the kitchen. To a stranger like Kai, Dad must come across as rude and hostile, but that's only because they can't see that he is really just grief-stricken and lost.

I continue up the stairs and silently pray that Kai doesn't

mention the encounter, but of course, he does. How could he not? Dad gives off a weird vibe. So cold, so stoic . . . It's unnatural.

"You're sneaking a guy up to your room at night and your dad doesn't give me *the look*?" Kai questions once we're upstairs and out of earshot.

"That's because he doesn't care," I say over my shoulder. I can't look back at him right now.

"Well, what about your mom?"

"Not here. Working late," I lie. My heart pangs with guilt. It's not a secret – I was the kid in the sophomore year whose grandparents had to pull her out of class in a frantic mayhem of panic because her mom had just passed away that afternoon. I was always surrounded by friends who invited me to hang out, who sat with me at lunch, who were always just *so nice*. I was the girl whose mom was dead, but the pressure of all of that pity got tedious. I didn't want to be defined by my mom's death anymore.

It wasn't long before I realized that it wasn't so difficult to get my peers to react toward me in a different kind of way, one that had nothing to do with pity. That's why I kissed Andy Donovan under the bleachers and made sure the news was on everyone's lips. It got me attention, but this time it was for a completely different reason than my mom's death.

We walk into my room and Chyna has managed to style her hair into a puff above her head, smoothing down her baby hairs with a toothbrush. She glances over at the door when we enter and immediately stops touching her hair.

"Kai, this is Chyna. My best friend and computer whizz

extraordinaire," I say, flashing her a grin as I close the door behind us, "and Chyna, this is Kai. My accomplice and tire-slasher extraordinaire. You sort of met at the party." We all share a laugh.

"Hey," Kai says, giving Chyna a nod, and she squeaks back a quiet hello.

"Make yourself comfortable," I tell Kai. I flop back down onto my bed, secretly hoping that he'll join me, but he doesn't. Instead, he sits down on my floor. When his back is turned for a mere second, Chyna and I exchange a look – her eyes go wide and her mouth pulls into a tight smile, a clear signal that she agrees with me on the fact that Kai is seriously hot. We didn't get much chance to discuss him at the party.

"So, did you charge the phone?" Kai asks, getting straight to business. He leans back against my wall and pulls his knees up to his chest.

"All charged," Chyna says. She yanks the charger out of Harrison's phone on the dresser and gets up, sitting down cross-legged on my bed next to me. She grabs her laptop too but doesn't turn it on yet. "I know it's obvious, but have you guys tried *guessing* the passcode?" She taps at the phone. "It's only a four-digit passcode. I'll check the obvious." I watch over her shoulder as she tries entering four zeroes, and then one-two-three-four, but neither of them gains us access to Harrison's life. Chyna thinks, then looks over at me. "Do you know his birthday?"

"Oh! I do, actually," I say, feeling surprisingly useful. "It was Labor Day because we hooked up ..." My words trail off when I remind myself that Chyna and I aren't the only two people in my room. I can't talk so freely about my time spent with Harrison when I have a guest.

Kai scoffs and pulls out his own phone. He scrolls for a second, checking his calendar, then says, "Labor Day was September third this year. Try that, Chyna. By the way, is it spelled like the country?"

"Nope, spelled like my name," Chyna says with a wry smile. She tries different combinations of dates on Harrison's phone, like zero-nine-zero-three for September 3rd, and nine-three-zero-one for September 3rd '01, but still nothing. She puts the phone down and opens up her laptop instead. "Okay, we can't guess it. And you want all the files, so I can't just reset the phone to factory settings," Chyna says, voicing her thoughts out loud. "Time to download all kinds of risky software, and if some virus blows up my computer, you guys are buying me a new one. This might take a while." She plumps up my pillows and gets comfortable.

"Absolutely," I promise. I do appreciate Chyna helping us, especially when I know she doesn't think what we're doing is *right*. Her moral compass is vastly stronger than mine, but she always puts our friendship first before anything else. That's why she's so willing to help out.

"Hey, Nessie," Kai says from the floor. "I added another idea to the list after I left the diner."

I scoot over to the edge of my bed and look down at him, raising an eyebrow. "And why *did* you leave the diner?"

"Saw someone I didn't want to talk to," he says quickly, brushing it off, "which gave me an idea. You said Harrison goes to Bob Evans every Wednesday night." I nod. "How do you think he'd feel if an unwanted guest turned up?"

"Go on," I say curiously, sitting down on the floor next to him. I don't know how much distance to keep between us. Too far might make it noticeable and awkward. Too close might *also* make it noticeable and awkward. I position myself a foot away, and wonder if the person he didn't want to talk to at the diner was the same girl who approached me after he left. She obviously knew who he was, after all.

Kai pulls out that little notepad from the pocket of his gym shorts and clears his throat, reading over the new notes he's added. "So we set up a fake profile for him on some 'no strings' dating app or whatever. An 'up for anything' profile, because sending his usual type his way seems like more a favor than an annoyance. And we talk to some people, then ask them if they want to meet at Bob Evans tomorrow night." Kai glances sideways at me and smiles. "We can discreetly watch as Harrison becomes hounded by chancers who think he's down for some fun."

"Isn't that cruel on the innocent people who get hurt in this too?" Chyna questions from my bed, eyeballing us over the top of her laptop, disapproval written all over her face. "And I've seen that prank happen in movies like a gazillion times. Not really original."

"It doesn't need to be original. It just needs to work," Kai tells her, his tone as nonchalant as ever. "And when it comes to Harrison Boyd, we need stuff that works."

"Hmm, okay. Point taken," Chyna grumbles, averting her eyes back to her laptop screen. "I just hope you're not leading my best friend astray."

Kai looks at me, taking in my features. The corner of his mouth curves into a tiny, knowing smile that's almost ... pitiful. "I think she was already astray when I found her."

My chest tightens when he says this. Is that a joke or is there meaning behind his words? Suddenly, in that exact second, I wish Kai could see straight through me, like he knows my mom is dead and my dad doesn't care and my sister needs me to protect her and I don't believe in relationships because I'm scared of being left heartbroken and I get drunk and stay out late and fool around with guys because I'm acting out to get attention and I say that I don't care when I *do* care. But then I remind myself that it's impossible for Kai to know these things.

"Don't worry, Chyna," I say, forcing down the lump in my throat and keeping my voice even, "I know the limits." Or at least I think I do.

She doesn't reply.

"So?" Kai urges. He sits up a little and holds up his phone. "Do I download some sleazy app or nah?"

"Let's do it," I say, biting back laughter.

"Man, I hope no one sees this on my phone ..." he mumbles as he downloads the app, and I let that laugh escape as we both huddle in closer around his phone.

Kai doesn't follow or have Harrison as a friend on any social media, so it becomes a team effort to essentially steal his identity. I snoop through Harrison's Facebook and Instagram accounts, picking out different pictures of him and then texting them over to Kai's phone where he adds them to the fake account we're putting together.

Harrison, young and hot, Westerville.

"Bio?" Kai asks, looking up from his phone. "Chyna, any thoughts on a biography for our friend Harrison?"

Chyna fires him a look, because Kai has yet to understand that she is simply here on the grounds of hacking a phone, and not because she wants to be part of our overall scheme. "*Hey, I'm not really Harrison, don't meet me,*" she suggests, smiling sweetly.

"I know," I say, taking Kai's phone from him. My thumbs hover over his screen, ready to type, when I notice that his phone is in airplane mode. It raises my suspicions – why doesn't he want any notifications coming through right now? And then it crosses my mind, for the very first time, that I don't even know if Kai is single. What if he has a girlfriend?

"You need to type something," he says into my ear, his breath tickling my cheek. I'm pretty sure all the hairs on my arms stand up.

I swallow hard and type a biography for Harrison:

What's up? I'm Harrison. I'm just testing the waters here so casual encounters only. Keeping it low-key.

"That'll do for now," Kai says, taking his phone back. His fingers brush over my hand, but all I can think is that there's a girl out there who will kill us both if she finds out her boyfriend is in my room. He finishes setting up the profile, then grins proudly once we're all set and ready to go. "Time to start chatting."

I know what we're doing is wrong, but I have a one-track mind right now. All I can focus on is screwing with Harrison, nothing else, so I'm incapable of worrying about the consequences of my actions. Kai and I spend a while talking to different people, striking up casual conversations, until eventually Kai gets up to head for the bathroom. It leaves me in charge of all the scandalous communication.

The second Kai leaves the room, Chyna lowers the lid of her laptop and gives me a scolding look. She slowly shakes her head, lips pursed. "Girl, he's an absolute *snack*, but he's also kind of a jerk. What nice guy would really be happy to do all this stuff?"

"And I kind of need him to be a jerk," I say. I pull myself up from the floor and sit down on the edge of my bed with a deep sigh. "No nice guy was ever going to slash Harrison's tires for me, or sneak into locker rooms with me, or set up a fake 'casual encounters' profile with me. I'm being a jerk too." My smile is tired, disheartened. "I know you don't agree with what we're doing, but . . . have you *seen* what everyone is saying about me online? Harrison did that to me. He betrayed me."

Chyna pushes her laptop to the side and crawls over to me, hooking her arms around me and burying her head into my shoulder. "Okay, Vans. You do what you need to do."

I reach up and squeeze her hand. I know screwing with Harrison won't make that video ever go away, but it'll at least offer some compensation. "Thanks. And I promise we won't take it too far."

"You better not, because I'm not bailing you out of jail

for committing a felony," she teases half-heartedly, pushing me away as she crawls back to her laptop, sinking back into my pillows. "Even though I'm pretty sure I'm committing a crime myself right now."

"And I love you for it," I say. I blow her a kiss, she catches it, and then I leave the room to go find Kai. I want a minute to talk to him alone, and I catch him out in the hall just as he's making his way back to my room. I close my bedroom door behind me.

"I don't think your friend likes me all that much," Kai says with a wary smile. He leans back against the wall and stuffs his hands into the pockets of his gym shorts.

"You're right. She doesn't," I agree. It's quiet out in the hall, only the sound of the static buzz of Kennedy's TV from the other room. There are no lights on up here, either. We keep our voices low. "This might sound crazy," I say slowly, "but it feels like I've known you for way longer than forty-eight hours."

Kai's eyes softly narrow as he looks me over, his gaze meeting mine. "Maybe because I'm already seeing your worst side and you're already seeing mine. Most people don't see this stuff until at least six months down the line."

I cover my face with my hands and let out a frustrated groan of self-defeat. "We're assholes, aren't we?"

"Only because we have to be," Kai says. I drop my hands and lift my head, searching his face for answers, desperately seeking a reason for why Kai is even here right now. He knows exactly what I'm doing, because he says, "You're wondering again why I'm doing this, aren't you?"

"I wouldn't have to wonder if you actually told me," I say.

I cock my head to one side and stare at him. "I mean, c'mon. Who am I to judge?"

Kai's gentle smile falters into a frown. He looks down at the floor and is silent for a few seconds, deliberating over whether to finally tell me the truth. He shrugs, but never glances back up.

"Harrison was texting my girlfriend behind my back," he says, his voice unusually gruff. "Knew she wasn't single. Kept hitting her up anyway and trust me, he's persistent – I read the messages he hounded her with. That's when I found out she was cheating on me back in the summer."

I know in that moment that I'm a selfish human being, because all I can think about is the relief that comes with the realization that yes, Kai must be single. "I'm sorry. You don't want to be with a girl like that, anyway."

He looks up, his face thunderous. "I was in love with her, but she wasn't in love with me. So yeah, you're right. I don't want to be with a girl like that."

The hurt in his eyes takes me aback. In the past forty-eight hours, I've only ever seen Kai's fun, playful nature and his mischievous smirks. It's like there's a totally brand-new person standing in front of me now – a boy whose anger is bubbling within him, a boy who is hurt.

"Then Harrison deserves everything that's coming to him," I say with a nod.

Harrison not only sent an explicit video of me out into the world, he also stole Kai Washington's girlfriend. Any morality I had left is now gone. Between the two of us, we're bringing Harrison Boyd down.

11

I wake at six the following morning to a text from Chyna telling me to check my email. Groggy and half asleep, I search for my laptop in the dark and boot it up. The brightness of the screen burns my eyes, forcing me to squint. It's too early, but my need to find out what exactly it is that Chyna has emailed me is desperate, irresistible.

Last night's process of hacking into the device ended up taking much longer than we anticipated. Chyna left at eleven with her laptop and promised to stay up as late as necessary until the slow extraction of Harrison's files was complete. Meanwhile, Kai and I, posing as Harrison, openly flirted with far too many different folk to count on that app. A handful of them now thinks they're meeting Harrison later tonight at Bob Evans.

I pull up my email: A list of unopened newsletters from websites I don't remember ever signing up for, and a new email from Chyna. My stomach lurches when I read the subject line: *Harrison's files.*

My heart is thumping as I open the email. It's blank except for a zipped folder, which I automatically download.

The next thirty seconds feel excruciatingly slow, but I'm wide awake now, hunched over the laptop and drumming my fingers against the keypad. Finally, a list of folders appears on my screen: *Messages, Photos, Videos, Music, Mail,* and *Notes.*

I stare at the folders, adrenaline flooding my bloodstream, deciding which to open first. It's so exhilarating, the thought of having Harrison's life at my fingertips . . . I decide to get the boring files out of the way first. I check his music, but it's mostly Drake and Post Malone albums, though there's also a Taylor Swift album in there, which makes me chuckle.

Then I check his email, but his inbox is as boring and as ignored as my own: hundreds of unopened spam emails, random newsletters, and the occasional stranger offering to transfer him three million dollars if he provides his social security number. Oh, and the portable loudspeaker he bought on Amazon was dispatched yesterday.

I open up his notes next. A couple of reminders about assignments that are due, a list of colleges I'm guessing he must be interested in, and then the first worthwhile thing I've found so far: names. Names that include my own.

Lizzie Avery 7/10
Madison Romy 5/10
Sierra Jennings 8/10
Vanessa Murphy 9/10

I stare dumbfounded at my computer screen, the names etching themselves into my retinas.

It's the girls he's hooked up with.

It has to be. There's no other explanation, especially because my name is the newest addition. It's so gross and it makes me want to claw at my skin. How could I have ever been attracted to a guy like this? And Madison Romy is on there too? Oh, damn. I would have never guessed that in a million years. Lizzie Avery, however? She's on the cheer squad, so that's no surprise. Even expected, more like. But Sierra Jennings? The name draws a blank in my head. I've never heard of her, and unless she's a freshman, then I'm convinced she doesn't go to Westerville North. Unless . . .

Unless Sierra Jennings is Kai's ex.

I grab my phone and take a picture of the list on my screen. This information is more intriguing than useful, and it's made me realize that Harrison is kind of a dog. I mean, seriously? *Rating* the girls he's been with? Like he needs to create a list to record his achievements? What a scumbag. I should have known that on Sunday when he told me I wasn't the only girl he had on speed dial.

There's nothing else of interest in his notes, so I move over to his messages. The messages are displayed as a thread of text, each conversation contained in its own subfolder. I open Harrison's messages with me first, even though I know exactly what they say. Our last messages to each other were on Sunday night before I ended things and he kicked me out of his truck. I scroll back through the thread, all the way back to our very first exchange on the first day of September. It was me who got in touch first.

VANESSA: Hey, it's Vanessa. Saw you at Polaris earlier. We should hang out sometime.

HARRISON: What's up? Yeah, maybe we should.

In hindsight, I wish I had never texted him. I was bored, having cooled things down with Nick Foster a month earlier, when I saw Harrison at the mall. He just happened to look hotter than usual that day and I wondered what it'd be like to kiss him. We hooked up for the first time that same night, embarking on what soon became a two-month fling.

I cringe as I flick through the rest of our messages. All the flirting and teasing . . . None of it was worth it. But how was I supposed to know that Harrison would turn out to be such a jackass? That he would have absolutely zero respect for me?

I brace myself – I don't know what I'll find this time – then read his messages with Noah and Anthony too, mostly focusing on what they all discussed on Sunday night and also Monday when the video was first leaked. They are all in one big group chat together with a handful of other guys from the team.

HARRISON: You were right, man. She just cut things off. Left her at Heritage Park lol. Girls like her will get picked up easily there.

NOAH: Told you she gets bored quickly.

ANTHONY: Who do you think she'll go after next?

NOAH: You if you're unlucky enough ;)

Then I can see that Harrison sent a file into the chat just after six the next morning, and I know exactly which file that was. In front of me is the exact moment Harrison broke my trust and shared that video. I can't bring myself to read the string of messages that followed, so I close that chat.

I then work my way through each subfolder of conversations with different contacts, reading mundane texts between Harrison and his parents, until I get to the exchanges between Harrison and Sierra Jennings. I hesitate before I open the folder. I'm suddenly aware that I'm snooping around Harrison's private life, and it feels wrong, but I mentally remind myself that he doesn't deserve privacy. He didn't give *me* any.

I check my phone for the time. It's 06:23. The darkness outside is beginning to lift. I inhale and open the folder, glued to my screen as I read over the most recent texts between Harrison Boyd and Sierra Jennings. They're from Monday.

HARRISON: A lot of shit happened today. Need you to make me feel better.
SIERRA: Oh, babe. Do you want me to come over?

Oh, babe indeed.

So. Sierra Jennings is the other girl then, which feels immensely awkward, given that she's Kai's ex. This feels like the worst love triangle in the world, the way we're now all linked.

For a second, I contemplate forwarding all these files

over to Kai. The texts date right back to January, message after message after message . . . but then I remember that Kai has already read them. These are the messages that led him to discover the truth about Harrison and Sierra in the first place, and he wasn't kidding when he said Harrison was persistent. At the beginning, the messages are pretty innocent. Harrison and Sierra talked about school – despite being students at different ones – and what they'd been up to that day. Harrison suggests they should hang out sometime; Sierra says no, she has a boyfriend. I skip ahead to their messages from March. Harrison has grown more full-on by then, begging Sierra to let him take her out, promising her fancy dinners and nights she wouldn't forget. She entertains the idea, and even seems amused whenever Harrison makes digs at Kai. He continuously tells Sierra that she can do so much better, and I decide I don't want to read the rest. I've already realized I don't really like Sierra Jennings, and that I'd be pissed too if I found out someone made such an effort to steal someone away from me.

I take a deep breath and decide that it's time to open up Harrison's videos. It's impossible to ignore the fact that one of the videos in this folder has caused total uproar. If Harrison had never sent out that video, we could have simply ignored one another. Nothing more than a fling that was done and dusted, rather than turning into the war that it is now.

It's the most recent video there is.

But the truth is, I can't even open it, let alone watch it, and I immediately delete it from my computer. I don't want that video in my life, and that includes on my hard drive.

I search through the rest of Harrison's collection instead. Blurred, out-of-focus videos from parties. Short clips of him and the guys at football practice. And then a video that I know could be lethal if it got into the wrong hands.

Hands such as my own . . .

A video of Harrison, Noah, Anthony and some other guys from the team. They're sitting in the bleachers of our football field, apparently late at night and after hours because there're no floodlights on. The image isn't clear – Harrison's moving his phone around too much – but there's no mistaking what's going on. Huddled in their circle up on the bleachers, the guys pass a burning joint around, each taking a drag. Getting stoned on school property . . . Not a smart thing to do in the first place. But *filming* evidence of it? Harrison has gone beyond the realms of stupidity here.

Which is utterly wonderful news for me.

If I *really* wanted to ruin Harrison's life, I could anonymously email these videos over to Couch Maverick. Harrison would be kicked off the team for sure without question, blowing up his chances of playing college football. It would be a severe, risky move to make . . . but just the power of knowing it's an opportunity I could grab is satisfying enough. I make an extra copy of the video, just in case I ever feel forced to use it as a weapon.

Finally, I open up Harrison's photos. There's thousands of them. I scroll quickly through page after page of files, skimming through the images for anything that jumps out at me. There's everything from pictures of juicy burgers to internet memes, too boring to bother looking at, but then something truly exciting catches my eye.

I enlarge the image.

And at 06:47, I let out a laugh so loud that it ruptures the morning silence.

"Oh, Harrison," I say, shaking my head at my screen, "you're making payback far too easy."

12

After Chyna and I arrive at school and she heads off to grab her books from her locker, I remain outside, lingering by the bike racks. I keep my head down and try to stay under the radar, and for the most part, it works. No one bothers me today, but it's still only day three of that video being out there in the public domain, so I would be naive to believe that everyone has forgotten about it already. The reality is that everyone is still talking about it – only behind my back this time, I bet.

I kick at the concrete for a while, pacing back and forth, until I hear the distinct sound of a bike's wheels spinning. I look up and let out a breath of relief when I spot Kai making his way toward me.

"Good morning," he says, squeaking to a stop. He swiftly gets off the bike and begins locking it up to the rack, eyeing me over his shoulder. We didn't plan to meet here. In fact, I think we're still supposed to be trying our best not to be seen together.

"Chyna got the files," I splutter. I'm bouncing on the balls of my feet, and I can feel the weight of both mine and

Harrison's phones in the pockets of my jacket. I reach out and excitedly squeeze Kai's elbow, unable to contain myself. I've been sitting on this information all morning and I've been dying to break the news to him. "I looked through everything as soon as I woke up, and there's so much stuff we can use."

Kai straightens up and glances down at my hand on his arm. I quickly let go. "Seriously? Damn, I need to give your friend more credit," he says. "What did you find?"

"Videos of Harrison and some other guys on the team smoking pot in the bleachers. Some photos that will be useful. And I think he's had a thing with Madison Romy."

"The girl from the diner?"

"Yeah. That might explain why she's so willing to help us out," I say as the realization dawns on me. There must be a reason why no one has ever heard about the two of them hooking up. It seems like the kind of thing Maddie would brag about – getting with a guy from the football team pretty much boosts your position in the school hierarchy – so why has she kept it a secret? "Meet me at the office after school?"

Kai nods. "And don't talk to me in class."

I roll my eyes as he turns and walks away, but I find myself rooted to the spot, staring after him. I didn't tell him *everything* I found – like those messages between Harrison and Sierra. It seems cruel to let him know that I've read them, because I'm sure those messages are really humiliating to him now. Harrison and Sierra made Kai look like a fool.

"Kai," I say loudly. He stops walking and glances back over his shoulder. I lower my voice and can't stop myself from asking, "Her name is Sierra Jennings, right? Your girlfriend."

Something flashes in Kai's eyes. Resignation, but also anger. His mouth twitches, his eyes narrow. He's silent for a few seconds. "*Ex*-girlfriend," he quietly emphasizes, then turns and keeps on walking, staring at the ground.

I watch him until he disappears inside the school building, then I count to thirty in my head before I make my way inside too just as the first period bell rings out. I head straight for my Biology class, but I do notice as I pass my locker that it has been scrubbed clean. None of the graffiti from yesterday remains and my locker looks brand new, shining a little more brightly than the rest. At least that's something.

Surprisingly, I don't end up rattled by nerves as I approach the science labs. I share this class with Harrison, and when I walked into this room on Monday, I slapped him. I haven't been in here since, but I feel relaxed, in control. It's because I have all the power now. Harrison has nothing more to use against me, whereas I have *everything* to use against him. He's blissfully unaware that when he and his father are enjoying their burgers at Bob Evans later tonight, a handful of so-called dates will be approaching him. He's also unaware that I'm not doing all of this on my own, that I have a kickass accomplice. And although Harrison *is* aware that I'm the most probable suspect in the theft of his phone, I doubt he has any idea that I have access to every single one of his files. Having the ball in my court feels empowering.

I walk into the lab, my head held high. Maddie Romy's

face is the first I see. She gives me a quick, small smile of acknowledgment for the first time in her life and then looks away. Even *she* doesn't want to be associated with me in public, but I don't take it personally. She's doing Kai and me a favor later, anyway, so as far as I'm concerned, she's one of the few people I can actually trust around here right now.

And then I see the face that was once so gorgeous but is now anything but – Harrison Boyd's.

He's at his usual desk, his eyes already glued to me, following my every move as I weave my way around the room. The desk next to him where I usually sit is still empty, so mustering up every ounce of courage that I can, I walk over and sit down a mere two feet away from him.

"Hi, Harrison," I say sweetly, my smile angelic. I angle my body toward him and reach into my jacket pocket, presenting him with his phone that went missing from the locker rooms yesterday. I find it so much easier to feign confidence rather than letting my anger push me to tears. "Were you looking for this?"

Harrison nearly bursts out of his chair and snatches the device from my hand. He gives his phone a quick once over, making sure I haven't smashed the screen, even though I now wish that I had. His eyes flash back up to look at me, completely enraged. "What the fuck are you playing at?"

"Oh, don't worry. I couldn't guess your passcode," I tell him, flicking my hair over my shoulder. I turn back toward the front of the class and remain silent for a few moments just to antagonize him, then shoot him a sideways glance. "But I didn't need to."

Harrison looks around the class as people continue to file in, then edges in closer to me and hisses, "What are you talking about?"

"I wonder what Coach Maverick would say if I sent him that video of you getting stoned in the bleachers," I taunt, my tone perfectly innocent.

Harrison's face pales. He looks down at his phone in his hand, perplexed as to how I've gotten access to it, then clenches his jaw. "You wouldn't dare."

"You like to send out videos." I turn to face him again, my expression entirely blank, acting disinterested in this exchange. "Why can't I do the same?"

Harrison groans and rubs his hands over his face, fighting to keep his anger in check. We're quiet so as not to cause a scene, though a few of our classmates are already tuned in. "Just don't, Vanessa. I swear to God. You slashed my tires – which are costing a fortune to replace, by the way – and next you took my phone hostage. Stop messing with me." His nostrils flare as he grows more exasperated. Desperately, he reaches out for my wrist, forcing me to keep my attention on him. "I'm sorry, alright? I shouldn't have shared that video. I was pissed at you."

"Harrison," I say, gently pulling my wrist free from his grasp, "I'm just getting started." I give him a tight, challenging smile, then turn away.

"Vanessa," he hisses, but I don't so much as glance at him for the rest of class.

He whispers my name every chance he gets. Even tries to pass me a note, which I promptly push off the edge of my desk. It's fun watching him beg, especially because I know he isn't actually sorry about releasing that video of us. He only wants me to stop playing tricks on him.

When class ends, I calmly gather up my books and strut out of the room.

All the while Harrison stares helplessly after me.

The hallways are silent. Kai stands ten feet away from me, pretending to text, keeping his head down. I sit on a chair outside the school's main office, one leg crossed over the other, staring at him. I should really be in detention right now, but I'm willing to accept double-time for skipping it. I haven't turned up once this week and I'm surprised it hasn't been brought to Principal Stone's attention yet.

"You do know that you're more than welcome to eat lunch at our table, right?" I ask Kai. Earlier today when I gave him a subtle wave in the school cafeteria, he totally blanked me and sat on his own instead.

"But then people will assume that we're *friends*," Kai replies quietly, refusing to lift his head as he speaks. He's doing that thing again where he takes our undercover mission way too seriously. Even though there's no one else around and classes ended twenty minutes ago, he's still worried someone will creep up and spot the two of us together.

"And you don't want to be friends?"

"Yes, I do," he says, trying to fight the smile that's growing, "but not until this mission is over."

I wonder for a minute when this *will* be over. How far do we plan to go with our mission to screw with Harrison? When will we decide that we've done enough? I'm about to ask Kai this when my thoughts are interrupted by the sound of heels clicking against the floor.

"Hi, hooligans," Maddie says with an air of superiority as she approaches.

"Aren't you technically a hooligan yourself now?" Kai challenges.

She sets her eyes on Kai, glowering at him. "Shut it, new kid."

God, this is an odd trio. I never thought I'd be spending my Wednesday staying late after classes to riffle through the school's filing system with Kai Washington, the new kid, and Madison Romy, the teacher's pet. I stand up from my chair and join the two of them as Maddie breezes straight into the main office. Honestly, it doesn't even surprise me that she helps out the office staff. She's a total brown-noser.

"Hi, Miss Hillman," Maddie says, greeting the woman behind the main desk. Miss Hillman has worked at this school for decades and is sweet, but sweet can also mean naive. "These two have lost their class schedules, so I'll print them some new ones."

Miss Hillman nods and gives us all a smile. I hope she doesn't end up in trouble for this.

Maddie guides the way across the main office, past

Principal Stone's office and toward the counselor offices at the back. There's not much staff still here, most of them gone for the day.

"Our files are kept back here," Maddie explains, placing her hand on the door handle of Mrs. Delaney's office. "And aren't we lucky none of the counselors ever work late? God forbid you ever have a mental breakdown after school." She double checks around us for any other administration staff that may be lurking, but the coast is clear. The three of us slip into Mrs. Delaney's office unnoticed.

Kai immediately throws himself down into the huge, plush chair. He swivels back and forth, touching all the items on Mrs. Delaney's desk. I eye him in disapproval – I'm pretty sure leaving fingerprints at the scene of the crime is a no-no in undercover missions.

"What can we expect to find in these files?" he questions Maddie. He sits back and stares her down, drumming his fingertips together like some fancy CEO of a billion-dollar company.

"For starters, we can find out why *you're* even at this school," she says, taking up position by the row of metal filing cabinets that line the wall. She bends to the floor and opens a drawer at the bottom, silently searching through the stack of files for a moment before she stands, a paper-thin file in her hands. She smiles at Kai and flicks the file open. "Ah," she says. "Expelled from Westerville Central for fighting. Doesn't surprise me, given that you were involved in a brawl at my house at the weekend. And Mrs. Delaney herself has noted that you're overly confident and charming."

She looks up from the page. "The overly confident part is true. Charming? I disagree."

Kai stands from the chair and grabs the file from her, reading it for himself. "I'm an acquired taste," he defends, skimming over the biography the school has put together about him.

While I stand by the door to keep watch, I realize I'm focused more on Kai again than I am on any possible witnesses. His dark eyebrows pull together as he reads, his lower lip caught between his teeth. He may be an acquired taste for some, but of all the different personalities in the world, his is my favorite right now.

"Vanessa, Mrs. Delaney thinks you might go off the rails," Maddie says, stealing my attention away from Kai. My gaze flickers over to her, and she tosses a file across the room to me. I barely catch it. "And given that you've partnered up with Mr. Charming over here to ruin someone's life, I think she's right."

I look down at my own file. It's thicker than Kai's, but he's only been at this school for three days, whereas I've been here for four years. I open it and skim over the first page. General details about me, like my date of birth and my address. Copies of all my report cards. A record of all my grades in each of my classes. A list of the colleges I've applied to. And then personal notes from each of my counselors over the years.

Mr. Williams, the freshmen year counselor, wrote that I was excelling in all of my classes. That I was a well-mannered, polite, hard-working student who had transitioned seamlessly into high school.

Mrs. Sinclair, the sophomore year counselor, wrote that my mom passed away during first semester. She notes that I missed an entire month of classes, and that I was now falling behind. That I needed extra support during this time, which, to Westerville North's credit, I did receive. By the end of the notes on my sophomore year, Mrs. Sinclair talks about how much happier I seemed to be.

Mr. Rogers, the junior year counselor, wrote that I was still falling behind in my classes, but that I was making no effort to catch up. I'd ended up in detention for the first time of many that year. Based on his notes, I was no longer a star student, but also not the worst either. I was somewhere in between, and not bad enough to be a cause for concern yet.

And as *if* Mrs. Delaney, my current counselor, has a note that I focus more on the social aspect of school rather than the academic aspect. Like, how the hell would *she* know? Do the counselors hang out in the hallways and stalk our every move? Mrs. Delaney is apparently worried that I'm losing it like some wild child who doesn't care anymore.

I grind my teeth and look at Maddie. "Are they seriously allowed to keep all this information?"

Maddie shrugs as she rummages through different drawers of the filing cabinet, presumably searching for Harrison's folder. "A school's got to know who its students are," she says. "That's how they keep tabs on who the potential psychos are. My bet is on Ryan Malone."

Kai and I exchange a look. He throws his file down on Mrs. Delaney's desk and sits up, demanding, "Just give us Harrison's file."

"Fine," Maddie huffs. She slams the drawer shut and hands Kai the folder. "Here."

The three of us huddle around the desk, Maddie and I leaning over Kai's shoulder, silently reading over the first page in unison. The entire office block feels eerily silent, as schools so often do after hours without the buzz of noise from its students, and it puts me on high alert. My body is tensed up and I'm trying not to breathe too heavily against Kai.

Harrison has good grades in all his classes, just like I thought he did, and there's lots of notes about his lifetime football stats, too. Kai flicks through the boring pages, desperate to get to the juicy stuff – and the juicy stuff is the personal stuff, the things only our counselors know about. Kai stops at a page of notes written by Mr. Rogers last semester.

Harrison cheated on his SATs back in the spring.

And the only reason Harrison wasn't kicked off the football team was because Mr. Rogers decided, for Harrison's sake, to keep things quiet because being caught cheating *and* being kicked off the football team would instantly ruin his chance at a scholarship – though it's not like his parents can't afford to send him to college. If it had been anyone else who was caught cheating, I bet Mr. Rogers wouldn't have hesitated to take the appropriate disciplinary actions, but it seems he didn't want Harrison's parents kicking up a fuss. So, all Harrison got was a month of detention.

Kai glances sideways at me, our mouths inches apart. He smiles. "Bingo."

Maddie gathers up the files from the table, both Harrison's and Kai's, then also grabs mine out of my hands too. She walks back to the filing cabinet and begins returning the folders to where they belong. I'd wondered why she was so willing to help us, but I think I know why. She has her own grudge against Harrison Boyd.

"Maddie," I say gently, but she doesn't turn around, only shoves Harrison's folder back into the "B" drawer. "Are you helping us because you hooked up with Harrison once?"

She stiffens at the filing cabinet. "What?"

"What?" Kai says, spinning around in Mrs. Delaney's chair to stare bewildered at me.

I continue to focus on Maddie. She's frozen in place, rigid and unmoving. Slowly, I move across the office toward her. "What happened?"

"He's a jerk," she mumbles, her voice cracking out of its usual high pitch. She speaks in a low murmur, blinking fast as though she's fighting back sudden tears. "I thought he really liked me. At least he told me he did, but that he didn't want anyone to know about us until we were official. And he said we weren't official until we slept together. He totally manipulated me. I was stupid, okay?" Her head snaps up to look at me, the sharp movement causing a tear to break free and roll down her cheek. "I wasn't even ready for that in the first place, and then he never spoke to me again after it. I tried to pretend it didn't happen, and I don't think he told anyone, because I *know* that news would have spread through this school like wildfire if he had." Her eyes narrow. "So how do *you* know?"

"I had a hunch," I say, only because I think it'll upset her even more if she finds out he has a record of their encounter in his phone. And that she's *rated*. I shake my head in disbelief. Harrison is worse than I thought. I feel stupid myself for actually believing he was a nice guy, but at least these new discoveries mean I can carry out my mission to ruin his life with zero guilt or remorse. "I'm sorry, Maddie. You're right, he *is* a jerk. That's why we're doing this."

As I look at her, I see something in Madison Romy that I've never seen before. I see . . . *myself*. I see a girl who's insecure and acts out to gain positive attention so that her peers like her, accept her, the same way *I* act out to gain *any* attention because I lack it from my dad. We aren't different at all – we are totally the same. We both just want someone to pay us attention. And, I realize, maybe that's why I've never particularly liked Maddie. Maybe all this time I've been projecting my thoughts about my own behavior onto her.

Maddie wipes the tears from her cheeks and looks away again, storing my own file back into the unit. "Just make sure he doesn't know I've helped, okay?" she sniffs, trying to get back some control. "I still like to be friends with him."

"You don't need to be friends with everyone," I tell her softly. God, I feel like a damn counselor myself. How did I go from feeling so hostile toward Madison Romy's needy personality to feeling sorry for a girl who's clearly vulnerable? It's almost like realizing I feel sorry for *myself*, because it's such a shame we're resorting to such desperate measures rather than just allowing ourselves to be vulnerable and open. "It's better to be loved by a few than liked by many."

"Wow, that was kind of deep, Nessie. Did you read that on Facebook?" Kai pipes up from the desk. I fire him a glare. Way to ruin the moment.

Maddie slots Kai's folder back into the bottom drawer and then straightens up, her gaze meeting mine. Her smile is fragile, her eyes wet with tears. "You know, I never really liked you all that much. I'm sorry."

"The feeling's mutual," I say, and we both crack into quiet laughter, finally taking notice of one another for the first time. At the end of the day, we're just two girls who have been screwed over by Harrison Boyd. We *should* be friends.

Kai gets up from Mrs. Delaney's chair and walks over, his stride as smooth as ever, eyes on Maddie. "It seems Harrison messes with everyone, so don't take it personally. Think of it as a lesson learned. You'll meet someone who does actually like you for yourself," he tells her, offering his own reassurance to cheer her up. "Perhaps someone who's overly confident and charming, like me. But I doubt you'd be that lucky." He winks at her and slings an arm around her shoulders.

Maddie laughs and rests her head on his chest for a moment. "Thanks, new kid."

How does he do that? How does he just do everything *right*, even when he's doing the wrong thing? He's so effortlessly charming, his sarcasm and wit so easily delivered, but he's also genuinely *nice* when he needs to be.

As the three of us leave the office block, the dynamic has changed, and I trail behind, struggling not to daydream of Kai's lips against my own.

13

"Oh, yeah, for sure the criminal justice system is corrupt. How do those cops sleep at night knowing they've tampered with evidence and thrown two innocent people in jail? It's so messed up," Kai says, staring thoughtfully out my windshield. He's become deeply invested in telling me all about his thoughts on the conspiracy theories involved in some crime documentary on Netflix. Also, he believes that Avril Lavigne died and was replaced by a lookalike. *Riiiiight.*

"Any theories on aliens?"

Kai looks over at me. "They exist. There's definitely a UFO at Area 51."

I roll my eyes and toss a chip into my mouth, scouring the parking lot. We're in the Green McRusty, parked beneath a row of trees outside Bob Evans. Harrison and his dad are already inside. We can see them from here, sitting in a booth by the window, eating burgers. Meanwhile, Kai and I are outside in the SUV with the heating up full, milkshakes in the cup holders, and a selection of snacks spread out between us. It's like live entertainment, lying in wait for these "casual encounters" to turn up at eight. Still ten minutes to go.

It's fun just listening to Kai talk. The minutes are ticking by too fast. He's so enthusiastic, his hands moving as he talks, and although I'm not completely sold on his conspiracy theories, hearing *him* talk about different subjects has made it the most interesting conversation I've had in forever. It's so refreshing, for once, to actually be talking about something other than who hooked up with who, and did you see what so-and-so wore to school?

I pull my legs up onto my seat and cross them, bumping my knees against my steering wheel. "Okay, new conspiracy: Harrison Boyd is actually the devil in disguise, and he acts like your typical sweet, popular kid with good grades in order to screw with girls."

"That's not a conspiracy," Kai says. "That's a fact."

I laugh and reach for my strawberry milkshake, sipping it while I scan the parking lot once more. It's a cold night outside, but it feels warm and cozy inside the car. Kai leans back in my passenger seat and kicks his feet up onto my dashboard where his phone sits propped up by CD cases. He's streaming a recap of Monday's NFL game, though he hasn't been paying much attention to it.

The Green McRusty has temporarily turned into our own personal campsite.

"All this surveillance work is tiring," Kai says. He reclines the passenger seat all the way back until he's practically staring at the roof of the car. He grabs the bag of chips from between us and plants them in his lap. "Have you ever done anything like this before? All the sneaking around?"

"No," I admit, "but it's kind of fun."

"That's because you're with me," he says, turning his head to face me. He wiggles his eyebrows and shoves a handful of chips into his mouth. All I can hear is the crunching of potato chips and the drone of the football commentary.

I stare back at him. "Yeah, it is."

"OH!" Kai leaps up from the seat, nearly spilling the chips all over the floor, and taps frantically at the window. "I recognize her from the app. That's Samantha, I think. The 'attractive older woman'. Ohhhh, man, this should be good." He gets comfortable with his milkshake, loudly slurping the remnants.

Talk about another ruined moment. It's like the universe is conspiring against me.

I rest my chin on the steering wheel and squint out the windshield at the dark parking lot. There's a voluptuous figure making for the door of Bob Evans, her walk confident and full of anticipation. Yep, Samantha. No doubt about it. My breath catches in my throat as she walks through the door – it's like watching an impending train wreck.

"Maybe Chyna's right," I whisper in the silence. "Maybe we shouldn't have dragged innocent people into this."

Kai casts a quick glance over at me. He puts his hand on my knee and leaves it there. "I mean, you're right. But we can't do anything about it now."

I stare at his hand on my body. My jeans are ripped at the knees, so I can feel his skin against my own. I feel like I'm twelve years old and my crush has just held my hand for the first time. I try to play it cool, try to focus on Samantha inside the restaurant, but all I can't think about is that I want to grab Kai's hand and pull him closer.

"Look!" Kai says, taking his hand back. He presses up so close against the window that his breath steams up the glass.

Inside the restaurant, Samantha has made a move toward the booth, which Harrison and his father are occupying. Although distant, we can see the scene unfold through the restaurant windows – Samantha stopping at the booth, leaning over it, while Harrison and his father turn their heads up to look at her. It would be sweet if we could hear the words being exchanged, but it's not hard to guess what's being said in there. Harrison starts making frantic movements with his hands, his father rising up from the booth. Samantha glances around, confused, reminding me yet again that I'm an awful person. Finally, she storms out of the restaurant and unlocks a car at the other side of the lot, before speeding off. No doubt completely pissed off.

"Can we, like, pay these dates for their troubles?" I ask Kai.

Kai relaxes back in the passenger seat and furrows his brows at me. "You wanna pay people off?" I shrug, and the smile he gives me is gentle. "Okay, Nessie. I'll message them later and apologize, but I don't think we need to give them a peace offering . . . Hey, look, I think that's another one!"

I look outside again and, sure enough, there's a figure in black skinny jeans and choppy bangs heading for the restaurant door – that must be Raven. It's like a repeat of the previous few minutes. Emo kid walks over to the booth, Harrison becomes visibly furious, using hand gestures until Raven has no choice but to escape, flicking the Vs back at Harrison as they go.

The third hook-up turns up immediately after. The same happens again, except Harrison gets up from the booth as if to shove his unwanted "date" away. But they don't need telling twice. Kai is shoveling chips into his mouth at full speed, engrossed as though he's watching a live fight on TV.

"Oh shit, they're coming out," he says, slouching down in the seat as though we'll be spotted.

Harrison and his dad are leaving the restaurant in a rush. They march across the parking lot to his dad's BMW, and it's clear from Harrison's body language that he's totally embarrassed. I can't imagine it's much fun having your meal interrupted several times by strangers looking to hook up, but that's the whole point. Harrison Boyd isn't allowed to have fun anymore. The BMW speeds out of the lot, disappearing across Uptown Westerville.

"I bet he's mortified," I say as I sit up. "And who knows what his dad must think."

"Good," Kai says. He whips out his little notepad and a pen, then scores a line through this task on the to-do list. We've slashed Harrison's tires, hacked into his phone, and sent a triple act of randoms his way looking for fun times. "Tomorrow night we're breaking into his house."

I look at him funny. Breaking into Harrison's house seems like a step too far. "You were serious about that?"

"Uhh, yeah." Kai's expression mirrors mine. He puts the notepad away. "Wear all black again, like that leather jacket you sometimes wear. It looks good on you."

"Kai . . ."

"Yeah?"

My lips move, but yet I can't find my voice. What I want to say is this: *Kai, this might be a little weird, but I really like you.*

But what I actually say is, "We should get going."

I adjust my seat then pull out of the Bob Evans parking lot. We've been parked here for over an hour, so my legs feel numb as I drive across Uptown toward Kai's neighborhood. The glow from the streetlights races across the windshield, lighting up our faces every few seconds.

"Stop worrying, by the way. I still think you're a good person," Kai says quietly, breaking the silence. His observation takes me by surprise. Is my guilt that obvious?

"You've known me for three days," I say with a small laugh. The past three days have felt like forever. "How could you possibly know I'm a good person?"

"I think we're all good people. Even Harrison, despite how shitty he is," Kai explains. "We all just do bad things."

"And how often do you do bad things?"

My eyes are fixed on the road ahead, but I can still sense Kai sheepishly smile next to me. "Not all that often. You've been a bad influence on me."

"Hey!" I abruptly swerve the car. "*You* approached *me* in that office, remember? If anyone's the bad influence here, it's you."

Kai grins at me, his blue eyes shining. I'm finding it difficult to concentrate on the road. "Are you glad that I did?"

"Well, you're not *that* bad." The past few days, although they've been hell, have also been a lot of fun. And that's because of Kai.

"Even though you're seeing the worst side of me? The

side of me that's choosing to do all the wrong things?"

I pull up outside his house and look at him. The car is in park, the engine still purring, the two of us gazing at one another in the silence. "I like this side of you," I admit quietly, glancing away from him as a flaming heat spreads across my face. I turn off the heating, but I don't think that's the problem. My stomach is doing somersaults.

"You do, huh?" Kai teases. I sense him sit up, twisting in the passenger seat to fully face me, but I can't bring myself to look at him. There's a sudden pressure in the air around us, tension that's brewing.

"Yes, okay?" I snap. I can't take it anymore. Exasperated, I swivel back to look at him, clutching the steering wheel. "I like this wrong side of you. I like *you*."

Kai's playful grin immediately falters. His face screws up with confusion as he stares at me, absorbing my words as though I've spoken a foreign language. He blinks a few times. "You know this is how action movies usually turn out, right? The female accomplice always falls in love with their slick counterpart."

"I didn't say I was in love with you," I defend. Not yet, at least, but at this rate, I might just be in love with him by Monday. Although Vanessa Murphy *doesn't* fall in love.

"Not yet," Kai says, voicing my own thoughts as if he can read them. He winks and reaches for my hands, removing them from the steering wheel. His skin is warm against mine. "Wait until you see my good side. I'm such a gentleman." Kai's smoldering gaze is locked on me as he lifts my hand to his mouth and kisses my knuckles. He's messing around, trying to lighten the mood after such a forward confession, but it triggers an impulse that's unstoppable.

Clasping his jaw in my hands, I crash my lips against his. My heart hammers in my chest as I kiss him in the darkness of the car. My mouth against Kai's, Kai's mouth against mine ... He moves his thumb to my chin, tilting my head up as he kisses me back, taking my lips between his own. Now it's so soft, so gentle, so innocent. I slide my hand to the back of his neck, working my fingers into the nape of his trimmed hair and up into his thick curls.

But then Kai reaches for my hands and tears his lips from mine. I freeze like a deer caught in headlights as he holds my hands still, both of us blinking at one another, our mouths parted open. For such a fragile kiss, I'm left breathless.

"I'm sorry, Nessie. I gotta go," Kai blurts, moving my hands away from him and scrambling to gather his stuff. He grabs his phone from the dashboard and reaches for his hoodie on the floor.

"What?" I squeak in disbelief as I watch him slide out of the car. Did I do something wrong?

Kai turns, one hand on the edge of the door. His expression looks stunned, almost panicked. "I'm sorry," he whispers, his breath visible in the air, carrying his words. He shuts the door and rushes into his house, never looking back.

I'm paralyzed with humiliation as I sit alone outside his home. *He didn't want to kiss me*, I realize. *Oh, God, why did I do that?* Kai never said he liked me back. He was joking around with me, because that's just how Kai is, and there I was, throwing myself at him like some crazed maniac.

I groan so loud I'm convinced the car rumbles and I slam my head down against the steering wheel, absolutely mortified. If the ground opened up and swallowed me whole right now, I'd send it a thank you card.

Kai was *in love* with a girl. He's the type of guy who does fall in love, the type of guy who kisses girls because he cares about them. I'm not the type of girl guys like Kai go for, and there's no doubting the fact that he *knows* the kind of girl I am, because he'll have heard what everyone is saying about me. And I kiss people because it's fun, because I want to, but I wish I could tell Kai that isn't what I was doing with him just now. I don't like him in the way of *I like you because you're hot and fun to hook up with.* I like him more in the way of *I like you because you're gorgeous, and funny, and your presence seems to fill my lungs with the fresh air I so desperately need.*

I lift my head from the steering wheel, my whole body still flaming hot with embarrassment, and my eyes widen at the sight in front of me. Flurries of snowflakes are landing on my windshield. I glance all around, looking out every window of the car, and now excitement fills me. It's snowing! Finally!

I remain parked outside Kai's house, watching the weather in true fascination, wrapped up cozy inside the car with my music playing on low. Snow is my favorite thing in the world. It starts off light, wisps of snow blowing in the air, then gradually grows heavier until I'm trapped in the middle of a snowstorm. My wipers aren't fast enough to keep the windshield clear. The streets around me turn white, beautiful and crisp.

I gaze helplessly at Kai's house, its roof and windowpanes dusted with snow, and think of how perfect it would be if Kai was still sat here with me. I imagine us watching the snow fall together, exchanging kisses every once in a while. But when I glance at my empty passenger seat, my heart sinks. Kai doesn't *want* to kiss me.

I turn the music up to blast my thoughts away, pull on my seatbelt and drive away from Kai's house, leaving behind fresh tracks in the snow.

14

"It was *awful*," I whine, throwing my head back to the dull sky, a groan building in my throat. "Not the kiss. The kiss was amazing," I say quickly. "But the circumstances . . . Oh God, I've never been so embarrassed in my life!"

Chyna raises a questioning eyebrow at me. "Didn't your sex tape just get leaked on Monday?"

"You're not allowed to make jokes about it until after Christmas," I warn, jabbing a threatening finger at her.

It's first thing on Thursday morning and we're trudging through the snow from the student parking lot toward the school entrance, wrapped up in warm coats. Even wearing boots feels weird, like suddenly we switched from fall to winter in the blink of an eye. It snowed heavily all night, covering the entire region of Columbus in a gorgeous white blanket for us to wake up to. Ohio weather doesn't disappoint. I *live* for this. I'm decked out in my new navy cotton hat with matching scarf and gloves that I bought months ago and have been dying to wear.

"I'm sorry," Chyna apologizes. She shoves her bare hands

into her pockets. "So, he really just got out of the car and left?"

"Chyna, you should have seen his face," I say, squeezing my eyes shut as I recall that awful moment last night when Kai was beyond desperate to leave. It was so clear he hadn't wanted to kiss me, like he regretted even letting it happen in the first place. "He couldn't have left quicker if he'd tried. Just grabbed his stuff and pretty much *ran* away."

Chyna thinks for a minute as we head through the school entrance and into the warm hallways. "Maybe it's not you," she says inquisitively, and we exchange a look. "Maybe he's still in love with that ex-girlfriend of his."

Her words take me by surprise, because I'd totally forgotten all about Sierra Jennings. I'm silent as Chyna and I walk down the hallway together. Kai did say he was no longer in love with Sierra, and that he doesn't want to be with a girl like her anyway, but he *could* be denying how he really feels. It's not like it was his choice to break up – by the sound of things, it seems Kai would have happily stayed in that relationship with Sierra if she hadn't cheated. Besides . . . why would Kai be going to such lengths in the first place to ruin Harrison's life if he *didn't* care about Sierra anymore?

"Crap," I whisper under my breath, my head spinning. I. Am. An. Idiot.

We stop by Chyna's locker – there's never been any graffiti on hers, because Chyna doesn't make mistakes like I do – and blow one another a kiss before separating. We'll meet up again at lunch as always. It sucks that this semester we don't share a single class together.

I head further down the hallway to my own locker – great, someone's drawn the outline of a naked woman on the door – but before I get the chance to enter my combination, someone's hands are on my shoulders. Firm and with a tight grasp, their thumbs digging into my shoulder blades.

"Vanessa," a familiar voice hisses in my ear, breath hot against my cheek. Harrison.

I steal a glance over my shoulder. Harrison's body is pressed close against mine, holding me tightly, and Noah and Anthony hang back behind him. Noah fires me a wicked smirk.

"Get off me," I order with as firm a tone as I can muster. I try to elbow Harrison away, but he doesn't budge.

Suddenly, he squeezes my shoulders even harder and pulls at me, yanking me away from my locker. We're in the middle of the hallway, surrounded by the final stragglers who have yet to make it to class, but no one is paying attention the one time I need them to. Noah lurches forward and wraps a hand around my wrist. Alarm bells are ringing in my ears and my chest tightens with an awful feeling of doom.

"We just want to talk," Noah says, but the laugh that escapes his mouth begs to differ. It's menacing and sadistic, borderline evil.

"Get the hell off me!" I demand, this time louder. I try to shake Noah's hand off my wrist, keep trying to elbow Harrison in the chest, but they won't let go. They're grabbing me too tightly, pulling and pushing me down the hallway. I feel powerless, and my mind's racing with terrified thoughts. Where are they taking me?

Anthony opens the door to the janitor's closet, and I'm dragged inside. The three of them join me, closing the door behind us and flicking on the dim light. I'm finally released from their grasp, but the lack of space in here feels suffocating. I glance around, surrounded by shelves and mop buckets, and decide that, if necessary, I *will* bear arms and use a mop.

"Did you think it was funny?" Harrison asks, folding his arms across his chest as he looks me up and down. His face turns ugly when he glowers like that. "Sending those weirdos to Bob Evans last night? I know it was you. Were you watching?"

"I really don't know what you're talking about, Harrison," I say as calmly as I can, my gaze evenly matching his. Feigning innocence seems like the logical path to take, but the snort of disbelief Harrison lets out makes it clear he already knows it was me behind last night's scheme. Who else would it be? But he still isn't aware that he has an enemy in Kai Washington too.

"Quit playing games," Harrison snarls, taking a step closer to me. His arms are still crossed, but I notice that his hands are balled into fists. "I've told you. You're going to regret messing with me if you don't stop."

"Haven't you thought just for a second that perhaps you're the one who should regret ever having messed with *me*?" I challenge, and I'm shocked by the power of my own words. They roll off my tongue so naturally, so confident and so fierce. I raise a daring eyebrow at Harrison and press my lips together. My hands are trembling, but he and his friends will *not* intimidate me.

"Is this still about that video?" Harrison asks. He lowers his head so that we are eye-level with one another. "It would have been kept private if I actually cared about you."

Noah reaches for my hat and swipes it off my head despite my best efforts to stop him. I can feel the static in my hair. "Yeah, that video was good though," he sneers with a wink. Anthony cracks a smile.

"You're a dog," I mutter, snatching my hat back. I shove it into the pocket of my coat and turn to Harrison. "And yeah, this is about the video. That video is going to follow me *forever*. Don't you get that or are you too self-obsessed to realize that what you did was wrong? I thought I could trust you."

"I don't care!" Harrison snaps. Noah's face lights with glee, entertained by the animosity. "I'm warning you . . . If you don't stop these games, I'll make your life a living hell."

"Maybe I should warn Sierra about the kind of guy you really are," I spit, glaring back into his face. It's hard to believe that last week I thought Harrison was a genuine guy, that I actually felt *bad* about not wanting to go on that ski trip with him. It's clear now that I had a lucky escape.

"Who's Sierra?" Anthony asks. His and Noah's heads swivel around simultaneously to look at Harrison.

Harrison's eyes widen. He looks at his friends, then back at me. I wasn't aware that his hookups with Sierra were a secret, but the stunned look on Harrison's face has me smiling. The realization dawns on him that I now know the name of the other girl he was seeing at the same time as me. "How the hell do you know about her?" he demands, his voice seething.

Suddenly I'm the one who's in control. "The same way I know you cheated on your SATs. Was that information supposed to be private? Private just like that video of us?" I taunt, smiling. "Yeah, sorry. No privacy around here."

Harrison lurches forward, grabbing my arm and moving his face to mine. His lips are inches from my own, spitting venomous words rather than kissing me. "I've warned you," he growls. His blue eyes are blazing with resentment, his expression so hard and cold, but still I see a flicker of panic cross his face.

"Stop touching me," I hiss, squirming beneath him. My back is pressed against the shelves and Harrison's body is trapping me in place. I feel threatened, just like he wants me to feel. As he bends my arm back, I realize that I am no match for Harrison. I'm just a little over five feet tall, and he's a football player. There's no real way I can fight back.

I try, though. I shake my arm, desperate to pull myself free from Harrison's hold, but the more I struggle, the tighter he squeezes. I curl my free hand into a balled-up fist and slam it into his chest as hard as I can, over and over again, until Noah grabs my wrist to stop me. The two of them pin me back against the shelves.

"Hey, c'mon," Anthony mumbles, but no one listens to him.

Harrison and Noah hold me in place, sneering down into my face, and my limbs stiffen. My heart is pounding in my chest, beating way too fast. Bile rises in my stomach.

I stare at Anthony, my terrified eyes silently begging him to do something. The three of them are best friends, always have been, but they aren't all equal. Noah is the alpha, the quarterback on the team, the leader in every group. Harrison is his second-in-command; important enough to have people listen to him, but also with enough of a spine to make his own decisions. And then there's Anthony, the nicest of the three, the one who tags along and doesn't say much, whether or not he agrees with what his friends are doing. If anyone is to put a stop to this, it'll be Anthony. He stands quiet in the corner, avoiding my eyes.

"I thought you liked attention from guys," Noah snickers, edging in closer. "Isn't that your thing?" His lips are so close I can feel his breath against me.

Harrison's laugh is vile as he holds me still, but I'm too paralyzed to move even if I could. I squeeze my eyes shut as I hold my entire body rigid in the face of their cruelty. Harrison is far too close to me, his hand is still bending back my arm.

Then there's the metallic click of a door handle being tried, and Harrison and Noah abruptly let go of me just as the door swings open. I'm panting as we all look over at the janitor.

Mr. Kratz scratches his bald head, deep lines of confusion forming across his forehead. "What's going on in here?"

I don't wait to offer any explanations. Instead, I take off, barging past Mr. Kratz and breaking out into a desperate run for safety. Classes have started, so the hallways are empty as I sprint down them. I burst out through the school's main entrance and dive into the snow, my footsteps weighed down as I drag myself away. The cold air bites at my nose and ears, but I don't waste time putting my hat back on. I just keep running, trudging through the snow toward the student parking lot until I'm off the school campus. My strides are long, my breathing heavy.

Forget school. I'm not going back there today. Screw Harrison Boyd. Screw Noah Diaz. And screw Anthony Vincent for watching on in silence. I know I can knock on Mrs. Delaney's door and tell her what just went down, but I'm already dealing with enough as it is, and I just want to *get out of here*. I'm shaking now, but I tell myself it's because of the cold.

I head away from school as fast as I can, past the elementary and middle school next door, past the fire station and the churches. I don't realize where my steps are taking me until I arrive at the cemetery gates.

I pick up speed again, pushing through the gates as I desperately try to remember where to go. It's been months since I last visited. The headstones are all dusted with snow, some of their engravings hidden completely, and I become frantic but also furious at myself for taking so long to find it. I come to an abrupt stop, take a deep breath, then look around again. Everything appears so different when it's covered in a white sheet of snow. I move slowly, taking the time to check each headstone, until finally I find the one I am looking for.

With a gloved hand, I wipe away the snow from the headstone to reveal the engraving beneath.

DEBRA MURPHY

SEPTEMBER 5TH, 1979 – AUGUST 18TH, 2016

A BELOVED WIFE, MOTHER, DAUGHTER, AND SISTER
DEEPLY LOVED AND SORELY MISSED

I drop to my knees in the snow. The tears break free before I can stop them, streaming down my cold, rosy cheeks. My chapped lips tremble and my chest rises and falls with each sob that escapes my throat.

"I'm sorry," I weep, my voice a whisper. "Mom, I'm so sorry."

I think of all the mistakes I've made in the two years that I've been forced to live without a mother to guide me. All the cries for attention from Dad, all the distractions, all the pretending to be someone I'm not. I don't know who I am. I've drank too much beer, I've skipped classes too many times, I've said and done too many things I regret. I look up at the cloudy sky through my blurred vision and imagine Mom watching over me. How disappointed would she be now? I'm not the daughter she raised.

Mom raised me to be a good person. To look out for people, to always smile, to do my best. And I tried. I really did, but this is hard. Dad barely remembers that I exist, too consumed by his own grief to realize he still has two daughters who need a parent. I let Harrison film that stupid video and now it's out there in the world, following me wherever I go. I even kissed Kai last night, a boy who did not want to kiss me, because I have no idea what I'm doing anymore.

I hear the crunching of footsteps in the snow behind me, then a body sits down next to me. I glance sideways, entirely numb, and stare blankly at Kai. It's so cold my tears feel frozen against my cheeks. Kai is staring straight ahead at the headstone, his knees pulled up to his chest. His gaze shifts to meet mine.

"Your grandma?" he asks gently.

My heart seizes and I look down at my lap, blinking back a fresh batch of tears that are brimming. He obviously hasn't processed the dates fully – it can't possibly be my grandmother – so I'm forced to correct him. To say it out loud. "My mom," I croak. "Brain aneurysm."

"Oh," Kai says. I can hear the surprise in his voice, no doubt taken aback. Just the other night I told him my mom was *at work*. He looks back at the gravestone.

A guttural sob rises in my throat. I even lied about Mom. I *denied* my mom her own truth. I'm the worst daughter in the world. I press my hands to my face, muffling my cries with my gloves. I'm shuddering uncontrollably, but it's long overdue. I always like to tell myself I'm strong, I'm someone who keeps her head up and just keeps on moving forward, but every once in a while, I lose it. I guess it reminds me that I'm human.

I drop my hands and look at Kai again. "What are you doing here?" I ask through my tears, sniffing. I thought I was alone. Just me, Mom, and the snow. I feel so vulnerable right now, so bare and exposed, more so than I did on Monday when that video was being watched by everyone. I'm stripped bare in a totally different way.

"Couldn't bike to school in this weather, so I had to walk, which made me late," Kai says quietly, though I notice the soft way his eyes are taking in my expression, trying to understand the pain in my eyes. "I got to school just as you were leaving. You looked upset. I'm sorry, but I had to follow you. What happened?"

I wipe away my tears and shake my head. "Just Harrison and Noah. They were trying to scare me. It was nothing," I lie, playing it down. Being assaulted and harassed inside a janitor's closet feels like a new low for me, but I don't want to talk about it. I don't want to get Kai involved.

He looks skeptical. "Nothing, but yet you're in tears?"

"I'm not crying because of that," I mumble, which is partly the truth. I'm crying because of *everything*. It feels like I've made too many mistakes. Nothing seems to be going in the right direction, but I'm pretty sure I'm the one to blame. It's like I can't drag myself off this train of self-destruction. "I'm just having a rough morning, okay?"

To my surprise, Kai inches closer to me so that our bodies touch. He slides a bare hand into my gloved one. I stare down at our interlocked hands, both of us silent as the breeze whips around us. It's such a small gesture, Kai's hand in mine, but it feels so warm and intimate. It lifts the weight off my chest.

"Okay, well, I'm here. Why don't you tell me about her? Your mom."

I force my gaze up to look at him through eyes full of tears, and I realize then that no one has ever asked me to talk about my mom before. Most people probably want to think I've moved on. I keep my head up in the hallways at school with a smile plastered across my face. I show up to parties and football games and am often the center of attention. I'm happy, right? Except, no, I'm not. Not really. I fake it, so no one ever asks how I'm doing, or if I'm okay, or if I want to talk.

"We lost her two years ago ..." My voice hitches and I inhale a fresh breath of air, staring back at her gravestone in front of us. "Completely out of nowhere. It was like the ground disappeared from under my feet. Mom was like the backbone of our family, and without her ... we haven't been doing too great."

I look down at my hand in Kai's again, and he is massaging soft circles against the back of my hand with his thumb, never taking his eyes off me. I can *feel* him watching me, even though I can't bring myself to glance over at him. He is listening carefully and giving me all the time I need to get my words in order. I'm grateful, because I've never really spoken these thoughts out loud. Never really admitted the truth to anyone.

"My dad ... my dad ..." I stutter. "He's not the same anymore. I don't even know who he is lately, and he's drowning so deep in his own grief that he doesn't care about my sister and me. It's like when mom died, a big part of him died too."

"You miss them, huh?" he asks, and it catches me off guard that he asks if I miss *them*, and not just *her*.

His words hit home at full force, because it's true – I don't just miss my mom, I miss my dad too. I *miss* my dad, which sounds insane when I see him every day. I pass him every morning in the kitchen while we silently navigate around one another, and I see him smoking in the armchair in the living room every evening, and I watch him slip further away from me with every day that passes, but I miss feeling safe. I miss feeling cared for and I miss feeling loved. That awful day two years ago, I lost both of my parents.

I nod in response to Kai and squeeze my eyes shut again as a new batch of tears wells up. I choke a little as I try to suppress my sobs, but then I let go and allow myself to feel the way that I do. I let myself cry and I don't care that Kai can see me; I don't care that he knows I'm not as strong as I make myself out to be.

Kai hooks an arm around my shoulders and pulls me in close. I collapse against his chest, burying my face into his coat while he rests his chin softly on my head. I can feel the warmth of his breath as he holds me tight, securing me in his embrace like a safety blanket. He holds me for a long time until I've wept two years' worth of tears.

"You're a nice guy, Kai," I murmur with a small smile as, at last, I dab at my eyes and sit up. "Do you know that?"

Kai's face brightens. "This is my better side," he admits with a breath of laughter. He gives my hand a squeeze and playfully nudges my shoulder. "And since we're both skipping school right now anyway, there's no point in going back there. Hot chocolate on me?"

15

Kai and I grab an Uber to downtown Columbus. It's totally random. We should be at school, but I'm happy to roll with Kai's reasoning – we've already missed first period, so there's no point going back. I don't want to go back anyway. I want to get as far away from Westerville North and Harrison Boyd as I possibly can, with or without Kai. But having him accompany me is a definite bonus.

We climb out of the Uber twenty minutes later, out into the cold city streets of Columbus alongside the riverfront. There's something about the city that's so refreshing, like it's less suffocating than the suburbs, even though it's way more crowded. Maybe it's knowing that all these people around me have no idea who I am. None of them know that there's a video out there of me. The city feels more freeing that way – I'm anonymous and invisible. No one can judge me.

"So," Kai says as we slide into a booth by the window of a café just across from the river. It's so warm inside that the glass in the windows is fogged up with condensation, blurring the passersby on the sidewalk outside. "Do you come downtown a lot?"

I shake my head as I pull off my hat and remove my gloves. My cheeks sting from the cold, like my earlier tears have frozen into my skin. "Only sometimes with Chyna," I say with a shrug. "Do you?"

"Nope," Kai says. He looks out the window, watching the figures outside. The café is bustling with people, but we're both resigned to silence. We're usually so playful around one another, but today there's no room for joking. We're both somber.

Our waitress approaches and we order two large hot chocolates, topped with marshmallows and whipped cream. They arrive a few minutes later and we both wrap our hands around the steaming hot mugs. We haven't fully defrosted yet.

"Vanessa," Kai says as he scoops up a mouthful of cream with a spoon. He looks across the booth at me, his gaze capturing mine, and shoves the cream into his mouth. "Do you want to tell me what happened this morning? With Harrison? He threatened you – how?"

I should have known Kai wouldn't believe me when I told him it was nothing. I look down at my hot chocolate, trying to waste some time, hoping Kai will change the subject if I stay silent for long enough, but he just stays quiet, waiting.

"He told me to stop messing around with him or I'll regret it," I say finally, not looking up. My voice doesn't sound like my own. "He got aggressive. He put his hands on me."

Kai sits bolt upright and lowers his spoon. "What?"

"It's fine," I say quickly. "I guess I deserved it. We *have* been screwing around with him. He's bound to get pissed at me."

"No," Kai objects, shaking his head fast. "You don't deserve it. You didn't deserve for that video to be sent out, and you don't deserve to be threatened, or touched. Harrison is the one who deserves everything he's getting."

I sit forward in the booth and hunch over my mug, touching the cream with the tip of my finger. I can't look Kai in the eye right now. I still feel a little shaken up, but I also feel . . . angry. The right thing to do would be to stop all of this now before we make it any worse, before we really push Harrison to the edge . . . but I also want to mess with him more than ever. It's a mental battle, and I find myself leaning toward taking the side I know is wrong.

I look up at Kai. "Are we still breaking into his house tonight?"

A touch of weariness runs over Kai's face. "Maybe we should stop, Nessie," he says hesitantly. "Sure, it's fun messing with Harrison, but not if it means he's going to retaliate. Remember he doesn't know I'm involved. He thinks this is all you, and I don't want you to end up getting hurt because of an idea I suggested."

I narrow my eyes at him. It's the first time I've actually heard Kai be sensible in regards to our whole revenge plot. It makes him look older, wiser. "I can handle Harrison," I tell him, though I'm not sure I believe my own reassurances.

"Are you forgetting that I witnessed you literally *fleeing* from school an hour ago?"

I lift my mug, taking a long sip of my hot chocolate.

I wipe the cream from my mouth. "Can I ask you about Sierra?" I say, changing the subject, sparing my own blushes. I know Kai probably doesn't want to talk about it, but I've been thinking about him and her since yesterday.

Kai shrugs and sits back in the booth, playing with his hands in his lap; it's clear he's uncomfortable. I know this isn't an easy topic for him to discuss. "What do you want to know?"

I pause. It's not an easy question for me either. "Did you love her?"

I stare at him, watching him intently. He looks pained and I wish I hadn't brought her up, but it's too late now. "Honestly? Yeah. I gave everything to that girl. Like, I really had this vision of us being together for real. High school sweethearts, you know? She just made me happy, I guess." He smiles a little as his eyes bore into the table, but his entire expression looks heartbroken.

I had no idea that Kai and I were such polar opposites – he believes in happily-ever-afters, whereas I doubt they even exist. "It was that serious, huh?"

"It was for me, but I was so caught up in it all that I didn't even realize she wasn't as into the relationship as I was, and in the end she totally played me." He lifts his head, clenching his jaw as he stares out the window. There's probably a thousand different thoughts floating around his head right now ... and I'm about to invade them with some more questions.

"So why aren't you screwing with *her*?"

He turns slowly to look at me, his expression solemn.

"Because I've already told her everything I needed to. She knows how I feel about her now, and there's nothing more that either of us can say. Harrison, however ..." His words taper off. "He did a damn fine job convincing my girlfriend that the grass was a million times greener on his side of the fence."

I smile delicately at him over the rim of my mug, but not for long, because soon a devious grin toys at my lips. "Well, that's why we're going to break into his house tonight. So that you can let Harrison know *exactly* how you feel. Are you in?"

"I'm in," Kai says, and he clinks his mug against mine.

16

We stand behind the oak tree outside Harrison's house, the same one we hid behind on Monday evening. It's now Thursday and it's four minutes to midnight. We're wrapped up in thick coats and hats to battle the elements, and I'm constantly rubbing my hands together to create warmth. It's been a freezing journey over here, biking across Westerville on the slushy roads, and we dumped the bikes five minutes down the street. We've walked the rest of the way, and my limbs feel like ice.

"First we should try every door and window around the back," Kai says, studying the house, deciding our best course of action. He peers around the trees, tapping his finger against his lips.

"Or we can just try the basement window," I say. Kai looks over his shoulder at me, raising an expectant eyebrow. "It's always left unlocked. It's how Harrison used to sneak me in."

"The basement?"

"What? You think Harrison let me use the front door?" I laugh bitterly and gently push past him, taking the lead.

It's late, so although every car is in the driveway and it's clear the Boyds are home, the house is also in darkness. There's not a single light left on except for the porch light. I don't know what Kai and I are hoping to find, except perhaps Harrison asleep in his room, but we've decided not to steal anything. At least not tonight. We're hoping to creep Harrison out instead. It's not about taking something of his – it's about letting him know that if we want to, we can. We'll move some furniture around. Rearrange some family photographs. Anything that makes it clear someone was sneaking around the house.

"It's now or never," I say, and I sprint off across the lawn, tracing a path from the tree to the driveway, using the cars as a shield. Harrison's truck is missing three of its wheels – it's jacked up, lopsided and forlorn, and Kai snickers under his breath as we pass it.

The basement window is just around the side of the house. I lead the way, sticking close to the wall of the house, like a true secret agent. Harrison never wanted his parents to know about me, so I would sneak around the house exactly like I'm doing now, then climb in through the basement window where he would be waiting for me on the other side.

"*That?*" Kai asks indignantly when we reach the window. "That tiny little thing?"

The window does seem smaller somehow, but perhaps it's because *we* seem bigger when we're wrapped up in so many layers of clothing. I cock my head at the window – it's about an inch above the ground, and maybe three feet wide by three feet tall. I get down onto my hands and knees in the snow – hardened ice by now – and reach for the latch. With bated breath, I pull on the window, and it freely lifts open.

I flash Kai a beaming smile over my shoulder, but he only groans.

"Can't you climb in there and then open a door for me?" he says, unconvinced by my plan.

"You're not going to get stuck, Captain Washington," I tease, rolling my eyes. Quickly, I pull off my coat to make my body slimmer and slide in through the window feet-first. I even give Kai a sweet little wave before I disappear fully inside the basement. It's dark in here, but I turn back around and stare at him through the window, the moonlight illuminating him. "Are you joining me or what?"

"Fine," Kai huffs. He tears off his jacket, gets down onto his back, and slides through the window with total ease. When he lands inside, his body bumps into mine, but we quickly step apart. "Sorry."

"Don't worry about it," I say nonchalantly, but I'm just relieved it's dark in here so that he can't see the blush flooding my cheeks.

We look around the basement in silence as our eyes adjust to the darkness, and I use the furniture to guide me toward the stairs that lead into the house. I find a light switch on the wall and turn it on, bathing the basement in an orange glow. It's really more of an extra lounge than a basement – there's a flatscreen TV mounted to the wall, a plush couch, a bookcase that's over-stacked, and even a small bar. It feels so long ago now, those times I spent with Harrison right here in this basement.

"So this is how the other half lives," Kai says as he walks around. He plucks a trophy off a shelf on the wall, reading the engraving. He puts it back, grabs another.

How many times has Sierra Jennings been in this basement? I wonder. Hell, I'm pretty sure she was here on Monday while we were outside slashing Harrison's truck tires. At least that's what those text messages suggested.

"Kai," I say, my back to him. I walk to the bar and run my fingers over the bottles of liquor. I keep my head down and take a deep breath, then quietly ask, "Really think about it. Are you still secretly in love with Sierra?"

The air in the basement thickens as silence crowds in the two of us. My gaze is burning holes in a bottle of vodka as my heart thumps in my chest, waiting for Kai to say something, and finally he answers, "No."

I spin around to look at him, surprised. He stares back at me from ten feet away. "You're not?" He shakes his head while I try to process this fact. If he isn't in love with Sierra, then why did he seem so desperate to get away from me last night after I kissed him?

"Why would I still be in love with a girl who broke my heart?"

"Oh," is all I can say. The way he talks about her . . . God, he must have really fallen hard. I believe that he *was* in love with her, but I also now believe that he no longer is. I sit down on one of the bar stools and frown. "It's not because you're still in love with your ex then," I mumble to myself.

"What?" Kai says.

"You obviously just don't like *me*."

"Nessie, speak up," he says, walking over. He stops a foot away, frowning at me. "What are you talking about?"

"Last night!" I blurt in frustration, then hide my head behind my hands. I'm too mortified to look at him, the guy who doesn't like me back. It's so embarrassing. "You didn't want to kiss me."

We've been around each other all day, yet neither of us has brought up last night's kiss until right now. We've been carefully tiptoeing around the subject, and I know it's hardly the time or the place for this chat, but I can't take it anymore. I need to know why Kai doesn't like me. I thought we'd been hitting it off this week. We've been laughing and having fun and joking around, and I guess I read the signals wrong. Perhaps that's just what friendship feels like.

Kai is laughing now. A full, hearty laugh that he tries his hardest to suppress. "Trust me, I did. I do," he says, reaching for my hands. He pulls them away from my face and looks down at me, his blue eyes locking on mine. His smile is gorgeous, inviting, but it always is. "I just didn't expect it. I haven't even looked at anyone since Sierra. You took me by surprise, that's all."

I stare into his eyes, trying to let his reassurances sink in. A jolt of electricity fires up through my body, spreading all the way out to my fingertips where Kai's hands are still holding mine. "What?"

"Truth is," he murmurs, "I've wanted to kiss you since the moment I first saw you riding my bike down the street."

My heart thumps in my chest at what he's saying. "Why that moment?"

His smile only grows wider. "Because any girl who'll ride around late at night on bikes with me is a girl I want to know."

As soon as the words leave his lips, his mouth is against mine. He kisses me deeply, and it's so much more intense than last night; it's a kiss full of passion and desire. He moves his hands to my face and skims his thumbs over my cold cheeks. I'm numb from shock for the first few seconds, frozen under Kai's touch, but then I break out of it. I kiss him back, my mouth moving easily in sync with his, blissfully allowing him to take the lead. I slide off the bar stool and get to my feet, pressing one hand to Kai's chest and the other to the nape of his neck. We stumble around the basement, only the sound of my heart pounding in my ears, our adrenaline fusing together. He's such a good kisser.

The kiss only breaks when Kai moves his mouth to plant a sweet row of kisses down my neck. It leaves me utterly weak at the knees. I lock my arms around his neck for support and fight the embarrassing gasp that's rising in my throat. I guide Kai's mouth back to my own.

We fall back against the wall, Kai holding me tight. We can't get enough of one another.

But suddenly there's a tremendous clatter and we are torn from the moment.

Kai and I abruptly pull out of the kiss. On the ground lies a pile of trophies that we've knocked off their shelves.

"Shit," Kai breathes.

We both turn to look at the stairs to the house, listening. We're both frozen in place, our hands still on one another. We're silent for several long seconds until we hear them: footsteps above our heads.

Immediately, we let go of one another. There's no time to attempt to lift ourselves back out the window. Kai dives behind the bar while I dash over to the couch and drop to the ground behind it. We both remain crouched in position, out of view but not from each other. Kai's eyes are on me as we listen in silence to the footsteps. They move across the floor above us, then my heart stops when I hear the door to the basement being wrenched open.

It dawns on me then that we've left the basement light on.

"Who's down here?" a deep voice bellows from the top of the staircase. It's not Harrison's voice – it must be his father.

Kai stares wide-eyed at me from his hiding spot behind the bar. We didn't prepare for this. We didn't even *consider* that we could get caught, because we've been too wrapped up in the thrill of it. But now I realize how stupid we are, and I'm absolutely terrified.

"WHO'S DOWN HERE?" the voice repeats, more aggressive this time. The staircase creaks as Harrison's father apprehensively makes his way down into the basement. "Show yourself. I'm armed!"

Fuck.

Screw Ohio and its rather lax gun regulations. Kai's expression pales and I realize that Harrison's father is much more likely to react badly against Kai suddenly popping into view than he will against me – a tall, muscular guy? Definitely a burglar. But a terrified, scrawny girl? Harmless.

That's why I slowly stand up from behind the couch, not making any sudden movements and with my hands held up.

Harrison's father is standing at the foot of the stairs, shirtless but wearing sweatpants. He's pointing a handgun in my direction, but instantly lowers it when he realizes I'm just some teenage girl.

"I'm … I'm a friend of Harrison's," I squeak, unable to get my words out. I step out from around the couch despite the ice in my limbs. None of this feels remotely like a game anymore.

"What are you doing in here?" Harrison's father looks me up and down, displeased now. Then his shoulders sink and he runs a hand frustratedly through his fading blond hair. "Jesus. Harrison, are you down here too?"

Oh, the complete irony of Harrison's father suspecting me of fooling around with his son in his basement the *one* time I'm not. If I wasn't frozen in fear right now, I think I might have actually laughed.

"Harrison isn't here," I manage to say. My words feel like sandpaper in my throat.

Out of the corner of my eye, I notice Kai slowly rising up from behind the bar. He reveals himself slowly and with his hands visible, but it doesn't stop Harrison's father from jabbing the gun in his direction, taken aback by the second intruder.

"Hey, hey," Kai says. He doesn't move an inch. "We're just here to see Harrison."

Kai and I exchange a look. We are in silent agreement that the best way to get out of this situation is to play it cool, to lie. I do steal a glance at the open window though and wonder just how swiftly I'd be able make a run for it, but I don't have the courage to even try. Kai and I stay firmly rooted where we are.

"Who are you?" Harrison's father demands, his eyes flitting between Kai and me.

"Vanessa and Kai," I splutter, and it is the most inappropriate time in the world to think of how nice our names sound together. "I'm sorry, Mr. Boyd. We're not trying to disturb you. Please get Harrison. We're his friends."

I'm planning our escape route – Mr. Boyd will head upstairs to get Harrison while Kai and I throw ourselves out that window at full speed before we take off running down the street. We'll jump on our bikes and pedal like we've never pedaled before.

But Harrison's father doesn't budge. He lays down the gun on a shelf, his hand still hovering over it, as he turns to the stairs and yells, "Harrison! Get downstairs!"

A minute of intense silence ensues. Kai and I are like statues, unmoving and unblinking, while Mr. Boyd stares us down. He's either angry because he *knows* we're lying, or he's angry that Harrison is letting friends sneak over late at night. It's after midnight by now.

We hear more footsteps – this time faster as they cross whatever room is above us, then rush down the staircase. "What, Dad?" Harrison asks, the agitation evident in his voice. He appears before us and stops dead in his tracks halfway down the stairs. He's wearing nothing but a pair of boxers, his blond hair tousled. "What the hell?"

"Are these your friends?" his father demands.

Harrison stares straight past his father to me. He blinks, as though he can't believe I'm really standing here in his basement at midnight, then slowly he narrows his eyes into a glower. I give him a pathetic smile.

"I've got this," he says, but his father tries to argue with him. "Dad! I've got this," he repeats, more firmly this time. "And put that thing away."

Reluctantly, Mr. Boyd lowers his handgun and huffs and puffs his way back upstairs. We all wait until his footsteps disappear out of hearing range, then Harrison sets his fierce blue eyes on me.

"What the fuck, Vanessa?!" he hisses through gritted teeth. "Was slashing my tires not enough for you? Are you here to set my house on fire next?" He marches toward me, stopping a foot away, then shifts his gaze over to Kai, only for him to go totally silent. Recognition flashes in his eyes. "And what the actual hell are *you* doing here?"

"Dropped by to see how your truck was doing. Total bummer about those tires, huh?" Kai taunts, stepping away from his position by the bar. He calmly walks over and stands by my side, facing Harrison. The smirk he gives him is full of hatred.

"That was you?" Harrison says stiffly, as it dawns on him now that I haven't been doing all of this on my own – I've had an accomplice the entire time. Kai Washington, to be exact, the ex-boyfriend of the girl who Harrison made sure to steal. Kai is no stranger to him.

Kai dares to take another step forward. He lowers his voice and says, "Yup. I hope Sierra is worth it." Suddenly, he tenses up and shoves Harrison backward. It's the first time I've seen Kai look so furious, his eyes glistening with loathing, like he's waited months for this moment.

Before Harrison can lunge forward to hit him back, I jump between the two of them. The testosterone in this basement right now is overwhelming – the two of them are glowering at one another, fighting the urge not to wrestle each other to the ground.

"Don't," I warn, looking between them both. As much as I'd love to see Kai slam his fist straight into Harrison's smug little face, I know it won't help our cause. We need to get the hell out of here unscathed. My nerves are shot from Harrison's father pulling out that gun. I've suddenly realized that what Kai and I are doing is serious. We're out here causing real trouble, and trouble has consequences.

"Get the fuck out of my house!" Harrison orders, exasperated now. He looks helpless, as though he doesn't quite know how to handle the situation. He has two people who hate him standing in his basement, and he *knows* we're out to screw with him. He slowly backs away.

Kai holds up his hands in surrender. "Alright, we're out of here."

I seize the opportunity for escape and spin around on my heels, scrambling over to the small window that we climbed in through. From the inside, the window is eye-level. I use my elbows – and adrenaline – to haul myself up, then pull myself outside on my stomach onto the snow. I turn back to offer out a hand to Kai, but he's already swiftly pulling himself up with total ease. He joins me outside in the cool, fresh air and then lowers his head back to the window.

"Bye, bye, Harrison," he sneers, just as Harrison grabs the window and slams it shut. We hear him lock it too.

We grab our coats and stand up, our breathing rapid, and look at one another. Talk about a wild ride. We know it now – we've taken things a step too far. My pulse races at a million miles an hour and my throat feels tight, and, judging by the unfamiliar, stunned expression on Kai's face, he feels the same way. It's like I've left our fantasy world and come back to reality with a thud, because now I realize we were *lucky* to get caught when we did. If we'd followed through with our plan, we'd have ended up in much bigger trouble. Harrison's parents would have called the cops if they woke up to the scene of someone having ransacked their home during the night. And my and Kai's fingerprints would have been all over that place.

How come it's so easy to throw all caution to the wind?

"C'mon," Kai breathes, and he slips his hand into mine.

We run from Harrison's house, dashing past the cars on the driveway again to make a speedy getaway. Kai pulls me along behind him, both of us watching our footing on the snow so that we don't break an ankle, and we stumble all the way back down the street until we reach our bikes that we abandoned by a tree. Of course, they haven't been stolen – this neighborhood is too nice for petty theft.

"That was insane!" I say, letting go of Kai's hand so that I can run my fingers through my hair. I'm shaking from the rush and fear of it all and I can't stay still, too hopped up on adrenaline. I bounce from one foot to the other while repeatedly glancing back over my shoulder as though Harrison and his father are going to come bounding after us, all guns blazing. Literally.

"I know," Kai agrees. He leans back against the tree and kicks at his bike tire as his adrenaline begins to fade and the true danger of our actions sinks in. "Thanks for standing up first, by the way. I was going to, but I didn't wanna get shot," he mumbles, looking at the ground. His cheeks flare. "I feel like an ass. So much for my chivalry."

"Don't worry about it," I say, waving away his apologies. I definitely don't mind covering for Kai when he needed me to. When the chill of the night hits me, I begin pulling on my coat and it occurs to me that we didn't achieve what we set out to do. "Damn. We broke into his house and had a gun pointed at us for nothing."

"For nothing, huh?" Kai says. He straightens up and steps around the bikes to join me, a coy smile playing on his lips. We're standing in the snow on the sidewalk in the middle of a residential street, everything around us quiet and still at such a late hour. Kai stops in front of me, his gaze intoxicating as his lips part slightly. He places a hand on my hip. "Maybe the best revenge," he whispers, "is kissing you."

And, as we stand there together in the midnight cold, Kai's mouth finds mine.

17

For the first time this week, I think I may actually arrive to first period on time. Chyna and I are walking from the student parking lot toward school still with five whole minutes until the first bell is scheduled to ring. The campus is an ice rink – it hasn't snowed again since Wednesday night, so the snow has now fully hardened into a sheet of ice that makes everyone look like Bambi as we skate toward the main entrance.

"He actually pointed a *gun*?" Chyna whispers under her breath. She looks sideways at me, her mouth an "O," shocked. Thank God I have a best friend who listens to my daily updates on the drama in my life. Chyna doesn't need reality TV when she has me for entertainment.

"Yeah! Like, sure, we *were* breaking in, but still," I say. "It totally freaked me out."

Just then, several people skid past us, scrambling in the opposite direction from the school entrance. There's lots of excited murmuring, mostly from young freshmen, as they skate off. I glance over my shoulder, back toward the student parking lot, and notice even more people heading back that way.

I catch a glimpse of Hailey Wilson among the crowd as she passes us, and I reach out and grab her arm. Last week, we were friends. She used to love talking to me, but just like everyone else, she has totally avoided me this week. This is now the first time I've spoken to anyone else in my circle of friends since that video was leaked. "What's going on?"

Hailey stares at my hand on her arm like it's a gross imposition, then mumbles, "I think there's a fight or something," before she continues sliding her way across the ice.

"A fight?" Chyna says, exchanging a look with me.

My stomach tightens with a sense of unease. There're a thousand kids in this school – anyone could be throwing punches right now, but it's usually only seniors who know to keep the fighting off school property. Just beyond the student parking lot is where the campus boundaries are.

"I just got a weird feeling," I say, swallowing hard as I stare at the crowds amassing off in the distance. People are sprinting past us now, desperate to see all the action.

"You think it's Harrison?" Chyna asks, and I nod.

I also think it could be Kai. If Harrison and his buddies dragged me into a janitor's closet and threatened me, then I can only imagine what they will do to Kai now that Harrison knows he's involved . . . It could be a coincidence that there's a fight breaking out the very next morning, but my gut tells me otherwise.

I am definitely going to be late for first period again.

Chyna and I take each other's hands and help one another

skate across the campus, back in the direction we've just trudged from. We weave around all the cars in the parking lot until we reach the crowd on the open field at the other side. My heartbeat's rocketing the nearer we get.

A circle has formed, everyone packed in so tightly, fighting to get a clear view. The noise is deafening – people are yelling and cheering, their Friday morning brightened up by a live-action fistfight. It makes it impossible for Chyna and me to see what's going on. We search for any weak spots that we can push our way through, but I only grow more desperate. I need to see who's fighting.

"Go!" Chyna yells in my ear, letting go of my hand and giving me a push into the crowd. She shoves me forward, ramming me through the thicket of bodies, but I don't even get a chance to thank her. Suddenly, she's left behind and I'm jammed in the midst of the crowd.

I elbow my way through everyone until I find myself at the front. We are circled around a group of guys like an impromptu boxing ring, and my heart drops into my stomach.

My gut feeling was right.

Kai is on his knees on the ground, fighting to get to his feet, just as Harrison slams a fist into his jaw. It sends Kai straight back down, but Harrison isn't his only opponent – Noah is involved too, of course, and he hurls his foot into Kai's ribs. There's no Anthony, but there are a couple other of Harrison's friend from the team. It's four against one, and Kai is already heavily roughed up. His lip gushes with blood, his cheeks are grazed, and he can't open one eye. It's serious. He's on his hands and knees, defenseless, coughing hard. Noah and the other two guys kick him again.

"STOP!" I scream, but my voice sounds strangled amid the noise of the crowd.

Right at that moment Harrison's eye catches mine. He stares at my horrified expression then smirks as he swings his fist into Kai's mouth, sending him flying back to the ground.

"Alright, we're done here!" Harrison yells just as I'm about to throw myself into the fight. His eyes roam the crowd, flickering all around the circle that's formed, and he threatens, "Remember, snitches get stitches."

The crowd disperses almost immediately. No one needs to be reminded to keep quiet about what they've just witnessed – everyone knows the score. Harrison wipes the sweat from his brow with the back of his hand and then slinks off into the distance, following the crowd back to school.

"Hey, sugar," Noah says, barging his shoulder into mine as he passes. I don't pay any attention to him because my eyes are set on Kai.

He's lying face down on the grass, his body heaving, and I run straight to him and drop to my knees by his side. I place a hand on his shoulder, but instantly retract it when he groans. He spits blood and then rolls over on his back, staring up at the sky with his one good eye.

"Oh my God!" I wave my hands in panic, unsure what to do to help. Kai's face is totally busted and there's blood dripping from his nose and mouth. His ribs are most likely bruised too; he's holding his hands to his sides and moaning as he tries to take a deep breath.

"Oh. Hey, Vanessa," he says through busted lips when he turns to me. "What's up?"

I stare at him, utterly horrified. Harrison would have never found out that Kai was involved if we hadn't gone to his house last night, and it was *me* who insisted we did. Kai suggested that we stop, that it could be risky to keep pushing Harrison . . . but I didn't listen.

"This is all my fault!"

"Shut up, Nessie," Kai says, trying for a laugh that quickly turns into a painful cough.

A few people are still lingering, most likely checking out the severity of Kai's injuries, and Chyna rushes over. Kai manages to give her a small wave, and it blows my mind that he can be humorous right now. He just got his ass kicked in front of half the school, but somehow his ego is the only part of him that hasn't taken a beating.

"Should we take him to the nurse?" Chyna asks me. She's chewing on her lower lip as she glances back over at the school building in the distance.

"Nuh-uh," Kai objects, his words muffled through his swollen lips. "I'll be fine, Chyna-but-not-like-the-country."

Madison also swishes over and kneels down on the grass, fumbling inside her bag. "Don't you guys carry first-aid kits?" she asks Chyna and me, her tone patronizing. *Of course* Maddie carries around a damn first-aid kit in her bag. She pulls out a neat box of miscellaneous items and edges in closer to Kai. "Not so charming when you're covered in blood, huh?"

"Yet here I am, surrounded by ladies," Kai groans jokingly.

Slowly, he manages to sit up, his hands still pressed to his ribs. He releases a long breath of air. "Man, fuck that Noah guy. Now I know why he has a bad name for himself out on the field. He's worse than Harrison."

"What happened?" I ask as Maddie gets to work on Kai's face, dabbing at his open cuts with disinfectant wipes, cleaning up the blood. I'm impressed by how calm and unfazed she is.

"Well, you see, Nessie, last night Harrison discovered I've been helping you—"

"Kai," I say sharply, cutting him off. I give him a serious look. Now isn't the time for him to be flippant.

"They pretty much ambushed me the second I pulled up," Kai finally tells me, dropping his playful tone. He's looking at me with his eye that's still open while Maddie gently cleans up the other. "Basically dragged me over here. I'm guessing this is where the campus ends?" I nod. "Oh, and if anyone spots a bike dumped in the bushes somewhere, it'll be mine."

My heart sinks a little. Kai loves biking around. "They took your bike?"

"Actually, *you* took my bike," Kai points out, his grin more of a painful grimace. "Those assholes took my dad's."

"I'll look for it," Chyna offers. "I'm late for class anyway." She heads off to search the surrounding area, doing her best to make herself useful right now.

Maddie sticks a band-aid to a cut just below Kai's eye while I sit and watch. I'm the only one doing nothing to help, because I don't know how to. It's my fault Kai is in this situation. I should never have come up with the idea of getting even with Harrison. Revenge seemed so fun at first, but now we're in too deep.

"What can I do, Kai?"

"Kiss me better?" he suggests.

"Stop moving!" Maddie scolds him. She reaches for his chin and holds him steady while she sticks another band-aid to his cheek. He'll be covered in them soon. She also hands him a cloth for his nose. "You should probably still go to the hospital. You could be concussed or something."

"And build up a hefty medical bill that my parents can't afford to pay?" Kai shoots back in disagreement. "No thanks. I'll just let you nurse me back to health then I'll go drink some coffee." Maddie sticks one final band-aid to his face and then he pushes himself up from the grass, his balance slightly off as he stumbles on his feet. "Thanks, Maddie." He straightens up, steadies himself. "I think I'm gonna head home, though."

I nod and stand up too, looking him over. It's probably best that he doesn't go to school today – this is all such a mess. This fight will be the gossip of the day, and if it were anyone else, I'd be thrilled that attention had finally shifted away from me. But this is all at Kai's expense.

Chyna comes rushing back over, shaking her head. "No bike around here. Sorry."

"That's alright. Thanks," Kai says, then looks down at Maddie who's still on the grass, packing up her stuff. "And thanks again, Madison."

She humbly waves away his gratitude. "It's nothing, but keep those cuts clean – yeah?"

I step toward Kai and put my arms around him, laying my head against his chest. My guilt feels like a ton of bricks pressing down on me.

"Ouch," he says, flinching.

I let go and jump back. "Sorry!"

Kai rolls his eye – perhaps I'll get him a pirate eye-patch – and then leans in to me, briefly pressing his lips to my temple. He turns around and walks off, his steps slow and pained, until he becomes nothing more than a distant figure. I know I should really skip class again and go with him, but when I look back at the school building, a new anger flares up within me.

How dare Harrison hurt Kai.

I walk with Chyna and Maddie back to the school. We have to stop by the office first to let them know we're late, and I get even more hours of detention piled on me. Miss Hillman from reception seems genuinely stunned to be handing out detention to Madison Romy, but Maddie takes it like a champ. She doesn't whine about it once, or even mention how much of a saint she is for sacrificing her attendance to help Kai. She just tucks the slip into her bag and heads off to class without another word.

"So *now* do you realize that perhaps this whole plan for revenge was a bad idea?" Chyna asks when we're alone in the hallway. Everyone is in class but us, and she gives me a condescending raise of her eyebrow, as though to say *I told you so.* And she did. She warned me that this whole thing was a stupid idea, that we could get ourselves into trouble.

But Harrison screwed around with me first. Harrison instigated all of this, and of course Kai and I retaliated. It's become an endless circle. But I can't let Harrison make the final move. I can't let him *win*. I just can't, not after he's hurt Kai like that. I need to end this myself. On *my* terms.

"Yeah, this was a bad idea," I agree with a sheepish smile, but I'm not done yet. The gloves are off now, and I don't need anyone's help anymore. This is between Harrison and me.

Chyna groans, reminds me that it's Taco Friday at the Tate house for dinner later, and then blows me a kiss as she heads off to her class. I catch it and safely tuck it away in the pocket of my coat, watching her as she disappears down the hallway. And then I spring into action.

I don't head for my History class. Instead, I take off down the hall toward the library, my steps quick. I didn't want to have to do this, but Harrison has pushed me to my limit. I laughed when I found these pictures on Harrison's phone the other morning, but then quickly realized I didn't want to take things *that* far. That's why I never told Kai about them. I've been secretly holding onto them, but not for much longer.

I burst into the library and totally blank the librarian when she asks me to sign in. I tell her I'm running late for class and I need to quickly print my overdue homework, and she tuts and shakes her head at me as I dive for the computers. The library is empty, thank God, but I still angle the desktop screen away for maximum privacy. My heart rockets around in my chest as I plug my phone into the computer and load up my files, some of which are also Harrison's that I transferred over to my own phone for safekeeping.

I find the photo I'm looking for.

I print it, then shut down the computer as fast as I can and race over to the printers in the back corner before the librarian can see what I'm doing. This definitely isn't homework I'm printing off, and I would most likely be expelled if caught using school property in connection with such a photograph.

"Thanks!" I say cheerily on my way out of the library, but the librarian's skeptical frown doesn't falter. As soon as I'm through the doors, I remember something else I need. I head back inside and stop at the desk. "Sorry. Can I borrow a marker? Oh, and a drawing pin."

The librarian looks fed up with me now. She mumbles some disgruntled words under her breath – she's probably sick to death of dealing with teenagers – and reluctantly fetches me a black permanent marker and a pin. I thank her again and, much to her delight, leave for good this time. It's about the first and last time she'll ever see me.

Armed with my photograph and marker, I make my way back to the locker hallway. First period ends in just under ten minutes, which means that soon these hallways will be packed again while everyone moves on to their next classes and stops by their lockers. And I want everyone's attention to be on Harrison's.

"Vanessa," a voice says, and I stop dead in my tracks and look behind me to find Anthony slowly approaching. I shove my printout and marker into my coat pocket and fold my arms across my chest, my stance hostile.

"What?" I snap. I don't even bother to ask why he isn't in class. I have better things to do right now than talk to Anthony.

He walks over to me and stops a few feet away, stuffing his hands into his pockets. He rocks back and forth on the balls of his feet and stares at the ground. "I just want to say that I'm sorry for what happened yesterday. You know, in the janitor's closet. It wasn't right," he mumbles, unable to look at me. "And I don't think it's right what they did to that guy this morning either."

"And yet you said *nothing* and did even less," I bitterly remind him. "That makes you just as bad as Harrison and Noah."

"I'm not like them," he says, his eyes flickering up from the floor. He's riddled with nerves. It's clear from the bead of sweat that trickles down his skin. I always knew Anthony was the nicest of the trio, but still. He's a jerk through association.

"Then get better friends," I say, and I stare him down until he sighs and gives up. I watch him walk away, his head lowered, until he is out of sight. I count to twenty in my head to allow Anthony enough time to be a safe enough distance away, then I immediately get back to business.

I pull out my weaponry from my pocket and continue down the hallway. Harrison's locker is easy to find. It's on the very end of the row. He pinned me against it and kissed me hard often enough. I stand in front of the locker now, listening closely for a moment to ensure no one is approaching in the distance.

If Harrison wants to screw with me, then fine.

But I'll fight back harder.

I slam the photo against the locker door and pin it in place, using all my strength to pierce the metal. Then I pop open the cap of the marker and in huge, capital letters, I write:

#SMILEFORTHECAMERA

I stand back to admire my work. On Harrison's locker, there's a picture. A picture he took of himself, a picture that was so easy for me to get my hands on. It was taken recently and it's only one out of a batch of them. It's of Harrison standing in front of his bathroom mirror, his phone shielding his face, two fingers up in a peace sign. He is totally naked.

If Harrison wants to leak that video of us to the world, then I'll give our classmates a bit more content to enjoy. He might not even care that much. He's already in that awful video with me, but this photograph is more personal. It's not his choice this time. How will *he* feel when he discovers something so private has been shared to the world without his consent? How will he feel to be as disrespected, mocked, and knocked off balance as I was?

And the hashtag? A nice touch.

I dump the marker in a nearby trash can and remove myself from the scene. I walk down the hallway and linger around by the noticeboard, a safe distance away from Harrison's locker, and wait patiently. I stare at the clock on the wall and watch the seconds tick by, counting down to the moment the bell rings out and my peers discover Harrison's nude selfie. My stomach is knotted with nerves and excitement. I'm terrified about how Harrison will react and what the fallout will be from this, because I *know* I'm taking it too far. I *know* I'm only adding more fuel to an already blazing fire. But I have to do this, because my ego demands that I'm the winner of this war, no matter what the cost of victory.

The bell blares out across the school, echoing down the empty hallways. It feels louder than ever as it rings in my ears. I lock my eyes on a poster on the noticeboard, something about a new after-school yoga class, trying to play it cool as the sound around me gradually amplifies from silence to a chorus of voices and footsteps. My heart feels like it's no longer beating in my chest – as if it's stopped completely, and my breath has caught in my throat. I want to turn around, to watch the stunned expressions of the Westerville North student body when they discover what's pinned to Harrison Boyd's locker, but I quickly realize I don't have to. I can already hear the gasps of shock and the bursts of laughter.

Subtly, I angle my head and watch the scene unfold out of the corner of my eye. A crowd is forming around the locker at the end of the row, everyone pushing and shoving to get a good view, just like they did thirty minutes ago outside when the fight was going down. I remain in my spot by the noticeboard, keeping out of the way.

Harrison's life hasn't changed at all this week, despite that video. No one has tormented him, or whispered behind his back, or refused to sit at his table at lunch. No one *cares* about him and that video, because a football player hooking up at a party? That's to be expected. It's *cool*. But the girl the football player hooks up with? A tramp with no self-respect, apparently.

Harrison deserves his fair share of humiliation too. He was the one who shared that video with the world, perfectly aware that *I* would be the one to receive all of the backlash.

"What the hell is going on?" I hear a voice yell over the buzz of commotion, and I recognize it instantly. He's here.

My curiosity is too hard to fight. I look down the hallway at the scene I've created. People are snapping pictures of the locker door with their phones. Others are pulling over their friends to show them the latest Westerville North High drama. And Harrison? Harrison is shoving people out of his way, panic flashing across his features, until his eyes take in the display before him.

I watch him closely, basking in the joy that fills me when his expression twists with horror. All the color drains from his face as he looks around the crowd of spectators, all catching a glimpse of his perfectly average package. He tears the photo from his locker, shredding it in half, and then slams his fist into the metal. Everyone moves out of his way as he pushes people to the side, storming off down the hallway. He's truly enraged, and it's oh-so-satisfying.

For, like, two seconds.

Because in that very moment, I realize Harrison and I are no different. We are both terrible people. How am I any better for doing to him what he has done to me? I'm not. It's the most gut-wrenching feeling in the world, the way my chest tightens with regret. Hurting Harrison doesn't make me feel better. It only makes me feel worse than I did on Monday morning when I first discovered his betrayal.

I can't stick around here. I shove my hands into my coat pockets and turn on my heels, striding down the hall toward the school's entrance. My eyes sting with tears again, the same way they did yesterday when I ran down this same hallway, and I push open the doors and step out into the freezing air outside. I suck in a huge breath, filling my lungs until they feel as though they'll explode, then I release it.

I walk all the way home to an empty house, my head down.

I feel like the worst person in the world.

18

"Hey, honey!" Kai's mom says as she swings open the front door. She immediately ushers me inside from the cold. The house feels like a sauna compared to outside.

"Did Kai mention I was coming over?" I ask as I kick off my shoes. I hope his mom doesn't think I'm just turning up uninvited. I've been texting with Kai all afternoon while the two of us both skipped school and stayed home, but not together, and I offered to come over and keep him company tonight. It's just after eight, and I've spent the past hour at Chyna's binging on chicken tacos while I built up the courage to come over here. When it comes to talking to Kai's parents, I feel a little on edge. Usually, when I go over to a guy's house, I avoid the parents at all costs because I don't want them to ever think I'll end up dating their son long-term. I have to remind myself that with Kai it's different. We're not like that.

At least I don't think we are. All I know is that whatever this is, it definitely doesn't feel like some fling.

"Of course," Cindy answers, but her smile quickly turns down into a frown. "Was he fighting at school again? He won't tell us what happened to his face. Maybe you know? Also, do you know why he skipped school yesterday? The school called me. He isn't making a good first impression for himself."

"Uhhh," I say, awkwardly looking anywhere but at her. Clearly, Kai doesn't want his parents to know the truth, so how do I answer? I imagine telling her: *Sorry, Mrs. Washington, but your son got his ass beat by a guy who we've been screwing with the whole week.* I imagine the complete look of horror on her face.

"Mom," I hear Kai say sharply, saving me from having to lie straight to his mother's face. I let out a breath of relief when I spot him descending the staircase. He narrows his eyes at her. One is still black and swollen, but at least both eyes are now open fully. The gray sweatpants he's wearing low on his hips look ridiculously attractive. "Don't interrogate the guest."

Cindy holds her hands up in surrender as she backs away. "Okay, okay!" she says, but she eyes Kai with deep concern, pressing her lips together. Kai's first week at Westerville North hasn't gone down well – he's skipped a bunch of classes *and* gotten into a fight, so I'm surprised his mom is even allowing him to have friends over. "Just yell if you guys need anything."

"We won't," Kai says, then motions for me to join him upstairs. As I fall into place by his side, he flashes me a reassuring grin. I can see the cut in his lower lip.

We pass the living room and his father gives us a wave from in front of the TV, and I make the effort to wave back and offer a polite smile. I can't help but like Kai's parents and it's comforting to know that at this moment in time, they have no reason to believe I'm a terrible person. But I am.

Kai leads me upstairs and into his room, and this time it's nowhere near as cluttered as it was on Monday. His bed is unmade, there's still laundry scattered all over the floor, and there are too many cans of soda and water bottles on his bedside table, but everything else has been pushed into one corner of the room. I notice the Netflix home screen on his TV.

"Are we Netflix and chilling?" I joke. The thought makes my skin feel hot, but I kid myself it's just the intense heat in this house. I pull off my coat and throw it over the back of his desk chair.

Kai grins and dives onto his bed, sprawling out. He props his head up with a pillow and looks at me. "I've been watching that crime documentary all day. The one I told you about," he confesses. "I'm still piecing together my conspiracy theory."

I sit on the edge of the bed, crossing my legs. I keep a certain distance between us for now. "How are you feeling?" I ask, my brows pinched together in sympathy. I still feel awful for being the reason Kai ended up getting hurt the way he did, and I haven't yet told him how I messed up *again* today. He doesn't know that I've made everything much worse than it already was, simply because I couldn't control my impulses. "By the way, I'm returning your bike. You need it more than I do, so I've put it in your back yard."

"Thanks. And let me think," Kai says, then lifts his shirt and prods at his ribs with his fingers. I try not to stare, but it's near impossible to stop my heart skipping a beat at the sight of his abs. The smooth curves of his waist, the hem of his boxers . . . "A little bruised, but I doubt I've fractured anything. And my face? Well, I guess it just looks badass."

I crawl across the bed and lie down next to him, staring up at the ceiling, my hands pressed to my face. "It's my fault," I mumble, my voice full of remorse. "You were right. We should have stopped all of this yesterday, and Harrison would have never found out that you were helping me."

I sense Kai shift from beside me, and when I drop my hands from my face, I find him propped up on one elbow and staring down at me. His smile is lazy. "And who was the one who suggested we do this in the first place?"

"You . . . But we never meant for it to get this bad, did we?" I sit up and cross my legs, anxiously fidgeting with my hands in my lap. I can't look at him. "Kai," I say. "After the fight . . . I was so mad. I couldn't stop myself."

Concern slowly fills Kai's tender gaze. "What did you do, Nessie?"

"I never told you about some photos I found on Harrison's phone," I admit. "I was holding on to them, but I didn't ever plan to use them. They were nudes."

Kai snorts, and I snap my eyes up to give him a firm look. This isn't funny right now. The regret is eating me up and I've spent the entire afternoon wishing I could take back what I did. In fact, I wish I'd never started any of this in the first place. I should have just dealt with Harrison face-to-face in a more mature manner. At least then I would have been the bigger, better person.

Instead I chose to retaliate.

"I stuck one of the photos on Harrison's locker," I say. "It seemed like a good idea in the moment. Sort of like we'd come full circle. I wanted to make the final move. But now ... now Harrison will just hit us back even harder!"

I shouldn't have printed out that photo, and I definitely shouldn't have taped it to Harrison's locker for the entire school to lay eyes on – it was a step too far and I hate myself for letting things get this bad. Kai and I should have never made this into a game.

"I'm sure my ribs can handle another beating."

"Kai!" I hiss. His sarcasm and teasing, for once, are getting on my nerves. I need him to level with me, to be serious and reassure me that we'll get through this, because right now, I really don't know if we can. I already burst into tears yesterday morning when Harrison and his friends cornered me in that janitor's closet, and today Kai has sustained too many cuts and bruises to count. We're done.

"Then we'll tell Harrison that it's over," Kai says calmly. "Like, we'll strike up a peace deal. He doesn't screw with you anymore, and we won't screw with him. He'd be an idiot to ignore that." Kai moves his body closer to mine and surprises me when he rests his head in my lap, staring at the TV. "Can you play with my hair?" he asks.

I gently weave my fingers through his curls, feeling their softness against my hands. I run my fingertips down to the shaved section of his hair at the nape of his neck, massaging as I go. We sit in silence for a few minutes while my hands move over his head, and I wonder if he's napping. "Did you ask me over so I could soothe you to sleep?"

"No," Kai says, "I wanted to see you." He twists his body around so that his head is still in my lap, but now he's looking up at me. The corner of his mouth curves into a smile. "I think this has been the longest we've gone this week without having seen each other."

One hand is still resting in Kai's hair, the other is on his chest. I look down into his eyes and I can't remember a time when they were ever unfamiliar to me. Monday feels like so long ago. "Right? We've spent so much time together that I feel like I've known you for months."

"You *wish* you'd known me for months," he says, his smile transforming into a grin.

"Thank God you got kicked out of Central," I say with a laugh. "Otherwise I may never have been anything more than that girl who spilled her drink on you."

"Aren't you glad that I worked up the courage to talk to you in the school office?"

"You know I am," I whisper, and I run my eyes over him, taking in his gorgeous features. I touch the tip of my finger to his eyebrow, then softly skim my thumb over one of the grazes on his cheek. He parts his lips a little, and I touch the cut on his lower lip too. His gaze is locked on me as I draw a map between every little cut and bruise on his face.

"Then kiss me," he breathes.

I lean down and tentatively press my lips to Kai's. I'm still holding his head in my lap and we remain still, our mouths together, until he reaches up and rests his hand on the back of my neck. He pulls me closer against him, kissing me harder. My heartbeat is pounding in my ears. Kai sits up, never breaking the kiss, his hand wrapped into my hair as he hovers over me. He presses his chest into mine, pushing me backward until my head hits the pillows. I lock my arms around the back of his neck, keeping him close because I never want to let go. Kissing Kai is much more than I've ever felt. It's electrifying, sending sparks all through my body. It makes me realize that *this* is what I want.

Kai is what I want.

The room is so silent, the beating of our hearts the only sound. His body is above mine, his hands are tangled in my hair, his tongue is in my mouth. The kiss deepens, quickens, both of us surging with desire. I can't get enough of Kai Washington. I wish I'd known him forever.

I push against him, arching my back and lifting my body off the bed. Kai rolls over, taking me with him so I'm on top now. Our lips never break apart. His hands are wandering. They're in my hair, they're on my hips, they're pulling at the belt loops of my jeans. I tug at his T-shirt and we separate for the first time while Kai helps me pull it over his head. He kisses my face, my neck, my collarbone. His lips are firm and moist. He sits up, holding me close against his bare chest as I weave my fingers back into his hair.

Kai's hands are under my top now. His hands are warm against my skin, sending goosebumps all down my back. We both know which line we're crossing here. We know what happens next.

And I'm desperate to cross that line. I want Kai to kiss his way down my body, I want to feel his skin against mine, I want to share this moment with him. But I also don't want to cross that line *yet*.

I don't want to rush things with Kai. For once in my life, I want to take things slow, to get to know him some more. Things are different with him. This isn't just a fling, or some new guy who I'll get bored of after a couple months. I feel ... *excited* about the possibility of Kai and me. And that's something I've never felt before. I don't want to ruin it. I want to wait a little longer. Now isn't the right time.

"Stop," I say, breathless. I cup Kai's face in my hands and hold it still, gazing back into his cool, blue eyes. They are glistening.

"Sorry," Kai says. He's holding me close, and he instantly drops his hands to my waist. I gaze down at his chest, almost sure I can see his heart beating. Concern crosses his features. "You okay?"

"Yeah. I'm great. You're perfect," I reassure him, pecking my lips to his. I hook my arms around his neck and let out a sigh. "It's just that ... I don't know if I'm ready for this yet. With you. And not because I don't want to," I babble, "because I do. I really do, but I want to wait. Is that okay?"

"Actually, I was kind of thinking the same thing," Kai says, glancing down as he grows shy. He runs his hands from my waist down my thighs, over the denim of my jeans. He sheepishly looks up at me from beneath his dark eyelashes. "And trust me, I want this too, but I'm a little old fashioned. It should mean something, you know?"

My face instantly falls. His words are like a punch in the gut. "What's that supposed to mean, Kai?" I say.

"Oh God," he groans, his eyes widening. He shakes his head fast and grabs my hips. "Nessie, I didn't mean it like that. I swear."

But I'm already pushing him away. I swing my body off his and slide off the bed, grabbing my jacket from the chair. My cheeks are flaming with a mixture of anger and embarrassment. I can't even look at him now, so I keep my back to him as I angrily pull on my jacket. "I know what you meant," I say bitterly, my voice quiet. I should have known that my reputation defines me, and that of course Kai can't ignore that. "You think I'm easy, right? I thought you were different, Kai. You told me you didn't judge me, but clearly you do."

"Vanessa," Kai says. He comes from behind me, reaching for my wrist. "I don't think that."

I spin around, my entire body engulfed in rage, and shake his hand off my arm. "Well, why not? It's true," I snap at him. So much for trusting Kai. I'm humiliated even just standing here in front of him, knowing that he thinks of me the same way everyone else does. He knows I don't believe in relationships, but that doesn't mean that I don't want sex to *mean* something. "I guess it doesn't matter that for you I wanted to wait. It's like you didn't even expect me to."

Kai blinks fast, his forehead creased with alarm. "Nessie, c'mon," he pleads, stepping closer to me. He's still shirtless. "I just meant that I've only ever been with a girl I was in a relationship with, whereas you're more casual. That's okay,

234

of course. But those other guys can't *all* mean something to you."

"Wow," I say. I blow out a breath of disbelief at the words I'm hearing.

"Shit," Kai mutters, pressing his hands to his face as though he wants to shove everything he just said back into his mouth. But it's too late now. His words have already stung, their poison spreading straight to my core. "I'm screwing this all up. You know I don't care about that stuff. Your past and stuff. It doesn't matter, Nessie."

"But yet it's so obvious that you do care. And my name," I say through gritted teeth, "is *Vanessa*. Only the people who matter get to call me anything else."

I snatch my car keys from the dresser, and turn for the door. I storm downstairs in a fit of rage. As if I let myself *feel* something for a guy who thinks I'm incapable of having feelings. I'm so embarrassed and disappointed, I have to fight to hold back my tears.

Kai is close on my heels as I stride down the stairs. He keeps trying to call out for me, to reach for my hand, but I'm too wrapped up in my own fury at him.

"Leaving already?" Cindy says as I cross the living room, surprise evident in her voice, but I can't even look at her. I slip on my shoes and walk straight out the front door, trying my best not to slam it behind me.

The second I'm outside, the tears break free.

19

I dump the Green McRusty out on the street and then run for my front door, still wiping tears from my cheeks. I could cry in the privacy of the car, out here alone in the middle of our neighborhood where no one will notice me, but all I want is my own bed right now. My own pillows. My teddy bear. And it's not like I'll need to hide from Dad. He didn't even notice me leave earlier, so why would he notice me return?

I throw open the door and keep my head down as I head for the stairs. Out of the corner of my eye, I spot Dad at the kitchen table, huddled over his laptop again. He'll most likely be carrying out more research for this vacation to Ireland he expects us all to take next summer, because exploring our Irish ancestry was one of Mom's big dreams that Dad never paid attention to while she was still alive. Now he's trying his best to make up for it. To honor her wishes, I guess.

I step one foot on the stairs, sniffing as the tears stream down my face. Kennedy is in the living room, staring at the TV while she strokes a blissed-out Theo. We are all so distant in this house, each of us trying to get by in our own way. Kennedy and I carefully avoid talking about Mom in fear that Dad will break down further, and I push the boundaries of a normal teenage existence in an attempt to have my father *notice* me.

"Vanessa?" Dad says. I freeze on the spot, my hand on the banister, surprised to hear Dad say my name. I look over, my eyes puffy and swollen. He immediately rises from the table and removes his reading glasses. "Are you crying?"

"Do you even care if my answer is yes?"

Dad blinks at me, taken aback. He sets his glasses down on the table and walks over. Why now, the one time I *don't* want him to notice me, he finally does? "Of course I care."

I've lost my grip this past week; everything is slipping out of control. My morality feels like it's in the gutter, my reputation precedes me, and now I've found out Kai thinks of me the same way everyone else does. I imagine Mom again, looking down on me now as I stand on our staircase with tears in my eyes. I don't deserve sympathy – I've brought this all upon myself, because I'm a shitty, shitty person. Right now, it feels like I truly have nothing to lose.

I've got stuff that I need to say to Dad. Why should I care anymore about protecting his feelings? Why should it take physical tears for him to realize that I need him?

I turn back from the stairs and take a few steps toward Dad, looking up at him. "Really? You care? Because you sure as hell don't act like it."

Dad blinks, stunned, as if my words are shocking information, like he genuinely believes he's a doting father rather than just some stranger who happens to live in the same house.

Surely, I think, *he knows how absent he's been in our lives?*

"Vanessa . . ." Dad says, but he immediately runs out of words.

"What, Dad?" I press, my words laced with exasperation. How can he not see it? "Where were you that time I got so drunk I threw up on the porch? Why don't you stop me from sneaking out after midnight? And how many calls from school have you received this week that you've ignored? Because I've skipped so many classes and yet you haven't said a single word about it. You know why? Because you don't CARE!"

I hear the TV pause, then slow footsteps. Out of the corner of my eye, I see Kennedy approaching, watching from a few feet away. She's still holding Theo against her chest, anxiously rubbing his ears. I don't want her to see me yelling at Dad, but I've already gotten myself too heated now. It's too late to stop the words spilling from my mouth, all these questions that I've never been brave enough to ask, all these truths I've never had the courage to say out loud.

Dad slowly shakes his head, his lips silently moving as he struggles to muster up an answer. "I care . . . I love you. I love both of you. How could I not?" He glances at Kennedy, then back at me. He gulps hard, but his expression still looks frozen, his eyes wide with shock. "You know I've just had a lot on my mind. I thought you were happy."

"Happy!" I repeat with a cold, sharp laugh. *Happy?* Is he blind too? I pretend Chyna's parents are my own, I'm constantly worried about Kennedy, I refuse to let any guy get close to me. How can I possibly be happy? I'm in survival mode. "That's a fucking joke, Dad. It really is."

"Don't use that language with me," Dad stammers.

I don't think I've ever sworn in front of him before, but what does it matter now? Maybe if I'd sworn at him when I was fifteen, he would have cared then. I almost laugh. If only I'd known it was that easy to get his attention.

I cross my arms, my glare challenging. I don't recognize the man standing in front of me. "So now you wanna scold me for cussing?"

"What's . . . what's going on here, Vanessa? Why are you acting like this?"

"Because I'm tired, *Dad*, that's why!" I snap at him, my voice growing louder. I take another step closer, getting all up in his face. My eyes still sting with tears. "I'm tired of tiptoeing around you. It's been two years. We miss Mom too, me and Kennedy, but you can't just stop *living*. You still have two daughters who need you to look out for them, but you're just too selfish to care about us anymore."

I may as well have slapped Dad across the cheek, because my words seem to inflict a physical pain upon him. He clutches at his chest, staggering a few steps back. He searches for words that never arrive. The tension in this house right now is about to overwhelm us all, and Dad shifts his focus to my sister.

"Kennedy . . . you know I care about you, don't you?" he asks softly, his voice almost pleading. He so desperately wants her to say yes.

Kennedy looks down at the floor and buries her face into Theo's fur. "Not really," she mumbles, unable to meet his eye.

Dad looks back at me, aghast. He rubs at his temple and I can see him break out into a nervous sweat. His voice is weak, shaky. My dad is a broken man. "I thought I was . . . I thought cutting you guys some slack was the best thing to do. I thought I was helping."

"*Some* slack?" I nearly laugh again. He is so, so oblivious that it hurts. How can abandoning your daughters after they've just lost their mom possibly be *helping*? "There's a difference between being a laidback parent and a non-existent one. You know that, right?"

"What do you expect me to do?" Dad asks.

"Stop letting me do whatever the hell I want, for starters. I'm only seventeen! I need my dad, okay? I need *you*. I need you to text and ask when I'll be home, and I need you to yell at me when I walk through that front door smelling of beer, and I need you to ground me when I backtalk you. I need you to act like a damn father, and to actually care about my well-being, because sometimes I wonder if you'd even care if I drove that ugly rust-bucket of yours off a bridge."

Dad's features flood with horror. "Vanessa, please don't say that."

"Well, would you?"

"Vanessa!" He lets out a frustrated groan as he runs his hands through his graying hair.

"Have you even noticed that I've had the *worst* possible week?" I question, arms still folded. I'm not backing down, and I continue to glower at him, piling on the pressure. I have waited forever for this moment. "No, you haven't. But let me tell you about it." I stare straight into his eyes and I tell him the truth: "I hooked up with a guy who filmed us and then sent the video to everyone in school. Yeah, Dad, that's right. There's a video out there of me stripping, and I don't even have a parent to turn to."

Dad's jaw literally drops. He stares at me, completely blown away. So many different emotions flicker across his eyes, too fast to pinpoint a single one. The color drains from his face at such speed I think he might faint in front of me.

"We didn't just lose Mom," I say quietly now, my voice almost a whisper. "We lost you too."

I leave him there at the bottom of the stairs, staring after his disgrace of a daughter as I run to my room. Fresh tears spring to my eyes. My heart feels too dense, too heavy, the weight of it crushing my chest. I slam my bedroom door and strip off my jacket, then throw myself onto my bed. My room is in darkness, but I prefer it that way. I burrow under my comforter and press my face into my pillows, then scream against the soft fabric. The scream is muffled, almost silent. I feel utterly helpless.

"Vanessa?" Dad's voice pleads at my bedroom door as he quietly knocks once, wary and apprehensive. And so he should be.

"GO AWAY!" I scream.

His footsteps fade down the hall and a few moments of silence pass where all I can focus on is my ragged breathing. Then I hear the click of my door opening and a sliver of light from the hall shines into my room. I grit my teeth, prepared to yell at Dad for having the nerve to barge into my room, to care *now*. But it's not him.

"Vanessa?" Kennedy gently says, but I'm crying too hard to reply.

My entire body is trembling and I'm squeezing my pillows with my fists. I hear the door close again, then sense movement in my room. My mattress shifts as Kennedy sits down on the edge of my bed. She doesn't say anything for a while, but then she finally asks, "Why did you explode like that?"

"Everything sucks. Couldn't get much worse," I mumble.

"Even that hot guy sucks?"

I lift my head from my tear-soaked pillows to look at her. "*Especially* that hot guy."

Kennedy frowns. She's left Theo downstairs, and now she's looking down at me with concern. It's like our roles have been reversed. Suddenly, my little sister is the one looking after me. "What happened?"

"He turned out to be just like everyone else," I whisper, then bury my face back into my pillows and pull my comforter up over my head. I want to disappear off the face of the earth right now. I don't ever want to go back to school. I don't want to ever face Dad again. I never want to see Harrison, or Noah, or Anthony again.

And I definitely never want to see Kai Washington again.

Kennedy climbs under my comforter with me and cuddles up close. She wraps her arms around me, squeezing me tight, and she doesn't have to tell me that she loves me because her actions say it for her. She stays quiet, never saying anything more, and holds me until I cry myself to sleep.

20

Every Saturday, I have breakfast with the Tates. It's become a weekly tradition over the years, ever since they first began inviting me after Mom passed away. It reminds me of what a loving, close family feels like. Rachel makes giant, fluffy pancakes from scratch, and always has too many toppings to choose from, and Tyrone always makes his own fresh orange juice. We all sit together around the table, stuffing our faces between the laughter. It makes me feel warm and fuzzy inside.

"And turned out, that girl he was dating? She's his distant cousin," Isaiah says, finishing his story about his buddy from college who's unknowingly been in a relationship with a family member, and we all share a chuckle around the table.

It was hard to drag myself out of bed to come here this morning. But if anything were to make me feel better, it would be breakfast with Chyna. I left my house and drove over here before Dad was even awake. I can't bring myself to face him after everything I said last night.

"Vanessa, what're your funny stories from this week?" Rachel asks, offering out the plate of fresh pancakes to me.

I hold up my hand to decline – I'm already on my second – and give her a tight smile. Not only do we follow tradition of having pancakes every week, we also follow the tradition of sharing anything humorous that may have happened in our lives recently.

"Nothing new," I lie, exchanging a quick glance with Chyna. I fork up another mouthful of pancake, banana, and Nutella, hoping if I chew for long enough she won't press me. The truth is, so much has happened this week – but it's all totally inappropriate to share over the dining table. How do I find the humor in a sexual video of me being released to the world? Or the humor in me running around town seeking revenge on Harrison? Or the humor in fighting with my father? And how do I even begin to find the humor in catching feelings for the very first time for a guy who doesn't deserve them?

Rachel lets out a sigh of dismay. "But you always have something to tell us!"

"I have something," Chyna cuts in from beside me, and I shoot her a sideways glance, silently thanking her before I continue to chomp down on my food. We all listen to her as she talks. "Okay, so the other day, I got paired with Malik Dorsey in Chemistry. Mom, do you remember him? He used to live across the street when we were kids and we'd play together in our yard and I was kind of in love with him. He finally confessed to stealing a bracelet of mine and he gave it back to me the next day, so maybe we *will* end up getting married after all."

Did that really happen this week or is she making it up

just to save me from having to share a story of my own? If it did happen, she hasn't mentioned it to me. Or maybe she did and I was too self-absorbed to remember. I think of my and Chyna's conversations over the past week, and I realize most of them have all been about *me*. My life. My plans for revenge on Harrison, my thoughts on Kai . . . Have I even asked Chyna anything about *her* life? Did I even ask her how her college application went? *No*, I think, *I didn't*. If I needed another reason to hate myself this morning, this is it.

"Oh, I've got a good one!" Tyrone exclaims, and he dives into telling his dramatic story of an awkward misunderstanding he had yesterday with a coworker, but I tune out and miss all of the details.

When we're finally all excused from the table ten minutes later, Chyna is quick to hook her arm around mine and pull me away. Another of the great things about Chyna's parents? They don't ever need us to help clean up. Chyna and I head upstairs to her room, and I collapse onto her bed and stare at the ceiling.

"Are we still going to Maddie's party tonight?" I ask. I'd pushed the thought of that party to the back of my mind over the past couple days, but now the time has come to decide whether or not to show up.

"I don't know," Chyna says. She mutes her TV and sits down on the bed next to me. "Do you want to? I do. Malik could be there."

"Would it make me look weak if I didn't turn up?" I sit up and look back at her, chewing my lower lip. Noah doesn't ever miss a party, and that means his sheep will be there too – like Harrison and Anthony and the rest of his asshole friends. And if the party is anything like last weekend's, then half the senior class will be there . . . All of the people who have laughed at my expense this week, all of the people who have posted cruel things about me online. But isolating me is what they want. It's how they win. "Like, would everyone think I was too scared?"

Chyna thinks for a moment. "If you want to go to the party, I'll come with you. If you want to miss it, I'll skip it too. We could catch a movie instead or something. Just you and me."

I don't deserve to call Chyna Tate my best friend. She's everything I want to be – quietly intelligent, caring and loving, with a strong moral compass. She has the crappy end of the bargain. Her best friend is selfish and self-centered, and reckless and corrupt. I don't appreciate her enough.

"Hey," I say. "How did your college application go?"

Chyna's expression turns puzzled. It's a drastic change in subject, that's for sure. I don't miss the way her eyes light up, though, like she has been waiting all week for me to ask that exact question, and it makes my chest ache. "Mrs. Moore said my application is great and there's nothing more I could do to improve it, so I finally sent it off. She thinks I'm in with a real shot. I have a good feeling, but maybe I shouldn't get my hopes up . . . Ahh, I don't know." She covers her face with her hands and releases a muffled groan.

"You have nothing to worry about," I reassure her, scooting closer and crossing my legs. I pull her hands away from her face and the smile I give her is sincere and genuine. "You're the most amazing person I know. Any college would be lucky to have you. Hey, you can even add to your application that you're skilled at phone hacking now too!"

Chyna rolls her eyes. "Yeah, right."

We laugh a little, but I'm quick to turn serious again. Anxiously, I play with my hands in my lap, twiddling my thumbs. Admitting to my flaws is tougher than I thought. "I'm sorry for being a shitty friend the past few days."

"You've had a weird week, Vans," Chyna says, still defending me even now. "Seriously, don't sweat it."

I look up from my lap. "That's not an excuse. I'm sorry, and I hope you're ready for the party tonight."

"So, we're going?" Chyna says, eyes shining with excitement. She loves parties. I know she's prepared to miss out on tonight for my sake, but I don't want her to have to make any more sacrifices for me. I want to go to this party with her so that she can sing too loudly to the music, bust a couple of her awful dance moves, and potentially hang out with this childhood crush of hers. It's the least I owe her.

"Yup! We're going."

I need to go to this party for myself too. I can't let Harrison think he's filled me with so much fear that I can't be seen in public.

It's time to come full circle. At Maddie's party a week ago, Harrison and I hooked up for the very last time, and seven days of hell have ensued. The video he filmed that night changed everything. This all needs to end now – no more messing with Harrison. I refuse to be terrorized by him any longer. He's hurt me and I've hurt him. There's nothing more to be done, and I know that if I don't turn up tonight, then he'll think he has won. The truth is, neither of us have won anything. We've both lost something. Mostly our dignity.

Chyna jumps up from the bed and twirls over to her closet. She begins rummaging through her clothes, pulling out different pairs of jeans and an array of cropped blouses. "I'm so unprepared. Do you wanna go to the mall? I need something to wear with these jeans," she says, holding up a pair of ripped, black jeans. Of course I say yes.

We park in the lot of Polaris Mall on the edge of Westerville. We've driven here in Chyna's car, because even she doesn't want to be seen rolling around in the Green McRusty, and we stroll toward the mall's entrance together.

Most of the snow from a few days ago has completely melted and disappeared by now. Only lumps of hardened ice remain in the gutters, but the sky above is full of thick, gray clouds that cast a shadow over the entire region of Columbus. It's forecasted to snow again later.

"Is Kai going to the party?" Chyna asks as we head into our first store. It's a casual, harmless question. I haven't yet told her what happened between Kai and me last night, mostly because I'm embarrassed by it, but also because I don't want to burden her with even more of my personal drama.

"No idea," I say, staring straight ahead as we walk. Chyna must immediately notice the forced nonchalance in my voice, because she shoots me a look that I ignore. Honestly, I *hope* Kai isn't going to the party tonight, and I can't imagine that he would be. His only friend at Westerville North is me. And maybe Maddie, at a push. It would be seriously bold of him to turn up alone, especially knowing that Harrison and Noah are likely to be there.

Chyna stops to search through a rack of discounted tops. "Did something happen?" she asks softly, her attention focused on the clothes in front of her. I know she's listening closely though. All I've done this past week is gush about how gorgeous and hilarious Kai is, and now I don't want to talk about him at all. She already knows something has so obviously happened, but she's gently coercing me to open up about it.

"Ooo, that's cute!" I say, pointing to the blouse in her hand.

"Vans," Chyna says, narrowing her eyes. She dumps the blouse back into the rack and angles her body toward me. "You can tell me."

I lean back against the mirror and shrug. "Well, usually when the guy you like insinuates that you're easy, it kind of ruins everything."

Chyna's expression mirrors mine from last night when Kai said the hurtful things that he did. First shock, then disbelief. She parts her lips, her jaw hanging wide. "No way."

I try to ignore the pain in my chest and play it off, to act disinterested. If I think about last night, I'll get upset again. It's easier to just rummage through the clothes rack, pretending to look for something, even though I'm staring blankly into the distance. "Yeah. The Kai thing is over."

And the fact that it's over before it even began is the worst feeling in the world. I'll never know what could have happened, if Kai really could have been the one to make me feel different about things.

Chyna knows not to linger on the topic. She returns to searching through the racks, asking my opinion on different items that she holds up, and by the time we get to our fourth store of the day, she finally finds a top she likes to go with her jeans back at home. Now it's time to stop for smoothies.

We're standing at the counter, watching the blenders while our drinks are made, when Chyna suddenly stiffens beside me. She grabs my arm and holds me still.

"Don't turn around," she says. She's staring at something over my shoulder, her eyes wide, and I do the exact opposite of what she tells me.

I crane my neck to look behind me and at first, I don't know what it is that I'm not supposed to be looking at. The food court is behind us, rammed with people and the babble of voices and screeching of trays. I scour the tables until my searching gaze lands on Kai.

Now my body goes rigid too. My limbs turn to blocks of ice like those outside.

Kai isn't alone. He's with a girl, and I recognize her immediately. It's the same girl who approached me in the diner on Tuesday, the one with the pretty makeup and blond hair, the one who asked if Kai and I were dating. It's Sierra Jennings. It's *her*.

"I told you not to turn around!" Chyna wails.

"Sierra," I mumble, but my throat has gone dry. I can't tear my eyes away from Kai and her. "That's the ex."

"The one he was in love with?"

I nod, and Chyna and I stare at the two of them, our gazes piercing straight through the pair. Kai and Sierra are sitting at a small table on the edge of the food court, neither of them eating. They're huddled together, heads bent close, wrapped in deep conversation. Their faces are serious, but neither joyful nor angry. It's hard to gauge the mood of the conversation, but Sierra appears to be doing most of the talking. She keeps playing with the ends of her straight, blond hair while Kai listens, his hands intertwined between his knees. He's wearing his Cleveland Browns' cap again, only forward this time, so the bill of the hat shadows his face.

"What are they doing together?" Chyna questions, her voice hushed as she leans in close to my ear.

"I . . . don't . . . know," I manage to say. It's a question I would love to know the answer to.

I thought Kai and Sierra were done. She cheated on him; she broke his heart. Kai told me he wasn't still in love with her, but could he have been lying just to spare my feelings the morning after he pulled away from our first kiss? Is that why he didn't want to take things further last night? Not because he wanted it to mean something, but because he was holding out to win Sierra back? Have I just been throwing myself at him while all this time he was still in love with his ex?

The girl working the smoothie bar presents our drinks on the countertop. I snatch mine and march away from the food court, never looking back again at Kai and Sierra while Chyna follows close on my heels.

Vanessa Murphy, chasing after a guy who doesn't want her.

Vanessa Murphy, catching feelings for a guy who has feelings for somebody else.

Vanessa Murphy, a complete fool.

21

I hear Isaiah blasting on his car horn outside.

It's almost nine, snow is falling fast and thick, and the cold air bites at my exposed skin when I swing open my front door. The wise thing to do tonight, after everything that has happened this week, would be to wear baggy jeans and a top with a high neckline, but the *brave* thing to do is continue to wear whatever the hell I want. That's why I'm wearing my favorite mini skirt and matching bralette, because I *want* to, and no amount of judging from my peers can stop me. I am, however, wearing an old pair of sneakers for trudging through the snow.

"So, you're going to a party," a voice says flatly from behind me.

I look over my shoulder, one hand still on the door. Dad is standing at the foot of the stairs. It's the first time I've seen him since last night, because we've been carefully tiptoeing around one another all day. The moment I got home from the mall, I locked myself in my room and only emerged to shower and grab a bite to eat, texting Kennedy from opposite rooms so that she could keep me updated on when the coast was clear. But even she has plans on a Saturday, so is no longer around to update me.

And obviously the coast isn't clear this time.

I give Dad a tiny shrug of my shoulders as we stare across the hall at one another in strained silence. With an outfit like this, a party is the only place I could possibly be going. "Yeah. I'll probably stay at Chyna's, so I'll be back tomorrow." I don't know why I even bother telling him the second part.

Dad shoves his hands into the pockets of his jeans and lowers his gaze to the floor. His mouth moves as though he is searching for the right words to say, like the rusty gears in his mind are slowly beginning to turn again after all this time, but he takes a long time to finally speak. "You should really be wearing a jacket. It's barely forty degrees outside."

"You're telling me to wear a jacket?"

"I guess I am," he says, looking up. He scratches at his temple and, again, he takes a few seconds to muster up the correct thing to say. "I'll grab one for you. Which one?"

I'm too stunned to reply at first. I stare at Dad, blinking in disbelief. Suddenly, he's telling me to wear a jacket because it's cold out? At least it's *something*, which is so much better than nothing. "Um, the black leather one," I manage to force out, my words quiet. "It should be on my floor."

Dad nods and turns, disappearing back upstairs.

I look out across the lawn at Isaiah's car still parked outside, its engine purring and the headlights casting a glow across the white streets. Chyna rolls down the window from the passenger seat and motions for me to hurry up, but I quickly throw up two fingers to let her know I'll be two seconds.

I don't even want to wear a jacket, but this is a moment that's too rare to ignore. Dad is actually telling me to do something for once. That's the only reason I wait by the front door until he returns, coming downstairs with my favorite leather jacket in his hand. He walks over and stops a foot away from me.

"Here you go," he says, and passes the jacket to me, his fingers brushing against mine. Neither of us is smiling. The interaction feels too foreign. "Have fun, Vanessa."

I squeeze the jacket tightly and step outside onto the porch as Dad closes the door behind me. I don't put the jacket on though, only carry it with me as I dash across the snow in my sneakers and dive into the cozy backseat of Isaiah's car. The heating is on full blast, his music playing loudly. I can smell the luscious scent of Chyna's perfume.

"What was the hold-up?" Chyna asks, turning in the passenger seat and peering at me from around the headrest as Isaiah begins to drive. Her hair is styled into a big puff and huge hoop earrings dangle from her ears. She's wearing the shirt she bought earlier.

"Dad wanted me to wear a jacket," I say blankly, still not entirely sure if the past few minutes really did just happen. All I've ever wanted for a long time is for Dad to give me some sign that he actually cares about me, but I didn't realize how awkward it would feel if he ever did. It's just so . . . unusual.

Even Chyna looks surprised. "He did?"

"Like you'll even wear it," Isaiah teases. I catch his eye in the rearview mirror and he gives me his usual goofy grin. Riding with Isaiah and Chyna is seriously like hanging out with my siblings, which means they have the right to taunt me.

"Watch me," I shoot back, and I pull on the jacket and wrap it tightly around me.

Isaiah drives us to Maddie's house, music blaring into our ears at full volume, and the familiarity of their mindless chatter instantly puts me at ease. Isaiah is heading to a party too, one that is probably way more cool than our high school one, but because he doesn't drink, he'll remain our designated driver for the evening. Soon I realize that I'm not worrying about Harrison or Kai, because I'm too caught up in the laughter inside the car. We stop by the convenience store en route so that Isaiah can score us some cheap booze, and soon we're skidding to a halt in the snow outside Maddie's house, armed with a positive attitude and hands full of hard cider.

"Remember, don't get in *anyone's* car even if they claim they're sober. I'll pick you guys up on my way home," Isaiah reminds us, shooting us a stern look as Chyna and I clamber out of the car. We both blow him a kiss, but he doesn't know that he's supposed to catch it and keep it safe.

There's a cool breeze tonight that makes the temperature feel so much lower than it has been the past few days, and the snow crunches beneath my sneakers as Chyna and I trudge toward the house. I can hear Isaiah driving off behind us and I can hear the music pumping from inside the house. There are two guys from school smoking cigarettes on the porch, watching us closely as we approach, and I'm convinced they exchange a smirk with one another when they realize it's me. That video is still on everyone's minds.

I take a deep breath, clearing my lungs, then walk slowly but with purpose to the front door with Chyna by my side. She must sense my fear despite how hard I'm trying to hide it, because she slips her hand into mine, and she stares the two boys down with a threatening look as we pass them. I imagine their looks and snickers will only be the first of many tonight.

We enter the house together and immediately, the music rings in my ears, mixed with the clinking of bottles and the cracking of beer tabs. The party is definitely a notch up from what it was last weekend. There are more people, that's for sure, and maybe Maddie is right. Maybe after last week's brawl and the scandal of that awful video being filmed at this same party, people don't want to miss out on any more potential drama. It's mostly seniors from Westerville North that are here, with a few of the more popular juniors here too. It's everyone that I know. Everyone that has laughed at my misfortune this week. Everyone that has flashed me dirty looks in the hallways. Everyone that has taunted me online.

Even now, I catch the looks people shoot me out of the corner of their eye as they pretend not to notice me, but really, I know they all do. I imagine people have been wondering whether or not I would have the courage to turn up tonight, and now they realize that yes, I do. Because

Vanessa Murphy won't let her mistakes – or Harrison's actions – ruin her life. She'll hold her head up high and keep moving forward.

"You okay?" Chyna asks, squeezing my hand more tightly. I just give her a tight smile and nod. "A drink?"

I nod again. Tonight, Chyna is the strong one. She's the one checking that *I'm* okay, the one protecting *me*. I'm not used to being out of my comfort zone like this.

We move across the living room toward the kitchen, still hand-in-hand, with the cider under Chyna's arm. A group of guys are playing beer pong in the kitchen as everyone carefully navigates around the game to get themselves drinks from the selection of alcohol that's spread across the counters.

"You're brave," someone murmurs as I pass them, and I can't decide if they're antagonizing me or complimenting me. I *am* brave for coming here.

Chyna and I set our cider down, grab ourselves a bottle each, then pop them open. I take a long sip, gulping down the alcohol in desperation to loosen up and relax.

"I'm going to go find Malik Dorsey," Chyna says, her voice slightly wary. "Are you coming?"

"Actually, you go ahead. I'm going to hang out in here," I say, taking another swig and giving her a reassuring smile. I want to prove to myself that I *can* survive on my own without Chyna quite literally holding my hand. Last week, floating around on my own never scared me, because I knew there'd always be someone who would strike up a conversation with me. It's different now. They're happy to talk about me, but no one wants to talk *to* me anymore.

Once Chyna reluctantly heads off to find her new love interest, I hover in the kitchen for a while, pretending to be invested in the game of beer pong, but really I'm just standing over in the corner hoping that no one will notice me. So many people come and go, but none of them are Harrison, and none of them are Kai.

"Vanessa!" Maddie says as she waltzes into the kitchen and spots me. She comes over, blond hair swishing around her shoulders, a grin plastered so wide on her face that it almost looks like it could hurt. "You made it!"

I have never felt so relieved to see Madison Romy before. "Hey! Did you invite half the school or something?" I motion to the packed kitchen, everyone brushing elbows with one another because the house is so full.

"I didn't need to," she says, proudly looking around. If her parents flipped at her for breaking some precious vase last weekend, then I wonder just how angry they'll be after *this* party. There'll definitely be some serious damage to this house by the end of the night. "Everyone was totally buzzing after last weekend! It didn't take any convincing to get people to come again. Thank you!"

I raise an eyebrow at her, questioning her gratitude. "For hooking up with Harrison Boyd in your little brother's bedroom?"

"Yes!" She grins, then leans in close and kisses my cheek. I think Maddie is secretly a middle-aged woman trapped in a teenager's body. She suddenly looks serious as a light bulb goes off in her head. "Wait. Where's Kai? Is he here yet?"

"Yeah, about that ..." I mumble. Does she seriously

believe that Kai and I were *actually* going to stir up drama on purpose, dragging ourselves into an even deeper hole than the one we're already in? Kai may have agreed to this twisted plan, but I certainly didn't. Besides, Kai and I aren't talking anymore. We won't be pulling off any teamwork tonight, that's for sure.

"Oh, look what we have here," a voice booms over the music, and my eyes flicker from Maddie's over to Harrison's. His gruff voice is so off-putting. I can't believe I ever thought his voice – or anything about him – was sexy.

Harrison weaves a path across the kitchen like he is Moses parting the Red Sea. Everyone instantly quits their game of beer pong and moves to the side, out of the way, as Harrison walks toward me, flanked by Noah. Anthony is nowhere to be seen. The music continues to play loudly, but the voices that were laced around it quickly die down.

Everyone's eyes land on me.

22

Harrison stops a mere two feet away from me and for a moment, I think of last weekend, when we both flirted with one another over in the living room. We were all teasing winks and seductive gazes back then, nothing else, and yet it has come down to this: two enemies standing face-to-face with an audience awaiting the fallout.

I glance over at Maddie, who looks torn between whether or not she wants this drama to unfold. She subtly steps away, removing herself from the situation, and hides behind some of the other guests. I don't blame her too much. I know she's intimidated by Harrison, and we weren't even friends a few days ago, so I can't expect her to jump in and save me.

"You have some nerve showing up here," Harrison says, folding his arms across his puffed-out chest as though his threatening stance will scare me. I can see the loathing in his eyes and the tension in his curled-up fists. There's no doubt he knows I was the one who taped that photo of him to his locker yesterday, and this is the first time we have seen each other since. Harrison looks rigid, like he's fighting the urge to lay his hands on me.

"It's brave of you to show up too," I throw back despite longing to curl up into a ball and cry. Fighting back was easy before, but now I don't want to play these games anymore. I want to admit that I can't do this for a second longer, that I don't want to keep arguing, but I can't break now. Not when everyone is watching. "How does it feel, Harrison? Being put on display to the world?"

A hush of snickers circles the room. The entire party is now crowding into the kitchen, everyone listening in, most likely thinking how great it is that drama is kicking off so early into the night. I used to love this type of pathetic entertainment, but being the school's punching bag really isn't a joke. It's awful and I feel so alone. The entire room is against me, and no one should ever have to feel like this.

Harrison casts a couple glares at the people huddled around us, then focuses back on me. "So, this was all about getting even with me?" he snorts, his laughter cold. "Great job, Vanessa. You did it. We're even now." He sarcastically claps his hands together, loud and slow while shaking his head pitifully at me.

All the air in here seems to disappear, suffocating me while I stare back at Harrison. It's not the reply I expected and now I can't seem to get words to form on my tongue. I feel so helpless, so trapped, and I know the longer I stand here without saying a single word, the more of an idiot I'll look. I search the kitchen for Chyna, hoping she'll appear to save me, but she is nowhere to be seen.

"It's a real shame," Noah pipes up, stepping around Harrison, "that you've made enemies of us." His voice is menacing, a warning. Noah smiles bitterly into my face, and I can smell the beer on him. It makes me wonder: Are they going to taunt me forever? Noah suddenly grabs my waist and pulls me forward, discreetly wrestling his body into position behind mine. He holds my hips tightly and we stare out into the fascinated expressions of our peers. I can feel Noah's breath hot against my neck as he loudly asks our audience, "Who else in this house has Vanessa Murphy seduced?"

"Stop it!" I hiss, trying to squirm my way out of his hold. I am mortified. Noah will always use my history as a weapon, making my past into something I should be ashamed of, and as a couple hands shoot up around us, shame is exactly what I feel. Nick Foster pokes up a hand from the back of the room. Blake Nelson sheepishly raises a hand then pretends to only be scratching his hair.

Harrison rolls his eyes and holds up his hand. "Worst luck," he says, as though the entire school doesn't already know.

I try to elbow Noah in the ribs behind me, but he is quick to grasp my arms, locking them in place. He pins my body against his. "See?" he murmurs, burying his face into the crook of my neck. He lowers his voice so that no one else can hear him, and he whispers, "No one likes a tramp."

I wish I could see the twisted expression on his face, and crush my fist straight into his nose. He's resting his chin on my shoulder and I look at him out of the corner of my eye. "Funny," I say quietly, my voice uneven. "You didn't have a problem with me when it was you I was hooking up with."

He snarls and tightens his grip on my arms.

"Let her go," a husky voice orders. "*Now*."

Kai emerges from the back of the kitchen, pushing his way to me the same way I had fought my way through the crowd to him yesterday morning. And, just like he was then, I am being taunted, abused at the hands of Harrison Boyd and Noah Diaz.

"Goddamn!" Harrison growls, throwing his hands up in exasperation as he turns to face Kai. One hand is balled into a fist by his side. "Did we kill some of your brain cells yesterday or what? You're insane to come here."

But Kai doesn't even give Harrison a second look. He shoves past him, ramming his shoulder into Harrison's, then stands before Noah and me. I'm still held in place, unable to move, and I stare numbly at Kai.

"Let her go," he repeats, more demanding this time. He's wearing all black, including a leather jacket that I would find knee-weakening if we were in any other situation right now, and his eyes are locked on Noah. I can see the worsening bruise beneath his eye, the cuts from the violence inflicted on him yesterday.

Noah's laugh echoes into my ears like the sharp shrill of a bell. "Alright, Prince Charming. Have her," he says, then pushes me hard toward Kai. I stumble, nearly losing my balance, but Maddie reaches out of the crowd and takes my hand, steadying me.

"I want to know," Harrison says slowly, falling into place by Noah's side. Their fiery eyes are set on Kai, each one prepared to back the other up. Harrison smirks, and I know exactly what's coming next: something that'll hit Kai where it hurts. "The tramp's hooking up with *you* now. So, who do you rate higher? Vanessa or Sierra?"

As soon as the words have left Harrison's mouth, Kai has hurled his fist through the air and straight into Harrison's jaw at just the right angle. A collective gasp fills the house, and everyone pushes against one another to get a closer view, but there is no fight to see – Harrison spirals down to the floor, his body like a long plank of wood as he hits the ground with a hard thud.

Uproar ensues. A chorus of voices erupt, people are pushing, Maddie is screaming. Someone asks if they should call 911. Noah kneels to the ground, pulling at Harrison's shoulders and demanding that he get back up. But Harrison is stunned and it's taking both his body and his mind a while to process what's just happened. Some of the other guys are quick to rally around their teammate, and between a handful of them, they manage to haul Harrison up from the ground. I look at Kai, but he's staring wide-eyed at his hand, carefully stretching his fingers. He seems surprised by the power of his single punch.

"I want you both out of my house," I hear Maddie say, and at first I think she is talking to Kai and me. But when I spin around to look at her, I realize she is talking to Noah and an unbalanced Harrison.

Noah has his arms hooked under Harrison's arms as he drags him backward out of the kitchen, but he pauses. "He just needs a bed and some water. He'll be up and running again in ten minutes. You can't kick *us* out, Madison," he says, and his tone is so self-righteous it's almost sickening. It's as though those guys believe parties are hosted solely for them.

"Yeah, I can," Maddie argues, her hands on her hips as she steps forward. For how timid she usually is, it's stunning to see her this resilient for once. "And I am. Take Harrison outside and get the hell out of here. I don't want bullies in my house."

Harrison tries to mumble something, but it's unintelligible. Kai's punch has rendered him dazed and unsteady on his feet. Noah glances down at his buddy, then back up at Maddie. "You don't want to be friends, Maddie?" he asks sweetly, innocently pouting his lips as he plays on Maddie's weakness. Everyone knows how hard Maddie tries to be on everyone's good side. That's why she was swept up into Harrison's world in the first place.

Maddie smiles, all the power in her hands. "Friends with *you*? No thanks."

Noah grits his teeth, shaking his head at Maddie as though she'll live to regret her decision, then continues dragging Harrison away. A few other guys from the team go with them while we all watch from the kitchen until they have left the house with Harrison still mumbling, but gradually finding his own feet again.

There is an odd moment that happens where everyone is totally silent and still, and then suddenly normality returns. The music bumps back up, loud and deafening, and bodies start moving around again, drinks clinking as people get themselves new beers and resume their chat. It's like the past five minutes never happened, and I think I prefer it that way. Noah and Harrison have humiliated me yet again, and I think I would die if everyone dwelled on it.

And Kai waltzing in like some hero in an action movie to save me like I'm some pathetic damsel in distress . . .

How dare he?

"You!" I hiss, pointing at Kai. He's still massaging his hand, but he looks up, his expression worried. The anger in my voice must be evident. I grab his other hand, and pull him with me out of the kitchen and over into the living room where it's less crowded. I grit my teeth, doing my utmost to hold on to my anger and ignore how gorgeous and badass he looks right now. "You don't get to just stroll in here and rescue me."

Kai frowns, cocking his head to one side. He looks at me gently, his voice soft. "You don't think you needed rescuing, Nessie?"

"No, I didn't. I could have gotten out of that situation on my own," I lie, blatantly, only because I don't want to give him any credit even though he *did*, in fact, save me. "I don't need you, just like you don't need me."

Kai frowns at my words, instantly understanding the point that I'm making. He takes a wary step nearer to me and holds up his hands in surrender. "Okay, I know you're still pissed at me after everything I said last night—"

"You're damn right I'm still pissed at you!"

He sighs at my interruption and rubs his temples, trying to think of the right words to say. "Please don't just cut me off completely because of some stupid shit I said when I was nervous. You *know* I didn't mean it the way I said it. C'mon, Nessie," he pleads, reaching for my hand. His knuckles are swollen. His gray-blue eyes pool with desperation. "Would I really have spent this entire week with you if I seriously thought those things?"

"You've only been hanging out with me because we shared the same goal," I argue, pulling my hand back from his. I'm so angry with myself. How did I fool myself into thinking Kai would ever be interested in a girl like me?

Now Kai is getting angry with me too. The muscle in his cheek twitches as he clenches his jaw tight. "Would I really have wasted every single night this week hanging out with a girl I didn't like being around? Would I really have spent all week thinking about you when we weren't together? Would I really have spent all day looking forward to the moment I saw you next?"

"And yet you're too embarrassed to be with me," I state. The words carry a sting that causes my heart to seize up, that feeling of suffocation returning again. I try to focus on my breathing as I shake my head. "But it doesn't matter anyway, because you're still in love with Sierra."

"Oh my God!" Kai exclaims, his hands flying to his hair in exasperation, pulling at it as he closes his eyes. He deeply inhales. "How can I possibly be in love with Sierra when I think I might be falling in love with *you*?"

I stare at him, wondering if I've imagined those words coming from his mouth, but suddenly Kai is reaching out for me. He clasps my face in his hands and touches his lips down against mine.

And he kisses me in such a way that brings back all of the memories of our earlier kisses, like they've all been fused together. He kisses me with the gentle fragility of our first exchange in the Green McRusty on Wednesday when our interlocked lips were so new and unknown. He kisses me with the same energy of the moment his lips found mine in Harrison's basement when the stakes felt so high. He kisses me with the same passion and care that he'd shown last night when things got heated in his bedroom, right before everything fell apart. And yet, here I am now: losing myself in Kai's embrace, in his scent, in his kiss.

But not for too long, because I will myself to pull away so that I can read the emotion in his eyes. Did he really mean what he just said?

And that's when I realize that everyone's attention is fixated upon us. First we were arguing in the middle of the living room, then we were kissing. Everyone's eyes are wide with fascination and, instantly, I feel like I could die with embarrassment. I look down at my sneakers and let my hair fall over my face so that I can hide.

"Perfect!" I hear Maddie say from beside me a second later. I steal a peek at her, and she is excitedly rubbing her hands together as she huddles in close to Kai and me. She keeps her voice quiet. "You guys did great! That looked so real and that kiss? Woah! Passionate. You should join the drama club! Oh my God. I'm putting your names down first thing on Monday!"

"That wasn't . . . We weren't pretending . . ." I stutter, but Maddie has already danced off across the room. I blink after her while Kai bursts into laughter by my side. I turn to him, amazed. No one is looking at us anymore.

"So now that Operation Harr-assassinate is over, it looks like we're focusing our energy on drama club," Kai says with that wonderful, devious look of his. He reaches for my wrist and skims his thumb delicately over the back of my hand. He glances up at me, almost shyly. "Can we go outside and talk?"

23

With my fingers intertwined with Kai's, I follow him through the house and into the back yard. The snow is thick out here and decorated with so many different footprints of the people who have slipped outside to grab a smoke. A couple people chill out over on the patio dining set, sharing cigarettes and laughing into the cold air.

Chyna is also out here. I spot her leaning back against the house, hugging herself to keep warm. She's talking to Malik Dorsey, her childhood crush who I've shared a couple classes with over the years, but she instantly catches my eye over his shoulder. Her expression grows perplexed as she glances back and forth between Kai and me. Last she heard, I didn't want anything more to do with him, but yet here we are, standing hand-in-hand. She quickly excuses herself from Malik and shuffles over to us. "I'm confused," she mumbles, looking expectantly at me for an explanation. Her dark eyes are glossy in the freezing air.

"How long have you been out here? Did you miss everything that just happened?" I ask. No wonder she looks frozen if she's been standing out here the whole time.

Her eyebrows furrow. "What just happened? Besides the obvious." She gives our hands a pointed glance and I feel my cheeks flush again, though I'm sure they're already too pink from too much blush and the cold.

"You missed Kai floor Harrison with one punch, for starters."

"What!" Chyna gasps, unfolding her arms and stepping forward. Her eyes go wide as she turns to Kai.

"He deserved it, of course," Kai says, glancing down at the snow.

"I always miss out on the good stuff!" Chyna whines. She sighs and glances back over to Malik. "You know what, you can fill me in later, Vans." The smile she gives me is kind and I know she does want the gossip, but she can see I'm busy with Kai, and she is busy with Malik.

I blow her a kiss, she blows me one, and we both keep them safe. She dashes back across the yard to continue her conversation with Malik.

"Come here," Kai murmurs, squeezing my hand as he guides me over to some abandoned deck chairs. They're covered in a layer of snow, but Kai swipes the snow away with his hands and then shrugs off his jacket. He lays the jacket down on one of the chairs and motions for me to sit.

If this is how we catch frostbite, I don't even care.

We sit down side-by-side, huddled in close, our body warmth radiating between us. My skin is dotted with goosebumps and I hug my jacket tight around my body. I look at Kai, unsure of what exactly to say. My head is still spinning from the declaration he made back inside the house.

Luckily, Kai speaks first. "I didn't mean anything that I said last night. It all came out wrong," he tells me again, his voice quiet yet firm. "And I'm not in love with Sierra. Why would you even think that? She screwed me over."

"I saw you with her . . ." I mumble. "Today at the mall."

Kai looks as though he could laugh, and I stare blankly at him, wondering what is possibly so funny. He shakes his head, still smiling, and looks sideways at me. "Yeah, she works at Sephora. She begged me to meet her on her lunch break, and I couldn't resist hearing what she had to say."

"And what did she have to say?" I press. Were they or were they not rekindling their relationship?

"She apologized. Told me she was sorry for what she did, that she regrets it. Told me she wanted us to give things another shot." He pauses for a moment, interlocking his hands between his knees the same way he had this morning when he was talking to Sierra at the mall, like he's thinking really hard about something. He stares off into the distance. "And you know, the crazy thing is that I probably would have believed her. *But*," he says, "I'm so not interested in her anymore. It made it so much easier to tell her to go to hell."

"Oh, shit," I whisper, swallowing the lump in my throat. God, why do I always jump to conclusions? Here I was, adamant that Kai didn't want me because he is still in love with Sierra, when he totally isn't. The guilt sets in, because now I know I've been angry at him all day for no valid reason, and that's not fair. Maybe I shouldn't have run away so quickly last night either. I should have stayed and given him the chance to apologize.

Hell, I *really* need to stop jumping to conclusions.

Kai turns his body toward me and frowns as he takes in my expression. I wonder what he sees in my eyes as he looks at me, because even I don't know how I feel. Everything is a total whirlwind. "You're so scared of getting close to anyone, it's like you just *have* to sabotage anything that has the potential to really be something," he says.

His change of tone surprises me. I don't like his accusatory statement. "What?"

"Admit it, Vanessa," he says gently. "You're trying to push me away. That's why you've convinced yourself of all this bullshit. You're telling yourself I don't care about you, that I'm not interested, that I'm still in love with Sierra . . . because that'll give you a reason."

I shake my head, even though his words ring true within me. "A reason for what?"

"For not seeing what could happen between us."

Is that what I've been doing? Subconsciously sabotaging things with Kai by conjuring up things that aren't real, like him still being in love with his ex, and him not being interested in me other than as an accomplice? Have I just been searching for a reason to cut him off because I'm scared?

The realization hits me like a ton of bricks. How did Kai notice what I couldn't? How does someone I've known since Monday already know me better than I know myself?

"Wow," is all I can say. I stare at the ground ahead, unblinking as my eyes begin to water. My teeth chatter too, but I clench my jaw to stop myself. I don't know how to reply. I am paralyzed by the truth.

I do want to see where things go with Kai, but it makes me anxious that I feel this way after so long keeping everyone at arm's-length. I'm so scared of getting serious with someone, of letting them in and then losing them, but I'm also scared of losing my *chance* with Kai. And it's an awful feeling, being so torn and wanting to take a risk for once in my life, but also trying to protect myself the same way I have for the past two years. Is that why I've been trying to blame Kai by telling myself that *he* doesn't want to take things further? Because that way, *I* wouldn't have to make a decision?

"Don't push me away, Nessie," Kai says, reaching for my hand. I let him, and even though his are still damp and raw from clearing away the snow, the touch of his skin on mine feels perfect. "Can't we just continue the way we are? Just hanging out and joking around together, and we'll see where we end up? And if you want to do the kissing thing, then I'm totally cool with that."

I finally look at him. His eyes are wide and hopeful, but also worried. He looks terrified that his words haven't gotten through to me, that I'm going to tell him there is absolutely no chance in hell that we'll ever be together like *that*. "Can I tell you something?" I ask.

"Only if it's something good," he says.

I give him a pathetic half smile and then drop my eyes to our hands. "You're the first guy I've ever thought there was potential with in the first place," I admit. Such a statement feels like a huge achievement. I don't do . . . *this*. I don't sit outside in the snow with a guy, holding his hand while we discuss *us*. It's terrifying and exhilarating all at the same time.

Kai's eyes light up, that fear disappearing, replaced with pure hope. "Then it's settled. Captain Washington is going to be the one who makes you believe in giving things a shot."

*

Kai and I leave the party. We catch up with Chyna first to make sure she'll be alright without me, but she's still bubbling with laughter with Malik, so she reassures me that she'll be fine. Isaiah will pick her up later, so I know she'll get home safely. I make a point of finding Maddie too, letting her know that Kai and I have decided to head home early, and she thanks us all over again for the amazing performance we gave earlier. Neither of us bothers telling her that it wasn't a performance at all.

There's nothing worth staying at the party for. I'm not in the mood for drinking and dancing on tables and all I want is to be with Kai, so we make our getaway just before 10pm.

We walk hand in hand and our pace quickens as we battle the elements. I can't tear my eyes away from him. I stare at the sharp lines of his jaw, the softness of his full lips, the shine of his glistening eyes. I even stare at that slit in his eyebrow and wonder when I decided that it was actually kinda hot.

"So how screwed do you think we'll be at school on Monday?" Kai jokes. His other hand is stuffed into the front pocket of his black jeans, and I can see that he's shivering a little. We're not too far from my house now, though.

"Whatever happens, I'm not going to fight back anymore," I say with a shrug. I'm so over this now – none of it is worth it. The five minutes of satisfaction I get from messing with Harrison isn't justified. It only ever makes everything worse. I'm going to be the bigger person from now on.

"Neither am I," says Kai. He pulls me through the snow, kicking it out of the way where it's been shoveled into piles at the end of driveways. "I think we've done everything we needed to. We caused an all-out war, but I'm game for a peace treaty at this point. I think I broke a knuckle." He lets go of my hand so that he can hold up his. He flexes his fingers and shows me his bruised, swollen knuckles. I stop walking and step in front of him, blocking his path. I take his hand and press my lips to those knuckles, the same way I kissed his injuries last night.

"Thank you," I say.

Kai looks down at me with a soft gaze. "I thought you didn't need rescuing."

"I didn't," I huff, pushing his hand away.

We laugh and sneak a kiss, then keep on walking, quickening our steps as the cold really begins to set in. We are absolutely insane to be walking home in this weather, but I guess none of our decisions this week have been good ones. We're a little bit too impulsive, and definitely reckless. But perhaps that's what has drawn us to one another.

When we finally make it to my house, I let out a sigh of relief and run for the porch. I've never been so happy to see my own front door before. I throw it open and pull Kai in, and – thank God – Dad has the heat on high. For once, my home feels warm and inviting. I kick off my ruined sneakers, and a huge shiver surges down my spine.

"Who's there?" Dad calls as he rounds the corner from the kitchen, poised with a frying pan and a dishcloth. He immediately relaxes and lowers the pan when he sees that it's only me. That's the difference between Harrison's family and mine – Mr. Boyd points guns at intruders; my dad wields a frying pan. "Oh. What are you doing back home so early? I thought you were spending the night at Chyna's. You usually do."

He *has* noticed that I spend most weekends at Chyna's place? All this time, I was convinced he just didn't care about my whereabouts, but maybe his lack of concern makes more sense now if he always thought I was safe over at the Tate house.

"I changed my mind," I say with a shy smile. I've never left a party early before. "We walked home."

"In this weather?" Dad looks flabbergasted at the thought of me walking home in such minimal clothing when it's thirty degrees outside. "Hot chocolate coming straight up!" He spins around with the frying pan and disappears back into the kitchen.

"What the hell?" I ask the air. Has my father been possessed? I have no idea who this man in my house is.

"What's wrong?" Kai asks. He carefully takes his snowy Jordans off and sets them down by the door, then joins me by my side again.

"My dad ... Never mind," I say, shaking my head. Kai wouldn't understand why it's blowing my mind that my dad is offering to make us hot drinks. Something so normal ... yet so strange in this house.

I grab some blankets from the living room and keep one for myself, then give the other to Kai. We wrap ourselves up in them, like two giant marshmallows, and then pad through to the kitchen to join Dad.

"I don't have any whipped cream. Sorry," Dad apologizes as he sets down two mugs of hot chocolate on the dining table. His glasses have steamed up a little, so he removes them and gives them a wipe with the hem of his T-shirt. "Sorry, but I was a little caught up in my own world the other night. Vanessa, do you mind introducing me to your friend again?" he says, studying Kai as he slips his glasses back on.

"Oh, yeah, right," I mumble as I slide down into one of the kitchen chairs. I wrap my hands around the mug of hot chocolate to hopefully bring back some feeling in them, because at this point, my hands are entirely numb from the cold. "So, this is Kai Washington. We're ... partners." I exchange a look with Kai and he tries to hide his smirk.

"On the school assignment?" he finishes, and I'm surprised to find he actually heard me the other night. Maybe he *does* listen.

"Yep," Kai says. "Nice to meet you, Sir."

"Oh, please," Dad says, holding up a hand. "Just call me James. And let me know if you guys need anything." He takes his own mug of hot chocolate from the countertop and leaves us in peace alone in the kitchen as he crosses over to the living room. He sinks down into his favorite armchair and pulls out his laptop. It's not hard to guess what he's looking at – probably more scenic non-negotiable sights in Ireland.

Kai sits down at the opposite side of the table from me and reaches for his own mug. We're both still wrapped in the blankets, pulling them tight around our shoulders, and we're silent for a few minutes as we let the warmth of the house, the blankets, and the hot chocolate melt the ice from our bones. We take long sips from our drinks while mirroring each other's smiles over the rims of our mugs. It's such a nice moment, the two of us perfectly content in the silence.

"I can finally feel my toes again," Kai says after a while. He gulps down the remainder of his hot chocolate, pushes the mug away, then pulls the blanket tighter around him. It makes him look so adorable, and the sight of this boy with the slit in his eyebrow and the bruised eye and the swollen knuckles wrapped up in Kennedy's favorite fluffy white blanket makes me giggle.

"And I can finally feel my face," I say. I reach up and touch my eyes just to double check that no icicles have formed on my eyelashes. I never would have imagined that I'd be sitting in my kitchen late on a Saturday night drinking hot chocolate – made by *Dad*, of all people – with Kai Washington, the enigmatic stranger who I spilled my vodka soda on.

I stand and collect our empty mugs, then dump them

in the sink and leave them there because I don't have the energy to wash them. I walk over to Kai and lean down into him from behind, wrapping my arms around his shoulders, pretty much covering him up with my own blanket. My chin nestles perfectly into the crook of his neck, and I inhale the scent of his musky cologne.

"I'm sorry for being angry at you," I murmur. I didn't need to go off on him the way I did. He's right – I was convincing myself of things he wasn't guilty of, so my anger definitely wasn't justified.

"And I'm sorry for being a complete idiot last night," he says, reaching up to take my hands in his own. We stay like that for a few moments, my body pressed into his as I hug him, my head resting on his shoulder, my eyes closed.

Is this what I've been missing all this time? All these special little moments that happen when you least expect them to? Is this what being with someone you really like entails? Are moments like this what makes the inevitable pain at the end of a relationship worth it?

"Let's go upstairs," I say, straightening up behind Kai. I'm reluctant to let go of him, but I finally unwrap my arms from around his shoulders and allow him to rise to his feet.

We head for the stairs, two giant marshmallows bobbing through the house, but I catch Dad's eye before I even step one foot on the staircase. He's watching us from his armchair, and he makes a dramatic point of checking his watch. He frowns, then shuts his laptop.

"It's getting late, Vanessa," he tells me with a subtle edge to his voice. "I think your friend should head home."

"Oh, yeah, of course," Kai says, his words babbling out of his mouth before he can stop them. For a guy who's usually so smooth and charming, he sure is awkward when it comes to meeting my father.

I raise an eyebrow at Dad. Kai was literally in my room four nights ago and Dad didn't even so much as bat an eyelid, yet now he's asking Kai to leave? What is even going on? I don't want Kai to go, but I also love that Dad isn't just sitting by and letting me take a guy up to my room. This ... *this* is what I have been waiting for all this time.

An actual parent, doing actual parental things, like reminding me to wear a jacket and making me hot chocolate and not-so-subtly kicking a guy friend out of the house when it gets late.

It's too glorious. Dad has really taken my feelings on board, and although his effort may be forced, I appreciate that he is already trying to be better within twenty-four hours of me exploding on him. Maybe all this time he wasn't non-existent because he didn't care, but rather he was absent because he *does* care. He said so himself – he thought giving Kennedy and me our own space and freedom was the right thing to do.

"Is it okay if I hang here for five minutes?" Kai asks. "Just until my mom picks me up?"

I laugh. As if Dad is going to say no and force Kai back outside into the blistering cold. Even Dad chuckles, tells Kai it's no problem, then opens up his laptop again and returns to his browsing.

Kai and I sit down on the bottom of the stairs together.

He texts his mom my address and she pings back immediately that she's on her way. Kai can't bike when the snow is as deep as it is tonight, and I doubt his vital organs could handle another walk out in that weather.

"So, can I see you tomorrow?" he asks, putting his phone away. His eyes dance with amusement and the same hopefulness that was in his expression back at the party, like he's waiting for me to panic and say no.

But the radiant smile I give him is nothing but reassuring. "Nessie would *love* to see you tomorrow, Captain Washington."

24

I open my eyes the next morning to Dad's hand on my shoulder, gently shaking me awake. Seeing him hovering over me first thing on a Sunday is enough to scare the absolute living daylights out of me, and I stare at him in terror for a few moments until the grogginess wears off a little. I prop myself up on my elbows and rub at my eyes, squinting at him. It feels too early for this. Plus, Dad *never* goes out of his way to wake me.

"I need you downstairs," Dad says, his expression solemn. An uneasy feeling instantly settles in the pit of my stomach. I don't like the serious tone of his voice, or the concern in his eyes, or the frown on his face. He has also shaved for the first time in months, so I barely recognize him without a straggly beard covering his jawline.

"What's wrong?" I ask, sitting bolt upright.

"We need to talk," he says, then leaves my room, expecting me to follow. His vagueness does little to appease the tightness in my chest.

I push back my comforter and climb out of bed. I'm only wearing gym shorts and a tank top, so I grab a hoodie from my closet and pull it on to keep me warm. I check my phone for the time – 9:16. *Definitely* too early for serious talks with Dad. I stick my head into Kennedy's room as I head downstairs and find that she's still fast asleep, snoring perfectly in time with Theo who opens one feline eye at me. It's not a family discussion. Dad only wants to talk to *me*.

My steps are quick as I make my way down the stairs and search for Dad. He's over in the kitchen, pouring two cups of instant coffee. If he'd paid attention to me over the years, he would know that I don't even drink coffee.

"Sit down," he tells me over his shoulder, having heard my footsteps approach. He turns around and slides a cup across the table, and I put my hand out to catch it.

"Can you please tell me what's going on?" I ask, anxiously chewing the inside of my cheek as I stiffly sit down on the edge of one of the dining chairs. Just last night, I was sat at this table with Kai drinking hot chocolate. Now I'm here with Dad drinking gross coffee.

Dad rests one hand on the back of a chair, but doesn't sit down. He studies me across the table, narrowing his eyes. "Harrison Boyd."

My throat tightens. "What?"

"Kennedy told me the name of the boy who posted that ..." He takes a deep breath, like he can't even say it. He pinches the bridge of his nose between his thumb and forefinger. "That video," he finally finishes, but he can't look me in the eye. "Was it Harrison Boyd?"

So now I can't even rely on my own sister to keep my

secrets. I'm going to kill her later for even discussing the matter with our *dad*. I shove my hands into the pocket of my hoodie so that Dad can't see the way I'm nervously twiddling my thumbs. I don't want to talk about this with my *father*. That video is humiliating enough as it is. "Yeah … Why does it matter? The video is already out there."

Now Dad sits down. "Because we are going to press charges against that boy," he says.

This was definitely not the kind of conversation I expected to wake up to. I have no idea where this has come from and now my head pounds as I try to absorb this new information. I stare at Dad, stunned and unable to reply.

"What he's done to you is a criminal offence," he continues, lifting his cup to his lips. He takes a slow sip, his sharp eyes still watching me over the rim. I realize then that this anger within him isn't aimed at me, but rather it's aimed at Harrison Boyd. This is Dad's ex-cop persona talking now. "He's been distributing explicit content of a minor, most especially without your consent. We'll see that Boyd boy in court. That Richard Boyd has a name for himself around here, so I can't say I'm surprised his son is a piece of work too."

I imagine it now – Harrison and me standing in a court room while I fight for justice, only for my whole case to be turned against me by mention of the vandalism of Harrison's truck, the theft of his property, the break-in to their house, the harassment … Not to mention the distribution of explicit images that I carried out too. Harrison has done wrong, but so have I.

"Dad . . ." I mumble, my words sticking in my throat. "We can't press charges."

"Why? Because you're scared Harrison will react?"

"No . . . because . . ." I'm so ashamed I have to pull the hood of my hoodie up over my head to hide behind it. "Because then they could press charges against *me*."

Confusion fills Dad's features and he stares at me in a silent, contemplative manner for a minute, trying to make sense of my statement, most likely wondering how on earth the Boyds could possibly press charges. "What are you talking about, Vanessa?"

I can't deny it now. I need to own up to what I've done before Dad persists on dragging the Boyds to court. I take a deep breath, clear my head, then slowly exhale. I push my hood back down and rest my elbows on the table, holding my head in my hands. "When that video got out on Monday, I was so angry . . . I started to retaliate."

"How, exactly?"

"I slashed the tires of Harrison's truck. I stole his phone and hacked into it. And then I sent random strangers to meet him at Bob Evans. And I . . . I broke into his house," I rattle off as the shame and the guilt only intensifies. I can't even bring myself to mention the photograph I taped to Harrison's locker, because that was such a lowlife move, even for me.

Dad's eyes bulge. If he thought he didn't really know his daughter before, then he definitely doesn't know her now. "Goddamn, Vanessa . . . What were you thinking?"

"Just please don't try and press charges against them, because I'll get in serious trouble too."

And so will Kai . . . But I keep his name out of my confessions. I don't want to drag him down with me. I'll take all the blame if I need to.

Dad presses a closed fist to his mouth as he stares at the refrigerator, thinking hard. I keep quiet, because I think I've said enough. "Have you and Harrison resolved this? Or are you still fighting with one another?"

"Still fighting," I say.

"Then get dressed."

Dad and I are in the Green McRusty, parked outside the Boyds' house at ten on a Sunday morning. Dad's wearing dress pants and a nice shirt, even wearing cologne, and he has tamed his unruly hair with gel for once. He looks . . . younger. It's as though my father has come back to life. He's still too skinny and his clothes still hang loose from his body, but already he looks more like the man he used to be back when Mom was still alive. He's making an *effort*, which is something he hasn't done in two years.

I don't quite look like myself today either. I'm wearing the clothes I used to wear to church a couple years ago when Dad first tried to drag Kennedy and me to weekly services in an effort to find peace with God after everything we'd been through. We all stopped going after a month, and this black pencil skirt and neat grey blouse have been lying in the back of my closet ever since. We need to look respectful in order to be taken seriously, Dad thinks. The more of an air of superiority we bring, the more likely the Boyds are to feel intimidated.

"I should probably mention that Mr. Boyd also owns a gun," I say in a last-ditch attempt to persuade Dad to abandon this whole idea of redemption and forgiveness. "And I know because he's already pointed it at me. It's totally high risk for me to go inside that house."

Dad looks over at me, blinks as though nothing I can say at this point can possibly faze him, and then gets out of the car. I groan and reluctantly step out too, slamming the door behind me. The streets are still covered in snow, but dirty and ruined with tire tracks and footprints now.

I follow Dad up the walk to the porch. Harrison's truck is still jacked up at a slight tilt on the driveway, so the tires haven't been replaced yet. I didn't realize it would have inconvenienced him this much – I thought he'd have fresh tires fitted the next day.

"You remember what you need to say?" Dad asks as he lifts his hand to the doorbell. I nod, and he rings the bell.

My stomach is so tightly knotted as we stand on that porch, waiting and waiting for what feels like forever, that I actually begin to heave. I also realize it's the first time Dad and I have gone anywhere together in months. It's just a shame that our first father-daughter outing in forever has to be this. I pace back and forth, hands on my hips, gulping in deep breaths of air.

Then I hear the click of the front door being unlocked, and I nearly collapse on the porch from nerves.

Richard Boyd only cracks the door open a few inches and peeks out to see who his Sunday morning guests are. A couple strangers dressed in church attire probably isn't what he expects to see. He snootily looks us up and down. "Are you doing charity work? Because if so, I'm not interested."

"Actually," Dad says, putting his hand on the door to stop Richard from slamming it in our faces, "my daughter broke into your basement the other night. You may recognize her."

This is what gets Richard to open up the door fully. He steps forward, lingering on the threshold, and runs his eyes over me in disdain. I bet I look different now compared to how I did the other night – conservative clothes, no makeup, hair pinned back, expression dripping with guilt.

"Yes," Richard says. "I recognize her. Why are you here?"

"We'd like to talk to you," Dad says. "And your son."

Richard looks reluctant to entertain our requests, but he finally huffs under his breath and motions for us to come inside the lavish house. It's the first time I've been anywhere other than the basement, and I look around in fascination at their exotic and vintage furniture. The Boyds are totally loaded.

We are led into the living room and told to take a seat. Dad sits down on a plush, crushed velvet armchair, and I sit down on the edge of the matching loveseat. The house is silent – no sound of the TV, no sound of food being made in the kitchen, no voices. It's like no one is home.

"Wait here," Richard warns. He fixes us both with a threatening glare before he disappears across the house, presumably to get Harrison. "And don't touch anything."

Dad and I exchange a look and we both know we're thinking the exact same thing – what an outrageous snob. We sit in silence, looking around at the luxurious house and inhaling the scent of citrus. It's an intense wait.

Finally, Richard returns with a woman by his side and Harrison trailing behind them with his head down. Is that his mother? She's gorgeous. Long, shiny blond hair that swishes around her shoulders as she walks in a way that reminds me of Madison Romy. She's wearing a silk robe and her cheeks are pink with blush.

"What is going on here?" she asks, crossing her willowy arms.

"Perhaps your son should tell you," Dad says coolly. He's playing hard ball, refusing to let the Boyds make a fool out of us, all while I cower over in the corner.

Mr. and Mrs. Boyd both crane their necks to look at their son, who's hanging back behind them like a dog with its tail between its legs. There's a bruise on the edge of his jaw from last night and his parents stare expectantly at him, waiting for him to explain what's going on.

"I don't know what he's talking about," Harrison lies. He looks on edge too, almost as anxious as I do, and I wonder if he knows that we're here to set things straight. I have nothing to hide now – *my* parent knows the full story. It's Harrison's parents who are still totally in the dark about everything, and it seems he wants to keep it that way.

"Are you sure?" Dad presses, his voice firm. Right now, he reminds me of the man that he used to be. Strong and certain, determined and powerful.

Richard and his wife sit down on the other couch directly opposite me, leaving Harrison standing alone in the center of the room, all the pressure on him as the four of us listen for a confession. Although, Mr. and Mrs. Boyd don't realize that it is a confession they're listening for. They're simply waiting for an explanation.

But Harrison stays mute.

"Your son," Dad says, clearing his throat and turning in the armchair to look over at the Boyds, "was involved with my daughter."

"Involved?" Mrs. Boyd repeats, her tone questioning. She gives me a look out of the corner of my eye as though she's already judging me, like I'm not good enough even when I'm wearing these damn churchy clothes.

"I believe they had sex together."

This is mortifying. Even Harrison's jaw drops a little, like he can't believe my dad is seriously discussing this. And with such a straight face too. I know it's awkward for Dad, but he's in cop mode, and cops aren't allowed to be ashamed or embarrassed. They just have to deal with the situation in front of them. Meanwhile, I'm dying for the ground to open up and swallow me whole.

"Okay," Mr. Boyd says nonchalantly, then rolls his eyes. "Thanks for reminding me to give my son a high-five. Anything else?" His wife tuts and shoots him a look of disapproval.

"They had sex," Dad repeats, his resolve unwavering, "and your son filmed my daughter. Not only that, he then shared it all around school."

"Harrison!" his mom gasps in genuine horror.

Richard drops his casual disinterest and presses his lips together. "Did you do that, Harrison?"

"Only because she screwed me around!" Harrison defends, his voice desperate. He's not so brave without his buddy Noah around. He looks more like a little kid who knows he's about to find himself in deep trouble and is prepared to throw a tantrum to get out of it.

"No," I say, talking for the first time since I got out of the car. I want to keep my chin held high and my voice strong, but my head is still lowered and my words sound like a garbled jumble as I say, "I had every right to end things between us if I wanted to. *You* had no right to post that video."

"Dad," Harrison says quickly, eyes flying over to his father, seeking help, "this is the girl who messed up my truck. She's been screwing with me all week. Why do you think she was in our basement? She was probably trying to burn the house down or something." Harrison is trying to justify his wrongdoings by highlighting mine, but I don't think his parents are falling for his distraction techniques.

"Yeah, and you dragged me into the janitor's closet and threatened me," I remind him, my voice growing stronger. Dad throws me a look – I hadn't mentioned that part – but I ignore him and look Harrison straight in the eye instead. "We can both play this game, Harrison."

"Sit down," Richard orders, and Harrison groans as he slumps down into an armchair. "I can't believe you would do something so stupid, Harrison. We raised you better than this."

"As you can see," Dad says, cutting in, "the situation has gotten out of hand. The two of them have been fighting all week and I think it's time that they cut it out and stop hurting one another. And, of course, we'll pay for the truck's new tires." Dad looks at me, disappointment in his eyes, and I glance down at the plush carpet. Now Dad has to fork out a small fortune to pay for my mistakes.

"I'm sorry for breaking into your basement," I apologize to Richard. How did I ever let things get this bad? "And for ruining your dinner at Bob Evans."

"Oh, don't worry about that. I'm more than furious at this idiot too," Richard mutters, glaring at his remorseless son. Harrison is staring at the floor now, his hands in his hair, perfectly aware that his parents are going to lay into him the second Dad and I are gone.

"Can I talk to Harrison?" I ask, and everyone looks at me, surprised. "In private, please?"

"That's a good idea," Mrs. Boyd says, nodding to give me the go-ahead. Her husband looks worried, like he thinks I'm going to tear his son's throat out.

I stand up from the couch, my legs wobbly, and walk across the living room. Harrison gets up too and follows me through the house. I have no idea where I'm going, but I walk through the kitchen and into a small study at the back of the house. It's far enough away from the living room that our parents can't eavesdrop.

"You seriously came over here with your dad, Vanessa?" Harrison mumbles, still pulling at the ends of his hair. At least he's not getting aggressive with me. He just seems abashed now, apprehensive, his face a picture of embarrassment.

"He didn't give me a choice," I say. "He knew everything."

He paces the study, unable to keep still. "And so what? You couldn't manage to ruin my life properly, so now you expect my parents to do it for you? Because they'll probably ground me – and worse – forever."

"No," I say, then sigh. I'm so tired of this. I step closer toward him. "Harrison, can we end this? I won't mess with you anymore, and you don't mess with me. We don't have to be friends or anything."

"And what about that friend of yours? Kai Washington," he says, and there's so much hatred in how he spits out Kai's name. "You expect me just to sit back and do nothing after last night?" He clenches his jaw tight and points at the bruise Kai inflicted with his killer punch at the party, then raises an eyebrow at me as he awaits an answer.

"Kai is done too," I tell him. "You *did* basically steal his girlfriend and try to beat him to a pulp, remember? I think you're pretty even now."

Harrison snorts, shaking his head. He pulls out the desk chair and collapses down into it, staring up at me. "So what? We just ignore each other?"

"Yep. Easy. And you're not allowed to have Noah do your dirty work for you."

We eyeball one another while Harrison contemplates the deal I've offered.

At the end of the day, all he has against me is that video, which has lost its power because everyone has already seen it – and will soon have moved on. But Kai and me? We have so much more. We have that video of him and his friends smoking pot in the bleachers. We know that he cheated on his SATs. Harrison has the most to lose and he knows it.

"Okay, Vanessa," he says at last. "Let's call it quits."

"Shake on it," I order, and he gets up, gives me his most challenging stare, then slips his hand into mine. We shake on our agreement that this fight is over.

"Just so you know," he says, swallowing hard as he tries to look me in the eye, "I really didn't mean for things to happen the way they did. I never meant for that video to spread as far as it has."

"Then why did you send it to everyone in the first place?"

He glances away. "I didn't."

"What?" I don't believe what I'm hearing.

Harrison sighs and scratches at his hairline, looking more awkward than ever, and my heart constricts in my chest. "I only sent it to the guys. And I know that's still a totally shitty thing for me to do, but I didn't realize that it would be out of my control after that. I honestly didn't *think*."

I stare at him, my body rigid. "So, who *did* send the video to everyone?"

He looks me in the eye now, imploring but silent.

"You need to tell me," I prompt. "I'm not going anywhere until you do."

"Noah," he mumbles at last.

I don't say anything. Who else but *Noah*? I wouldn't be surprised if he'd held a deep-rooted grudge against me ever since I ended our fling. That would explain why he'd do something so drastic to hurt me. Sharing that video must have been all too easy for him; he'd have got off on the power that making me so miserable gave him.

Harrison is still a jerk for sending the video to his friends, but at least I know now he didn't *choose* to share it with the entire school – and the rest of the world. In a way, Noah betrayed us both. He shared that private video of Harrison and me with everyone without either of us consenting to it. He took that video out of our control.

And I've spent the entire week unleashing hell on Harrison, when in fact, Noah Diaz is the enemy. He's the one I should have targeted.

But I've learned my lesson. Revenge wins you nothing, and it's often hard to weigh the consequences of your actions until it is too late. I'm not going to take the fight to Noah. This mess is *over*.

"I'm really sorry, Vanessa," Harrison says, and this time he looks me in the eye.

"So am I," I tell him. And I mean it.

Together, we head back to the living room where Dad is warning the Boyds that he's not afraid to press charges if Harrison doesn't leave me alone, and the Boyds are telling Dad that *they'll* do the same if I keep on committing misdemeanor crimes. I clear my throat to make them aware of our presence.

"Vanessa," Dad says, jumping to his feet. There's a giant question mark written on his face.

"Harrison and I have resolved our issue," I state, and Harrison nods in agreement to back me up.

"Great! Now he can go to his room and unplug his Xbox," Mr. Boyd deadpans, and he gives Harrison a stern look that I can't quite read. Harrison must know that look though, because he mutters something under his breath before stalking his way upstairs.

"We'll get going," Dad says, joining me by my side. "I'm glad this mess is sorted."

Mr. and Mrs. Boyd apologize for their son's actions, wish us a pleasant Sunday, and then walk us to the front door before slamming it behind us. Dad and I climb back into the Green McRusty and as he starts up the engine, he looks at me funny.

"Now see?" he says, with more than a hint of smugness. "When you behave like adults, problems get resolved much quicker."

I roll my eyes and prop my elbow up on the window, weaving my fingers into my hair and massaging my scalp. The weight of the burden that I've been carrying around has lifted and I feel so much lighter, like there's a new spring in my step and even the colors outside look brighter.

"Can I see Kai tonight?" I blurt. "You might have realized we're not really just partners on a school assignment."

Dad turns to face me. "Absolutely not," he says, indignant. As he starts to drive, he tells me, "You're so grounded."

And it's like fireworks explode in my chest, because I have never, ever been grounded before. Dad has never cared enough to punish me, but I have waited for this moment so long. I've waited for Dad to save me from the holes I've dug myself into, and I've waited for Dad to feel let down and disappointed by my actions, and I've waited – oh, how I've waited – for him to ground me like any other normal parent would.

My expression lights up with relief as my mouth transforms into a huge grin. I lean over and wrap my arms around Dad, burying my face into his thick coat and hugging him so tightly that he almost crashes the Green McRusty once and for all.

25

Being grounded was almost fun at first.

I took a long bath, complete with a rainbow bath bomb and raspberry-scented bubbles, and I padded around in my fluffy bathrobe and slippers. I styled my hair, taking the time to practice a new curling technique, and I even painted my nails a deep red for the approaching festive season. I watched *A Cinderella Story* twice, once with Kennedy and once on my own. I even tidied up my room, packing away clothes and decluttering all the trash I've let accumulate. It's all so therapeutic, the perfect chilled-out Sunday, but when it grows late, the boredom sets in.

I'm grounded for a month. *A month.*

I don't know if I can do this every day up until Christmas.

My phone buzzes and I roll over on my bed to grab it from my bedside table. There're only two people I'm currently messaging back and forth with, and that's Chyna Tate and Kai Washington. The only two people I need in my life right now.

The text is from Kai. He asks:

Do you think your dad will ever let us hang out while you're grounded, or do we have to wait until next year to get some alone time?

I fluff up my pillows and get comfortable. It's just after nine and I'm already in my pajamas, not quite paying attention to my TV anymore. Dad has taken Kennedy out for a late dinner and I'm not even mad that they've left me behind, because I do so deserve this punishment. I've been scrolling through social media for the past hour, filtering through everyone's posts to see what people are talking about. A couple people have called Noah a total jerk, and a few others are talking about the fact that Harrison was floored with *one* hit. There is absolutely nothing about me, and nothing that could possibly even be *about* me. The gossip on everyone's minds has already shifted forward to something new, like that video never even happened. I know now just how toxic it is being on the receiving end. I'm *so* over high school drama.

There's a smile toying at my mouth as I type back a reply to Kai:

ME: We can still hang out at school. That's if you'll finally talk to me in public ;)
KAI WASHINGTON (PARTNER): The secret mission is over, remember? We can be friends now. I'll even sit at your lunch table.
ME: Just friends?
KAI WASHINGTON (PARTNER): Yep, you don't like the word

"friend" to have the word "boy" in front of it.

ME: We are undefined, then.

KAI WASHINGTON (PARTNER): I like being undefined with you.
Your bedroom is at the front of the house, right?

ME: Yeah???

KAI WASHINGTON (PARTNER): Cool. Rocks incoming.

The next moment, there's a clatter that makes me jolt upright and causes my heart to skip a beat. I stare frozen at my window as more little stones and gravel are hurled against the glass, then finally snap out of it and scramble out of bed. I press my face to the glass and shield my eyes with my hands as I peer out into the darkness.

Kai is standing on my front lawn, his bike dumped in the snow next to him, waving up at me.

I slide open my window and stick my head out into the cold air. "Throwing rocks at my window? This move has been *so* overdone," I call down to him, and I hear his laughter echo up through the night and into my room.

"And so has climbing up the trellis to get to the girl," he calls back. I even catch the wink that he gives me, then watch in amazement as Kai climbs onto the trellis that runs up the corner of my house.

It's covered in prickly shrubs and roses, but Kai carefully works his way up, his movements swift. He slides onto the roof of the porch and stands up, carefully balancing in the wind as he walks over to my window. He crouches down to his knees, holds his head a few inches in front of mine, and smiles. "Hey, Nessie."

"You're insane, Captain Washington!" I say, laughing as I grab his arm and yank him inside. He squeezes through my window and straightens up when he lands inside my room, brushing himself off. "You can't be here."

"But yet here I am," he says, smirking. He's wearing jeans and a thick jacket, but also gloves because he's actually wrapped up warm in this cold weather for once. He pulls off his gloves and shoves them into his pocket. "I didn't want to break our streak of seeing each other every day. And—" he looks at the silver watch on his wrist "—there was only three hours until the day was over, so I raced over here, sliding all over the sidewalks on my bike, even fell off at one point and may or may not have sprained my ankle, just to see you."

My heart swells in my chest, reminding me how I felt last night when I hugged him from behind at the kitchen table. That comfort, that feeling of security . . . these moments. I want to experience these moments forever. I wrap my arms around Kai and rest my head on his chest, his jacket cold against my cheek.

"I've missed you today too," I tell him, my voice muffled against him. "How is it that we've only known each other for a week, yet I already miss you when we aren't together?"

"Do you know what that means?"

I tilt my head back a little and look up at him. "No. What does it mean?"

The corners of his mouth softly pull up into a smile. He's looking down at me, his lips only inches from my own, and he delicately rests his thumb on my chin, using his index finger to lift my head a little higher. "It means you might be falling in love with me too," he whispers.

"Maybe you're right," I breathe, and then I stretch up on my tiptoes and kiss his cool lips.

The kiss is so fragile, so innocent and pure, the two of us standing completely still with my mouth against his. The silence around us drums in my ears and my heart thumps around in my chest. My eyes are squeezed shut and I place my hand on top of Kai's, the one he's holding my chin with, and he kisses me back, his lips capturing mine this time.

We part for a second, opening our eyes to look at one another. His eyes are sparkling with a warmth in them that I haven't seen before.

"Kai . . ." I say, exhaling. I squeeze his hand beneath mine, and he tilts my chin up even higher. We are still so close, neither of us willing to let go. "I'm still not sure that I can do the relationship thing."

"But we're not in a *relationship*, Vanessa. We're teammates. Partners. Accomplices," he says with a smile, looking deep into my eyes, and when I think of it that way, a relationship suddenly doesn't seem that scary anymore. Kai and I, the perfect team . . . *Just like we have been this entire time already*. He skims his hand along the curve of my face and weaves his fingers into my hair, then presses his lips to my mouth. I can feel his lips tilt into a grin, one that is full of mischief, just as he murmurs, "Captain Washington and Nessie versus the world."

26

SIX MONTHS LATER

"Vanessa Murphy," Principal Stone announces, and I rise from my seat.

My legs are stiff from being seated for so long, and as I stand, I feel a little unsteady. I follow Bruce Munro along the row and into the center aisle. I'm surrounded by a sea of faces, though most of them aren't looking my way. Most of my classmates have grown bored by now, some picking at their nails, some resting their head in their hands. I can't blame them – we've been here for over an hour already.

I walk up to the stage, anxiously climb the steps, and walk straight past Principal Stone as he continues to read out names, his throaty voice echoing around the expo center. I look out over the thousands of empty seats and imagine them tomorrow night when they'll be full. We don't need to bother shaking Principal Stone's hand right now, because this is only our rehearsal. Our real graduation is tomorrow.

Brittany Nelson is behind me as I step back off the stage at the opposite side, making my way back to my seat. I see

Noah Diaz on the edge of the second row as I pass, but he doesn't notice me because he's too busy trying to use his phone without being spotted by any of the volunteer teachers that are coordinating the rehearsal. It's a miracle Noah is even sitting here right now, because everyone knows that he scraped through by the skin of his teeth. A few months ago, Noah was – unsurprisingly – suspended for being caught with weed on him on school property. He lost his prestigious football scholarship, is now attending a community college, and is lucky he's even being allowed to walk on stage at the ceremony tomorrow. Sucks to be him.

I follow Bruce Munro back into our own row and sink down into my seat again, relaxing. Unless we're all forced to repeat the practice run all over again, my part is done. I watch everyone else's names get called, and the worst part about the alphabetical order of things is that it means Kai will be one of the last people up. I crane my neck and try to search for him, but my class has four hundred students. I can't see him through everyone else, most likely because he's in the very back row.

Madison Romy's name is called out. I roll my eyes as I spot her popping up from her row across the aisle, hair and makeup already styled as though this were the real graduation ceremony. She keeps her chin up, yet her smile remains perfectly modest as though she's even rehearsed her expression for tomorrow. I hear her heels clicking against the floor as she walks to the stage and I find myself smiling as I watch her shake Principal Stone's hand even though she's not supposed to, because Maddie just has to do everything right. Her upbeat personality is contagious and although we'll never be best friends, I do think I'll miss her. She's going to Stanford, because *duh*. She used to drop by our table in the cafeteria sometimes, but she would never stay for long, because she had too many other friends to catch up with too. She even tutored Kai in English Lit for a few weeks, and Miss Hillman never did find out that she'd once snuck Kai and me into the office for all the wrong reasons.

Maddie catches my eye on her way back to her seat. Her smile grows more sincere, then she disappears out of sight again as she finds her seat.

It's strange, the way life turns out.

Noah Diaz, our star quarterback, keeping his head down in shame.

Madison Romy, the wannabe, heading off to Stanford.

Chyna's name is eventually called out and I sit up in my seat, making myself visible so that I can catch her attention as she shyly scuttles down the aisle toward the stage. When she notices me, she pulls a face that shows her nerves – she would happily stay in high school forever if she could – and I blow her a kiss that's full of reassurance. She catches it and holds it to her heart. She's studying computer science at Carnegie Mellon over in Pittsburgh, so she's anxious about moving out-of-state. I keep reminding her that she's only moving next door. She's literally only going to be three hours away from Columbus.

As I watch Chyna cross the stage, I catch sight of Harrison through the crowd. He's down near the front and has already been called up on stage, and I sigh so audibly that even Bruce and Brittany on either side of me turn to shoot me a look. I can't help it – Harrison walked down the aisle with such deliberate swagger, jokingly popping his collar and moonwalking across the stage in an effort to get some laughter out of his classmates. After Noah was suspended, Harrison seemed to take over the class-clown act, but I've never found him funny. We haven't talked much since Thanksgiving, except the one time he asked to borrow a pen in Biology. He's dating Sierra Jennings now and it seems to be serious, so I guess I wish him all the best. I do regret the things I did to him, and I know he feels bad about leaking that video of us, but you can't erase history. You can't blur out your mistakes and forget that they ever happened. You just have to learn from them and keep moving forward. Luckily, that's exactly what Harrison and I have done. I have no idea where he's going to college, but I do know that he isn't staying in Ohio.

When it's Anthony Vincent's time to walk, I feel oddly . . . proud. He stopped hanging around with Noah and Harrison not too long after I told him last year to get better friends. I've always guessed that he never really liked those guys anyway, and he became a much nicer person to be around when he wasn't trying to fit in with those jerks. He switched to a different table in the cafeteria and started hanging out with the swim team instead. He isn't going to college yet, because he's going backpacking around Europe for a year first, which makes me so, so incredibly jealous.

"Kai Washington," Principal Stone says, and my eyes

immediately flicker from Anthony to Kai, who gets up and follows behind him.

My heart pounds a little faster in my chest as my gaze latches onto Kai. He strolls down the aisle, quietly confident, but I see him searching the rows. I know who he's looking for, and when he finds me, his eyes sparkle and a beaming smile stretches up his entire face.

Kai never ended up taking up Coach Maverick's offer to join the football team for the rest of the season – he joined the basketball team instead, and they *killed* it. His friends are mostly the guys from the team, but he always made time to drop by our table at lunch to say, "*Hey, Nessie and Chyna-but-not-like-the-country.*" Chyna has a love-hate relationship with him, and I know that deep down she does think he's *slightly* funny, though she'll never admit it. He still bikes everywhere too, and for my birthday in January, he bought me my very own bike so that I could join him. A personalized one that has my name on it. Or rather, my nickname. Explaining to my dad why my new bike was named after the Loch Ness Monster was no easy feat.

Kai moves smoothly across the stage and salutes Principal Stone as he passes him, and it earns him a chuckle among the Westerville North High Class of 2019. I roll my eyes and press a hand to my face.

Kai is attending Cleveland State. And as for me? I'm attending Ohio State in the fall, right here in Columbus, because my sister needs me, and my dad needs me, and even Theo the cat needs me to feed him sometimes. It means Chyna is only three hours away, and Kai is only two. Everyone that's special to me is within perfect reach.

The rehearsal wraps up forty minutes later. We're all prepared for tomorrow night – we know the order of the speeches, we know our seats, we know what to do when our names get called out across the hall. It's when we're all dismissed that the nerves truly sink in.

Tomorrow night we really do graduate for real. We'll leave Westerville North behind and we'll all head off in different directions, forging our own paths in life.

The expo center fills with noise as everyone scrambles to their feet, chairs screeching against the floor and voices booming around the hall. Everyone wants to get outside into the morning sunshine, and there's an excitement among us all because the first of the graduation parties is tonight – *not* hosted by Maddie, much to her dismay. It's hard to ruin anyone's mood this weekend, and I, for one, am in exceptionally high spirits.

I spill out of expo center and into the heat of the day outside in the parking lot where everyone congregates. I search through the crowd until someone finds me first, because a pair of arms wrap around me from behind. I inhale the musky scent of his cologne and close my eyes, reaching for his hands as Kai buries his face into my neck. A smile spreads across my face.

The other thing about Kai? We've been together for six months. It's just like having a teammate for life instead of just for a temporary assignment. A relationship didn't seem so terrifying when I started looking at it from that perspective. We don't *officially* have a label on our relationship, but in my head I do call him my boyfriend.

And it makes me giddy every time the word crosses my mind.

I turn around in Kai's arms so that I can face him. He gives me a lazy, cute smile, his arms still wrapped around me and holding me close. We're still standing in the middle of the crowd while everyone continues to mingle, but no one pays attention to us. My relationship with Kai has been public knowledge for months now.

"How about," he says, "you come over to my place and help me pack? I'm still confused on what the weather will be like over there. Plus, my mom misses you."

I nod, unable to suppress my grin.

All Dad's planning and research finally amounted to something – we are heading off next week on the long-overdue Murphy vacation to Ireland to explore our family's ancestry. It's something Mom always talked about doing once Kennedy and I got older, and now we're finally making that trip in her honor. We're leaving for an entire month. The best part? Kai is coming with us.

I helped him search through thrift stores for cheap goods that can be easily flipped on eBay and I helped him mail all the packages, and we made sure all the cash he makes goes to help out his family first. Meanwhile, I picked up a waitressing job solely to earn cash on Kai's behalf. I quit after a few months because the manager kept yelling at me for having my nails done, but still – the money I made was enough to ensure Kai joined us on our trip.

"Kai, I have a proposition for you," I say slowly.

Kai raises one eyebrow, the one that he once cut the slit into. It has filled in by now. "What's the proposition, Nessie?"

"Race you to your house," I challenge, then plant a soft kiss on his lips before I push him away from me and take off running. I weave my way around my classmates as I sprint out of the crowd, and when I glance back over my shoulder, I see Kai close on my heels.

Our bikes are where we left them, chained up to the racks outside the expo center. I fumble in the pocket of my jeans for my key as I run so that the moment I reach my bike, I can unlock it and pull it free from the rack. I swing myself onto the seat, but before I can set off, Kai jumps in front of my bike and grabs my handlebars, squeezing my brakes so that I can't move.

"I'll give you a head start. I'll get the better view," he murmurs, then leans forward on my handlebars and kisses me before we race all the way across town together under the warm sun, our laughter the only sound I hear.

Acknowledgments

First and foremost, thank you to my readers for your endless support, passion and enthusiasm. You keep me going, and I hope you enjoy Vanessa and Kai's story.

Huge thank you to the Black & White Publishing team. It's been so much fun working with you on six books over the past four years. Thank you to Campbell Brown and Ali McBride for your guidance. And to my superstar editors, Emma Hargrave and Janne Moller, for working your magic and shaping this book into exactly what I wanted it to be. Thanks to Alice Latchford and Kristen Susienka for your invaluable help.

Special shout-out to Emma Ferrier for being such an amazing writing buddy. I'm so sorry for all my ramblings, but thank you so much for listening to my ideas.

Mum and Dad, you're the most amazing parents I could have asked for. Thank you for supporting me every step of the way, for putting up with my stress during those tough writing times. Thank you to my grandparents, Fenella and George, for being full of warmth and love. And finally, this year wouldn't have been the same without the arrival of my gorgeous nephew, Anders, who has made life so special. You put a smile on my face each and every day.

Also by
ESTELLE MASKAME

BOOK 1 IN THE PHENOMENAL **DIMILY** SERIES
THE INTERNATIONAL BESTSELLER

Did I Mention I Love You?
ESTELLE MASKAME

BOOK 2 IN THE INCREDIBLE **DIMILY** SERIES
THE INTERNATIONAL BESTSELLER

Did I Mention I Need You?
ESTELLE MASKAME

BOOK 3 IN THE SENSATIONAL **DIMILY** SERIES
THE INTERNATIONAL BESTSELLER

Did I Mention I Miss You?
ESTELLE MASKAME

from the author of the international bestselling DIMILY series
ESTELLE MASKAME
DARE to FALL

FROM THE INTERNATIONAL BESTSELLING AUTHOR
ESTELLE MASKAME

TYLER'S STORY
Just Don't Mention It

www.blackandwhitepublishing.com